To Steve

enjoy
Best Wishes
Lord R. Benson.
X

ABOUT THE AUTHOR

A war baby born in the UK to refugee parents from Vienna and Warsaw, Lord R Benson is mostly self-educated. At age five when his father died, he and his sister were placed in an orphanage. Beginning work at fifteen, he successfully completed a five-year apprenticeship as an electrician. At twenty-three, he began working for himself. Eventually his love of movies led to the opening of his own film company in 1981, which he still operates today. Lord R Benson and his wife of forty-six years live in London, and have two daughters and six grandchildren. Still very active in sport, he plays badminton, and has participated in the London Marathon, completing the race twice under three hours, raising money for the UCH hospital.

iPlot

An Apple a day will not keep conspiracy at bay.

Lord R. Benson

Copyright © 2013 Lord R. Benson

The moral right of the author has been asserted.

Apart from any fair dealing for the purposes of research or private study, or criticism or review, as permitted under the Copyright, Designs and Patents Act 1988, this publication may only be reproduced, stored or transmitted, in any form or by any means, with the prior permission in writing of the publishers, or in the case of reprographic reproduction in accordance with the terms of licences issued by the Copyright Licensing Agency. Enquiries concerning reproduction outside those terms should be sent to the publishers.

This book is a work of fiction and, except in the case of historical facts, towns and countries, any resemblance to actual persons, living or dead, is purely coincidental.

Matador
9 Priory Business Park,
Wistow Road, Kibworth Beauchamp,
Leicestershire. LE8 0RX
Tel: (+44) 116 279 2299
Fax: (+44) 116 279 2277
Email: books@troubador.co.uk
Web: www.troubador.co.uk/matador

ISBN 978 1780883 663 (Paperback)
978 1780883 670 (Hardback)

British Library Cataloguing in Publication Data.
A catalogue record for this book is available from the British Library.

Typeset by Troubador Publishing Ltd, Leicester, UK

Matador is an imprint of Troubador Publishing Ltd

Printed and bound in the UK by TJ International, Padstow, Cornwall

The actual swapping of our own iPad at Heathrow security when travelling to Australia inspired the development of this story.

I give special thanks to my wife Marion, and friend Nannette Holliday, for their invaluable support and encouragement during the writing ordeal.

CONTENTS

1. Death Bed — 1
2. Getaway — 3
3. Pages — 9
4. I spy ... — 23
5. Plans — 31
6. The dilemma — 42
7. Decisions — 46
8. Homeward bound — 60
9. X = CE — 62
10. Alpha, beta, gamma ... — 70
11. Next steps — 77
12. Friendships — 80
13. Find delete — 86
14. Arrivals, departures — 93
15. The interview — 99
16. Catching up — 113
17. Meetings — 125
18. Actions — 135
19. Questions — 147
20. Answers — 161
21. Solutions — 170
22. Upheaval — 187
23. Struggles — 202
24. Power — 217
25. Rewards — 236

1. DEATH BED

Canberra, Australia, 15 December 2011

"I'm going to give it to you straight, gentlemen. You do know she could die? Her vitals are decreasing." Dr Kelly was pulling no punches. "Truthfully, I have no idea what is causing her condition. To date, we've done every test possible. With nothing to go on, it's making it extremely difficult to know how best to treat her."

Registering their stunned looks, he could fully understand what they were thinking. The last thing he wanted on his record was the death of a Prime Minister. To be honest, it certainly seemed the likely outcome, especially if he couldn't find answers soon.

Dr Kelly was head of Mother of Mary Private Hospital in Canberra, where he'd worked for the last nine years. Becoming head only in July, it was a position he wanted to keep for a few more years, and then perhaps a more prestigious hospital till his retirement. While it had only been twenty-four hours since Carla Moore's admittance, her condition was baffling. She continued to be physically sick, and was now drifting in and out of consciousness. He'd never seen anything like it. Even consulting a few trusted colleagues around the country and overseas had not provided anything positive. If she hadn't been the Australian Prime Minister, he knew he wouldn't be panicking quite so much. She'd only recently turned fifty. She was still young, and until a couple of days ago was seemingly fit and healthy.

He looked at the two men seated on the other side of his large white desk. Dick Francis, the current caretaker Prime Minister, was the first to speak. "Thank you for your honesty, Doctor. How many people have you discussed this with?"

"Only you two know the full extent of what we know. Or should I say, don't know. Various members of my staff know bits and pieces, but no one knows it all, or our apprehensions. Naturally, we need answers in order to treat her correctly. In the meantime, I'm sorry to say, but it's pure guesswork and not how we usually operate."

"I'd appreciate if you can keep it that way, Doctor. The only statements released will come from my office. I'm sure you understand."

Nodding in agreement, he fully understood and was relieved he wouldn't be placed in the spotlight.

Strangely, only a mild "Thank you," escaped Greg Peterson's lips. He was clearly in shock. He was her partner after all. They weren't married, not even engaged, but they lived together in The Lodge. With such a high profile situation being flaunted in the public arena, Dr Kelly was having a hard time explaining to his eighteen-year-old daughter that it was not ok for her to move into an apartment with her boyfriend of just six months.

"If you like we can set up a room for you beside Ms Moore's?" he offered Mr Peterson.

Even then he couldn't give a definitive yes or no answer. "That's kind ... thank you. But I'm not sure." He smiled weakly.

Shaking his hand shortly afterwards, it felt like a limp fish. Dr Kelly had expected more gumption from him. After all Carla Moore was an extremely positive and forthright woman.

After seeing both men out, Dr Kelly's thoughts quickly re-focused on the mammoth task at hand – finding answers to what was causing Carla Moore's decline. He wasn't going to be beaten. Not yet anyway.

2. GETAWAY

London, thirteen days earlier

Butterflies were running wild in her stomach as she concluded the final check of the bathroom and bedroom. Looking in the mirror, her mind asking no one in particular, "Why is it always so hectic and nerve-racking just prior to going on holidays?" Sighing loudly, like millions of others who always experience the same angst, Beth knew all would be fine once they'd checked in, particularly when relaxing in the British Airways Club Lounge before departure. While Derek, her darling husband of thirty-nine years still travelled for work, it was the little bonuses of his Club Lounge and Business Class that made these long haul flights, to visit family and friends now living in Australia, all the more pleasurable.

"Charlie, where have you put the *iPad*?" she heard Derek ask their youngest grandson. At just eleven-years old, like all youngsters these days, he was a whiz with technology. He'd shown her how to use their new *iPad2* for so many things over the last few weeks that her mind whirled at all the things it could do. She knew she'd be lucky if she remembered half of it, so hopefully Derek would. If he didn't, their son and his children in Sydney would surely know. It seemed easy enough though. Simply touch what you wanted on-screen, and spread your fingers to expand it. Secretly she had to admit playing with it had been fun. While it seemed to have a mind of its own, her efforts had created loads of laughter between her and Charlie.

"How's it going darling? You got everything together?" asked Derek. His slender six-foot frame poised in the doorway. At fifty-nine he was still a stunningly handsome man, with a full head of dark grey wavy hair in classic Gary Grant style, honey coloured olive skin, high cheekbones framing deep-set blue eyes and a lighter grey, but not white, pencil thin moustache perched above perfectly formed full ruby lips. His classic film star looks had always melted her heart.

He was such a fusspot, but she loved him dearly. They'd met at school, in the fifth grade. Marrying young, Derek had always supported her and their family, a true gentleman in every sense of the word. Their sons had inherited all his wonderful traits: tall, good-looking, a firm but gentle hand with the children, and stable marriages too – a rarity in this day and age. Beth was very thankful for the cards life had dealt her. Now in their late fifties, she and Derek were also blessed with good health, wonderful children, grandchildren and a firm circle of friends. She cherished every day.

Gliding purposefully to her side, he leaned over to kiss her. She smiled, almost giggling at his suave manner. It's what she'd always loved about him, his ability to make light of these stressful situations.

Gently brushing a few stray golden locks from her forehead, he looked longingly into her blue eyes. "You're looking as lovely as a picture my darling, but if we don't leave shortly we may miss the flight. James has already put everything from downstairs in the Land Rover. Have you anything else?"

Turning her petit body to face him, she wrapped her arms around his waist. "No, sweetheart," she said, pulling him even closer, "I just need you." She knew this made him squirm, especially if one of the grandkids walked in. They'd always begin giggling uncontrollably, exclaiming, "They're at it again."

Quickly, he pecked her on the cheek. "Ok, let's get out of here."

Hand in hand they walked down the grand oak staircase towards the front door. She picked up her large black leather, Chanel handbag from the hall table and slung it over her shoulder on the way out. They both turned, casting one last look down the hallway as Derek pulled the solid blue door closed. The ancient brass knocker made a little clank as if to say goodbye. It would be three months before they'd return to their central London terrace house. Actually this was the part she liked the most. Leaving London at the height of winter for a glorious Australian summer, returning in March – perfect timing for preparing her spring garden. Plus spending quality time with the other half of their family and grandchildren.

Today only their son James, accompanied by Charlie, had come to take them to Heathrow. James's wife, Julia, had taken the twins, Lisa and Len, aged fourteen, to judo. Thankfully, as there's no way they'd have all fitted in the car with their extra luggage – mostly stacked full of Christmas presents.

With less traffic than James or Derek had estimated, they arrived at Heathrow with ample time to spare. Rather than hanging around, once James and Charlie had helped them check in, they decided it was best to head back home while the going was good.

"Have a great trip Nan and Pop. I'm going to miss you, but remember we can chat on Skype just like we do with uncle Don and the others now."

"Take care you two. Have fun and we'll see you in March." James wasn't as openly affectionate as Derek, but he still cared.

"You know we will. We'll call you once we're at Don and Sue's. Love you both. Safe drive home." Hugs and kisses all round and they were gone.

Derek smiled lovingly at her, "Come on precious, let's get to the Club and relax."

Perfect. She didn't need any further convincing.

Even though six lanes were operating, as usual the security lines were spilling into the corridor. Fortunately, they had the fast track lane. A woman shouting at the next security gate as she placed her handbag on the belt diverted Beth's attention. Following Derek through the scanner, all she could think of was the champagne and relaxing with him in the Club Lounge.

Waiting on the other side, everything had halted. Nothing was coming through. The line-up around them gathered. Starting up again, a dark, burly security guard approached just as Beth was about to collect her handbag. "This your bag, madam?" his deep, husky voice questioned.

She was surprised. "Aahh, yes," as she winced, wondering what could be wrong with her handbag.

"Do you have a computer in there?"

"I ... eer ... don't ..."

"Of course, the *iPad*." Derek butted in. Opening her bag, he quickly removed the *iPad* handing it to the guard who placed it in another plastic bin and popped it back up through the scanner.

Turning, she buried her head in Derek's chest, trying to conceal her flushed cheeks and the red blotches burning her neck. "Sorry darling that new *iPad* is so light, I didn't even think about it."

He held her tight. "It's ok, they're not going to put you in jail. Anyway I told Charlie to pop it in there. I should've remembered." He turned around, "Look here it is now."

Tucking it firmly under his arm, Derek took Beth's hand in his and led her directly to the British Airways Club Lounge. Still shaking, she knew that drink would go down extra well now.

While Derek organised their drinks and some food, Beth repacked her handbag, marvelling at how light the new *iPad2* was. It was stylish with its bluish-grey leather cover, and extremely compact. What would they think of next?

Returning with enough food to feed an army and two refreshingly crisp South African white wines, they soon forgot the security ordeal. The conversation quickly focussed on the additional things they'd do in Sydney during this trip. A sunset walk on Sydney Harbour Bridge was definitely on the list. Derek had a way of comforting, without being overly controlling.

On boarding the plane they settled into their spacious business class seats on the Qantas Airbus A380. Marvelling at the room, and the fact that the seat reclined to a fully flat bed complete with in-built back massager, Beth was in ecstasy, and they hadn't even taken off. It was times like this that made her appreciate her life with Derek even more. All the pent-up excitement was now overflowing. Beth couldn't wait for them to be airborne and dinner served, so she could enjoy the back massager while lying down.

Meanwhile, Derek was his usual pedantic self, strategically organising his book, glasses, the blanket and pillow, even taking the *iPad* from her handbag. Chuckling quietly to herself, this was definitely a man who travelled regularly and one who liked to be in control. It was so cute. Even as a woman, she'd never have thought quite like this.

After more drinks and a delicious dinner, Beth didn't waste a minute changing into the comfortable grey designer pyjamas they'd been given by the steward and reclining her seat, instantly hitting the massage button. Oohhh, that was so nice … within seconds she was in another world.

As the cabin lights dimmed, Derek's mind was still racing. It had been a hectic week both at work and home, and while he was pleased to now be on their way to Australia, his mind and body needed more time to adjust.

Checking out the movie line-up he wasn't overly impressed, having either seen most on offer, or not wanting to. Pulling out the *iPad* he wondered what movies Charlie and Beth had loaded. Lifting the smart leather cover the screen illuminated instantly. He was impressed. This was much better than waiting for his laptop to start up. Folding the cover back into a neat triangle underneath, it created a stand so the screen was at the perfect angle for viewing. He smiled to himself – technological advancements really were amazing these days.

Touching the movie icon it sprung to life, but to his surprise there were no titles. Strange. Days had been spent downloading a variety of movies and adding some from their own collection, even music. Reaching for the music icon, it filled the screen with nothing – again. How weird.

Glancing across at his wife, he watched as her rhythmic breathing raised and lowered the hands on her chest. She was so peaceful. Sighing, his thoughts turned to her. She was a honey. He was blessed to have such a wonderful, caring partner and family. Not many women would put up with his regular work trips away each month, plus the time spent with his mates watching football, or playing darts and badminton. Whenever possible she accompanied him to functions, and she was an excellent hostess. He felt proud and lucky. He wouldn't disturb her now. It could wait till later.

Taking another sip of the dry, full-bodied Australian red wine, he swirled it gently around his tongue and mouth before slowly letting it slide down his throat. Staring at the *iPad's* illuminated screen his attention was drawn back to it, rather than the wine. The movies had to be there somewhere. Still holding the glass in his right hand he began opening and closing each on-screen icon systematically with his left hand, making sure he didn't miss a one. But as he progressed, the more puzzling it became. Each program icon was blank – like a new *iPad* with applications but no personal data files. Sure their *iPad* was new, the very latest *iPad2*, but he knew Charlie had made sure all their personal data had been loaded. Charlie had also spent hours working with Beth showing her how it all functioned. While Derek personally hadn't taken that much notice, they'd briefly shown him what they were doing.

Touching the second-last icon while downing the last of his wine, he was no longer taking much notice. About to close the *iPad*, his mind clicked. Blinking to look more closely, this one was full of files, but not movies or music. Each was a document, numbered, not named. Certainly not something he, his wife, or even Charlie for that matter would've done. Placing the empty wine glass carefully on the side table he stared open-mouthed at the screen, trying to digest the thoughts his mind was forming. Surely not. It couldn't be.

Tentatively opening one of the documents in 'Pages', the words spewed forth. Scanning them quickly, this couldn't be true. Staring, his heart beat hard against his chest. Following suit, his breathing became heavier, pumping intensely. He glanced around – the cabin was in darkness. He couldn't even hear, or see any flight stewards. Yes he was sure now – this definitely wasn't their *iPad*. No way. So whose was it? Who had theirs? And where was it?

3. PAGES

A million questions occupied Derek's mind, with no real solutions. His mouth was parched. Should he press the call button, or walk to the galley? Choosing the latter he closed the leather cover on the *iPad*, tucking it into the magazine holder beside his seat before heading off with his wine glass in hand.

Pensive, Derek was unable to be his normal jovial self with the flight stewards. Thanking them politely for the wine and assorted nibbles, he walked back to his seat on autopilot. Where to begin? Never easily flustered or distracted, this had Derek puzzled. Hopefully a closer look at this *iPad* and those files would give him a clue to whose it was, and possibly some form of contact. Surely, they must have their *iPad* too. Why don't these things have a simple ID tag, like your luggage? Maybe that's a suggestion he could make to *Apple* for the next one.

Pulling out the *iPad*, he folded the cover back like a book page this time, and rested it on his lap. Opening the Pages icon again he stared at the various documents trying to figure out the numbering system of the folders. Drawing a blank, he took a sip of the new red wine. Deciding to begin with the top folder, his methodical nature took control. Holding a bite size morsel of cheese on rye, his hand hovered in front of his open mouth, his brain mesmerised by the words burning into his eyes.

From: Tom
Sent: Friday, January 28, 2011 5:57 PM
To: The Office
Subject: Opinion

I watched you on TV tonight, and listened to you on radio the other day. I can honestly say I disagree with you 100% of the time. I don't know how somebody like yourself can have the views, which in the long run, will destroy our great nation. Why don't you see and hear what the people are saying? The majority disagree with you. How about listening and thinking about their views? Surely we can't all be wrong, and you the only person right. Sure you can debate, but it is clearly no longer for the good of us as a whole. I think you just like to hear yourself speak, which shows me your views are phoney and that you are full of crap. Open your eyes and ears! Then let something out of your mouth other than lies and bullshit.

PS Your recent facelift didn't help you in the fashion stakes either, you look like a stuffed porcupine and that's insulting a porcupine. Suppose it was our money you wasted on it too? Let's face it nothing's going to help you ... but you could start by pulling your head out of your arse, and really see what is happening to what was once our great country and begin telling the truth too.

From: Fred
Sent: Friday, February 04, 2011 1:47 PM
To: The Office
Subject: Formaldehyde ...

Hey Two-Faced Liar:
I just saw you on The Morning Show ... ALL TALK and NO ACTION ... STILL. Typical of you and your brown-nosing 'greenie friends'. I, like millions of viewers, prayed for Scottie to lean over the desk and slap some sense into that mummy-head of yours. You are so fucking wrong on everything ... the economy, carbon tax, immigration, the war, education, health, you're even wrong about a free country. You're divisive and have nothing but your own ego to stand on. FUCK YOU! PLEASE go back to the cemetery and sell graves, where you belong. NO ONE wants to hear what you have to say anymore. You are the biggest mistake we ever made. NO

ONE TRUSTS YOU. NO ONE! You're just a two-faced liar – Carliar hope your hair catches on fire!

From: Jonesy
Sent: Saturday, February 12, 2011 11:49 AM
To: The Office
Subject: Rude and unattractive

You certainly didn't get your job because of your good looks, charm, wit or intelligence. You are a twit of the highest degree, just like many of your peers that work in that region of our country. You all need to get out of the box and see how the rest of the country really lives, works and thinks. You are also very rude by interrupting the host with your crap! You have nothing decent or new to say, so why bother sticking your face where none of us want to see it. We can't believe a word that comes from that scheming, conniving mouth anymore. I used to switch channels when you were on, now I just mute it. You need to get out of your ivory tower and start thinking in terms of reality instead of theory, because your theory clearly isn't working! You are killing a good nation. We'd all be better off without you in it!

From: David
Sent: Tuesday, April 26, 2011 8:51 PM
To: The Office
Subject: I find you a phoney!

I know it is just my opinion but to me you seem to be a phoney. I see you laugh while in a discussion with one of the TV show hosts as one of their guests. That shows you're not taking your discussions seriously. I watched while you make fun of other people, trying to make yourself better than them. It only makes you smaller. I won't lower myself and call you names even though it is deserved. I do listen to you so I can find out what you are thinking even though you are not totally honest. So it truly amazes me how you can get on your high horse and preach such a load of rubbish to us, and expect us to bow and scrape and praise your every action. I'm still baffled how you got to where you have ... it certainly wasn't through me or my friends. We just hope you'll wake up and come to your senses, before you drag us and the country all down to your level. If I ran my business the way you do, I'd be dead tomorrow. Wake up you phoney, and please do us all a favour and get out before it's too late for all of us.

Derek was taken aback. He'd never read anything so denigrating in his life. What sort of person would keep stuff like this on their *iPad*? What's 'The Office'? Was it political? Possibly. Perhaps some activist? This only created more questions than answers. Looking over at Beth, she was still soundly asleep. He desperately wanted to talk to her, but knew she wouldn't take kindly to being woken up for something that he had no solution for yet.

He took a deep breath and leaned back into the seat. It helped steady the anxiety pitting in his stomach. He stared at the screen, apprehensive about continuing. Although, he knew if he could find the answer, he'd then be able to sleep peacefully. He looked at his untouched food and wine; it beckoned, saying let's relax a little first. He closed the *iPad* cover. Out of sight out of mind, albeit briefly.

He automatically reached for the wine. It was mellow and soothing as it rolled gently down the back of his throat. Closing his eyes, he was unable to comprehend that people even wrote this stuff, let alone kept a computer file of it. Surely it needed destroying immediately.

After finishing the nibbles and a bit more wine he plucked up the courage to continue, hoping that it couldn't get any worse. Tentatively he touched the second file. It sprung to life, filling the screen.

> According to major studies about assassination attempts in the US in the second half of the 20th century, most prospective assassins spend copious

amounts of time planning and preparing for their attempts. Rarely is an assassination attempt a simple case of 'impulsive' action. However, about 25% of the actual attackers were found to be delusional. This figure rose to 60% when taking into consideration 'near-lethal approaches' (people apprehended before reaching their target). This shows that while mental instability plays a role in many modern-age assassinations, the more delusional attackers are less likely to succeed in their attempt. The report also found that around two-thirds of attackers had previously been arrested for other offenses, (not necessarily related), that 44% had a history of serious depression, and 39% had a history of substance abuse.

Derek reached for his half empty wine glass, finishing it in one mouthful. This obviously came from some sort of report – fairly straightforward – but not your everyday subject matter. However, still no name, or indication of the person's work or business. Moving to the next file he was praying for an answer, even though he wasn't particularly religious.

[19/07/11 10:03:21 PM] Jimjam: Hi Co ... Are you online?
[19/07/11 10:04:30 PM] Coco: Hello yes – doing the Tour de France stuff ... will send pics when I have gone through them. It certainly is so much more fun here than you see on TV. Had a huge storm early this morning but thankfully cleared in time for start, but got bad again just before finish. Where are you?
[19/07/11 10:04:58 PM] Jimjam: Sounds great ... Look forward to the photos!!! In Townsville at the Casino hotel ... getting ready for bed.
[19/07/11 10:05:12 PM] Coco: Yes, will go thru the 100s in a minute.
[19/07/11 10:05:51 PM] Jimjam: Your day seems like a really great one.
[19/07/11 10:06:10 PM] Coco: Nice to be in Tville?

[19/07/11 10:06:34 PM] Jimjam: Mine was a day of dramas ...
[19/07/11 10:06:51 PM] Coco: Like what? Sorry to hear that.
[19/07/11 10:08:36 PM] Jimjam: We had 100-knot headwinds rather than the 60 forecast ... So plane diverted into Townsville for fuel. Then just as taxiing for departure, a USA F-18 had a hydraulics failure and cable engagement. Another hour. But beat Virgin and Qantas Link into the air to get to Cairns for the required meetings. Back here about four hours late. Great dinner though, compliments of hotel. Then some of the others conned us into 10 mins in casino and we won straight up – split the winnings, so not too bad.
[19/07/11 10:09:23 PM] Coco: Well at least not your fault and you ended with good night. How much did you win?
[19/07/11 10:09:55 PM] Jimjam: Won $1000, paid for dinner and drinks plus gave us $150 each. At least it wasn't with BF – we'd have got nothing!!
[19/07/11 10:10:12 PM] Coco: Cool ... sounds ok in end.
[19/07/11 10:10:29 PM] Jimjam: Yes !!!
[19/07/11 10:10:39 PM] Coco: Great stuff. $150 ok for nothing.
[19/07/11 10:10:58 PM] Jimjam: Big day tomorrow ... three more ports ... and all of the defence exercise hassles down the coast too.
[19/07/11 10:11:10 PM] Jimjam: Funsville.
[19/07/11 10:11:25 PM] Jimjam: Anyway need some sleep ... just been checking schedules and squaring things away.
[19/07/11 10:11:45 PM] Coco: You know how to handle all that – you'll be fine. Have a great day tomorrow – suppose you need the beauty sleep now too :-)
[19/07/11 10:12:27 PM] Jimjam: Up at 0530 for a 0700 departure!!
[19/07/11 10:12:41 PM] Coco: Sweet dreams – thanks for the chat – take care tomorrow – hear from you when you get back x
[19/07/11 10:12:58 PM] Jimjam: Yep ... Enjoy your day ... Look forward to seeing the photos!!! x
[19/07/11 10:13:38 PM] Coco: Ok will put some up on FB – you'll see in morning x

Just a chat copy. Why though? This person certainly keeps strange files. Who were Jimjam and Coco? Perhaps this belongs to one of them.

He glanced sideways at the empty glass and plate. "Would you like another wine, sir?"

The flight attendant surprised him: he hadn't heard her approach. "Oh, yes please, that would be wonderful. Thank you." It was like she'd read his mind. He just hoped she couldn't read the millions of other things still whirling around in there.

After returning with the bottle, she filled his glass. "If you like, I'll leave the bottle. There's only a small amount left and you're the only person awake."

"Thank you. That's very kind of you. I still have a bit more work to do." Well, little lies don't hurt, and he did have work to do. He needed to find out whose *iPad* this was.

As soon as the attendant disappeared he quickly touched the next file. On a roll, he felt confident there would be no more nasty pages, and the owner's identity would be revealed this time.

[21/07/11 10:34:16 PM] Jimjam: Are you online?
[21/07/11 10:34:49 PM] Coco: Yes just sent you a heap of messages – with my new contact details in London.
[21/07/11 10:35:57 PM] Jimjam: Ok ... Just got about a five-minute download of all yesterday's messages and now two conversations with you open. This Cloud stuff is annoying sometimes.
[21/07/11 10:37:39 PM] Coco: Ok – how was your day?
[21/07/11 10:38:37 PM] Jimjam: Just tried to close the other conversation and it won't let me. Don't understand Skype!!
[21/07/11 10:39:58 PM] Jimjam: Quiet day thankfully. When do you leave?
[21/07/11 10:41:12 PM] Coco: Monday – will drive over – means I can take some nice French wine with me too.
[21/07/11 10:42:08 PM] Jimjam: Sounds cool, shame you can't bring it back here too ... maybe I just have to come over and help you drink it.
[21/07/11 10:42:58 PM] Coco: Ha, you better hurry.

[21/07/11 10:43:46 PM] Jimjam: Even got time to go to gym tonight ... am soooo happy!
[21/07/11 10:44:26 PM] Coco: Cool ... you sounding much happier.
[21/07/11 10:44:45 PM] Jimjam: Yeah, enjoy it while I can hey?
[21/07/11 10:45:27 PM] Coco: Well that's life unfortunately ... not always perfect for any of us sunshine.
[21/07/11 10:45:49 PM] Jimjam: Yes Mum! I didn't call you for a lecture.
[21/07/11 10:46:57 PM] Coco: Ok ... have had a hard day, in fact been a very busy few weeks, then back to London. Have a few hectic months before coming home to you briefly.
[21/07/11 10:47:37 PM] Jimjam: What are you doing with all your gear?
[21/07/11 10:48:39 PM] Coco: Am dividing it up into seasons as I have several suitcases here and am ditching anything I don't need. But will need winter gear when I'm back here next year!
[21/07/11 10:48:56 PM] Jimjam: So it will all fit in the car? What are you keeping?
[21/07/11 10:49:30 PM] Coco: Yes no worries. Only my clothes, papers and books really ... a few souvenirs, you know me. All easily fits in car – and some will stay there too. Car is undercover off-road in London.
[21/07/11 10:49:59 PM] Jimjam: That's all good then.
[21/07/11 10:50:35 PM] Coco: Yes I'll use car in UK now and when I come back.
[21/07/11 10:50:51 PM] Jimjam: That's good, you can garage it. Shame I can't come back with you too.
[21/07/11 10:51:08 PM] Coco: Yes have thought of that.
[21/07/11 10:51:22 PM] Jimjam: Too much happening here ... impossible.
[21/07/11 10:51:48 PM] Coco: What's the latest?
[21/07/11 10:52:12 PM] Jimjam: Same ol'... hard days at the office, nothing's changed ... unfortunately.
[21/07/11 10:52:38 PM] Coco: Do you expect it to?

[21/07/11 10:52:40 PM] Jimjam: Ha, pull the other leg!
[21/07/11 10:52:48 PM] Jimjam: You've seen the news? No way ... is only going to get worse ... am sure of that.
[21/07/11 10:53:04 PM] Coco: Why? Others have been in worse and got out.
[21/07/11 10:53:41 PM] Jimjam: True ... but I can't see that happening this time ... BF is not really listening.
[21/07/11 10:53:52 PM] Coco: That's tuff ...
[21/07/11 10:54:08 PM] Jimjam: You tellin' me ... makes it twice as difficult for me ...
[21/07/11 10:54:21 PM] Jimjam: I must be tired ... hit return by accident sorry.
[21/07/11 10:54:34 PM] Coco: Oh yeah forgot about that ...
[21/07/11 10:55:03 PM] Jimjam: I am going to have to go to bed soon ... Almost 2300 over here. Have a good day.
[21/07/11 10:55:57 PM] Coco: Will try ... but it's not too difficult. Will have a French wine for you later too!
[21/07/11 10:56:18 PM] Jimjam: Thanks gorgeous ... talk later x
[21/07/11 10:56:32 PM] Coco: x

Pondering the conversation, Derek let the red do its work. Are they friends or lovers? Hard to tell with the way young ones talk these days. Did one of them own the *iPad*? With nothing concrete, he moved to the next file.

> The government today announced that it's changing the flag to a CONDOM, because it more accurately reflects the government's political stance. A condom allows for inflation, halts production, destroys the next generation, protects a bunch of dicks, and gives you a sense of security while you're actually being screwed. It just doesn't get more accurate than that!

Releasing a tiny snort, Derek struggled to contain the belly laugh that wanted to erupt. This related to just about every government around these days. It was of no help, but it had certainly brightened the evening. He moved right along.

BIO

- Born on September 1961 in Wales.
- Suffered bronchopneumonia.
- Parents advised to live in warmer climate.
- Family migrated to Australia in 1966, settling in Adelaide.
- One sister, 3 years older.
- Father was psychiatric nurse.
- Mother helped out at Salvation Army nursing home.
- Dropped out of Adelaide Uni in 1982.
- Work in Australian Students Union in Melbourne.
- Became their second female leader.
- Graduated with Bachelors in Arts and Law in 1986, Melbourne Uni.
- Worked in law.
- Made partner 3 years later.
- Left after fraud scandal.
- Total 6 years in private enterprise.
- Chief of Staff for State Labor Opposition Leader.
- Interest in politics since 1980 when joined Labor Club.
- Formerly the secretary of the left-wing organization Socialist Forum.
- Elected as Federal Member for Lalor, Melbourne in 1998.
- Gave first House of Representatives speech 11 November 1998.
- 2001 elected to shadow cabinet and unopposed as deputy leader.

A politician's biography, albeit 10 years old? Not overly au fait with politics, he couldn't guess whose, although obviously Australian. With little or no interest in his own country's politics, he certainly didn't know or care about any other country. He considered his opinion was similar to the majority of people. With nothing concrete he pressed on.

They sent my census form back! Again!!! In response to the question: "Do you have any dependents?" I replied – "10,000 asylum seekers, 100,000 dole bludgers, 20,000 prisoners, half of Afghanistan and 535 politicians in Canberra. Apparently, this was NOT an acceptable answer.

Another joke. At this rate he'd have no answers and also no sleep. The wine long gone, Derek decided it was best to get some sleep. After going to the toilet and cleaning his teeth, he felt much better. The rest would have to wait till the morning. Beth hadn't moved a muscle all evening. He couldn't wait to tell her when she woke though. Before putting the *iPad* to bed, like a gambler, one more file beckoned him to open it.

[24/07/11 3:44:45 PM] Jimjam: Hey you there?
[24/07/11 3:46:30 PM] Coco: Am back – how's ur weekend been?
[24/07/11 3:46:59 PM] Jimjam: Working with BF – what else. In Brisbane.
[24/07/11 3:47:49 PM] Jimjam: Got out to the Brekky Creek on Friday night with Todd, Sue, Mandymoo, Slushbucket though.
[24/07/11 3:47:52 PM] Coco: Gr8. How's the crew? Was it good meal there still?
[24/07/11 3:48:21 PM] Jimjam: Stuffy black tie do with BF last night at Riverside.
[24/07/11 3:48:48 PM] Jimjam: Good food at both places and good to see crew, made my w'end. Brekky Creek is expensive for what you get these days.
[24/07/11 3:49:30 PM] Coco: Wow, must remember if I come visit again.
[24/07/11 3:49:44 PM] Jimjam: $38 for a good pub steak. Probably $25 else where.
[24/07/11 3:50:03 PM] Coco: Long time since I've been there … 5 – 6 years maybe.

[24/07/11 3:50:24 PM] Jimjam: I believe the Norman is better now. Tis run by the original owners of Brekky Creek.
[24/07/11 3:50:30 PM] Coco: They were always known for their good and extra large steaks though.
[24/07/11 3:50:52 PM] Jimjam: Yes ... Still good ...
[24/07/11 3:50:55 PM] Coco: Where's the Norman? Is that in town at cross roads near Grammar?
[24/07/11 3:51:18 PM] Jimjam: Yep.
[24/07/11 3:51:23 PM] Coco: Nice to know you almost had a good weekend!
[24/07/11 3:51:50 PM] Jimjam: Yeah, if not for BF would be fine – on my case all day today.
[24/07/11 3:52:33 PM] Coco: Why?
[24/07/11 3:52:43 PM] Jimjam: Things not going the way proposed – bags of horrible stuff.
[24/07/11 3:52:58 PM] Coco: You mean you see it all?
[24/07/11 3:53:20 PM] Jimjam: Sure, really brightens my day no end.
[24/07/11 3:53:27 PM] Coco: So any exciting reading? Give us the juicy goss.
[24/07/11 3:53:56 PM] Jimjam: Peel you off a few when I get a chance ... unbelievable. But water off a duck's back for BF!
[24/07/11 3:54:19 PM] Coco: Can't wait. You know me and goss ... delich.
[24/07/11 3:54:35 PM] Jimjam: Yes you'll love ... but I'm soooo over it all.
[24/07/11 3:54:50 PM] Coco: You're not giving it up are you??? I'd miss the titbits. What would you do anyway?
[24/07/11 3:55:25 PM] Jimjam: Actually been talking with the other side yesterday ... serious ... could be worth thinking about ... more talks after I'm back.
[24/07/11 3:57:51 PM] Coco: Wow you're not kidding? You'd change – really?
Just can't see you doing that ... but hey if it makes you happy again ... and pays the bills ...
[24/07/11 3:59:27 PM] Jimjam: Don't you dare say a word!!! Anyway gotta go lovely.

[24/07/11 3:59:36 PM] Coco: Ok, cool kiddo, Mum's the word. Luv ya 2. And wouldn't surprise me from what you've been saying anyway. Bye x

So who's BF? It also wasn't perfect in Tullabrook, or wherever these people lived. Derek's mind was egging him to open another one. His fingers reacting before he'd even fully thought it through. Hey presto, it appeared.

LESS DETECTABLE and more easily denied.

1. Georgi Markov, a Bulgarian dissident was assassinated by ricin poisoning. A tiny pellet containing the poison was injected into his leg through a specially designed umbrella. Widespread allegations involving the Bulgarian government and KGB have not led to any legal results. However, it was learned that after the fall of the USSR, the KGB had developed an umbrella that could inject ricin pellets into a victim, and two former KGB agents who defected said the agency assisted in the murder.
2. The CIA has allegedly made several attempts to assassinate Fidel Castro, many of the schemes involving poisoning his cigars.
3. In the late 1950s, KGB assassin Bohdan Stashynsky killed Ukrainian nationalist leaders Lev Rebet and Stepan Bandera with a spray gun that fired a jet of poison gas from a crushed cyanide ampule, making their deaths look like heart attacks.
4. The 2006 case in the UK concerned the assassination of Alexander Litvinenko who was given a lethal dose of radioactive polonium-210, possibly passed to him in aerosol form sprayed directly onto his food. Litvinenko, a former KGB agent, had been granted asylum in the UK in 2000 after citing persecution in Russia. Shortly before his death he issued a statement accusing then President of Russia Vladimir Putin of

involvement in his assassination. President Putin denies he had any part in Litvinenko's death.

OMG, what sort of work did this person do? He couldn't think of an occupation that required this sort of knowledge. This was becoming weirder by the minute. Looking at his watch, he still had several hours before they'd land in Singapore. And to think, all he'd wanted to do was watch a movie and unwind before sleeping. He should've stuck to reading his book. He just hoped that once he could find the owner of this *iPad* that they'd have his. Thinking more of theirs, thankfully there was nothing strange on it. He hoped the person was enjoying their movie, or music selection.

He wanted another drink, but not wine. He never normally drank this much, particularly on flights. He really wasn't a tea, or coffee man at this time of night either. One coffee in the morning and a couple of cups of Earl Grey tea during the day, sometimes three, then maybe a couple of glasses of wine over dinner with Beth, or a beer or two if he was with his mates, that was it. Boring some might say, but he didn't care what others thought, he enjoyed it that way. Then his eyes spied the water bottle. Perfect. Unscrewing the cap he took a large gulp. Then another. After replacing the cap and tucking it back in its holder, he focused on the *iPad* again.

Fighting with his thoughts – no more – just one more – no, get some rest – the next will be the last – not likely. It'll still be there later – ok you win. Picking up the *iPad* from his tray, he turned the leather cover over the screen, putting it to sleep. Nice looking gadget. It looked exactly like theirs. Even with the same coloured leather cover. How coincidental. He couldn't help wondering how often this sort of thing happened. And why to them?

Reclining the seat flat, he stretched out, placing the small plump pillow under his head and the soft woollen blanket neatly over himself. Searching for the massage button on the controls – yes, oh yes, that was nice. Closing his eyes, the gently pulsating knobs kneaded his weary shoulders and back. Succumbing to slumber was easy. Why hadn't he done it hours ago?

4. I SPY ...

Sunlight streamed through the expansive floor to ceiling glass panels and reflected off the highly polished marble floors, highlighting the massive colonnades. The blinding whiteness made him squint. Everywhere he looked it was the same, making his head spin.

Clip, clop, clip, clop. Someone was coming. Turning to face the direction of the sound, a burst of flaming orange-red assaulted his eyes. So this must be what they call a sight for sore eyes he thought, blinking feverishly. He hoped it would wash the image away. No luck.

Purpose in her stride, she swept by, leaving a sweet perfume trail that he found himself unwillingly following down the vast corridors.

Her slender pink hand with perfectly manicured bright red fingernails touched the keypad, springing the door lock. Pushing it open, she strode over to the massive oak desk placing the files down to one side. The dark suited man that had been silently following her had remained outside the door.

The room was mellow, allowing his eyes to refocus. From his position at the back of a preposterously large, floral covered armchair in the back corner of the room, he watched her every move. There was one large window and four doors off this enormous and palatially decorated room.

The woman in red paused, looking out the rear picture window. Several wallabies were grazing on the dewy spring grass they'd found under the shade of the scrub wattles and ghost gums. She appeared lonely. Was she reminiscing, perhaps even wishing she shared their uncomplicated life? He wondered if she had much of a life outside of her office; she looked very important. With these grand surroundings, she had to be a big boss.

He watched her intently as trance-like she ran her hand lightly along the edges of the highly polished oak desk. Walking along the front, down the right side and across the back, she only lifted her hand to swivel the large, brown leather chair before turning and backing into it.

He noticed she was taller, perhaps around five foot ten-ish, thin faced framed by short straight ginger-red angular-cut hair, which only accentuated her sharp pointy nose and slanted eyes. Her posterior however, was much more rounded than the rest of her, although the tailored red suit jacket did a good job of covering most of it. She wasn't what he would have called stunningly beautiful, but not totally unattractive either. Her skin was smooth and milky white. She interested him enough to stay a while.

Grabbing the top file, her mood appeared to change as she opened it and began reading. Pen poised in the right hand it pounced, making forceful scratches from time to time. Within no time she'd completed one pile and was on to the next, neatly stacked on the other side of the desk. He was getting bored, but just as he was about to move, the door closest to him burst open. This wasn't the one they'd entered through earlier.

"Good morning Miss Moore," a strikingly dapper suited young man announced. "Here's your tea and the morning dailies. I've highlighted a few possible issues, which I'll follow up. Other than that, nothing new to report, just a continuation from last week."

"Thanks Jonathon. Here, take these. You'll see what needs doing." Pushing the group of completed folders in his direction, she returned to what was open in front of her, not interested in any further conversation. He scooped them up and retreated, quietly closing the door behind him.

Well, that was short and sweet he thought. But before he could consider his next move one of the three telephones on her desk rang. It was the first time he'd noticed there was more than one and he wondered which one it was. She knew, snatching it immediately. "Moore."

"Yes, that's what I'd ordered." Silence. It was annoying not knowing the other half of the conversation. "I don't see that as an acceptable reason. It will be done as I've requested and in the office by eleven this morning. Understand?" As she slammed down the receiver he doubted the other person had any chance to answer.

Burrrrrrrrr. "Jonathon, get in here now!"

Instantly, light flooded in from the outside offices. Now humming, the workday was well underway. "Yes Ma'am."

"Get me the Indonesian file. Also, where's the activity sheet for today? Quickly."

Without closing the door Jonathon disappeared briefly, returning with a clear plastic folder, holding a neatly typed calendar-style sheet. Placing it squarely in front of her she glanced down, fingering one around the middle of the page. "Why didn't you let me know Hull was back?" Opening his mouth, she blasted forth before he could say anything. "Downey and Scott also appeared on the Morning Show. Why didn't you get me there too? You better have a copy. Anything important?"

Drawing a deep breath he burst into action. "They didn't want you this time. I tried. Nothing substantial was discussed, just the normal formalities and pleasantries about how they'd do things differently, better. I have a copy on my desk for you." He appeared uncomfortable telling her this. Did he know more? He guessed she didn't handle bad news well either. This guy was acting so scared. "And I didn't know about Hull until this morning."

"That's not good enough. Make an appointment for Hull to be here this morning." She quickly continued, "His job is out of the country, and as much as possible."

"Yes Ma'am."

Instantly she changed the subject. "What are the ratings like today?"

"Urr, not the best Ma'am." He could see Jonathon wincing ready for the berating. "You're down to 25%. Scott's 48%. Rest undecided."

Fists clenched on the desk and lips pursed, her nose became

even more pronounced making her look like a magpie, with a long slender beak topped with deeply set suspicious eyes. But like a simmering volcano smouldering below the surface, she wasn't ready to explode just yet.

"Ok. Just get that appointment with Hull."

"Yes Ma'am."

As Jonathon turned, he decided to make a quick exit too. Things were getting a bit hot in there, plus he wanted to see where the heart of the action was – the engine that drove this mean machine.

Now perched on the top of a cupboard in the back corner, he could see everything. Jonathon's neat, orderly and well-stocked desk was directly beside Moore's office door below him. In front of Jonathon sat a young woman, with another equally tidy desk piled high with various coloured folders. Cutting them off from the rest of the room was a counter that stretched the width of their area. A secure door at the left side ensured their imprisonment. Seated behind the counter were two female receptionists attending to a switchboard, with more flashing lights than a Christmas tree. Beyond the counter was a light airy room with a brown leather lounge, two armchairs, two large potted palms, a square glass coffee table with a couple of large books strategically placed to one side on it. The colourful Aboriginal dot painting covering most of the wall behind the lounge, created a warm glow amongst the formality of the reception area.

The girl in front of Jonathon turned, "You ok? Need a hand?"

"Thanks Nicole, I'm right for the minute. Just the usual start to another thrilling week." Acid leached from the last sentence, but not directed at her. It was obviously something they both knew quite well.

"Well don't let her get to you. It's not worth it."

"Yeah, I know. But I can fully understand why most guys never wanted her. Goodness knows what that faggot hairdresser sees in her either."

"Image JJ. It's all about image. She needed a partner to be accepted by the masses, and it was good for his ailing business.

Gosh, he doesn't have to work any more, plus his empire has trebled in the last year alone – probably the only thing that is prospering around the country at present. One wonders if they're sharing the profits."

"Do you think she's like this at home too? Cause she never changes, even when we're travelling."

"Birds of a feather stick together … and a leopard never changes its spots. I believe there's truth in both these," recited Nicole.

"Yeah, you're right there."

"Hey don't worry, one day her karma will catch up with her. In the meantime, we've gotta have patience until something better comes along. Just let me know if you need a hand later, ok? I'll keep tackling this pile of love letters from her adoring fans," she smirked.

"Oh, and excuse me while I'm being sick," he mocked.

"Yeah, both of us!" Laughter filled the room just as the office door sprung open.

"What's so funny?" she demanded. But before receiving any answer, "You got that appointment with Hull yet?" she snapped at Jonathon.

"No Ma'am. They're getting back to me."

The door slammed. He immediately picked up the black phone on his right, as he'd not yet contacted them. "Hi Justine. Moore wants to see Hull in her office as soon as possible. When do you reckon? – Thanks mate. Bye."

He knocked on the door before opening it, but remained in the doorway, "Minister Hull will be here at 10:30 Ma'am."

"Good. Get coffee, my tea and cakes too."

He closed the door, slumping back in his comfortable office chair and sighed loudly. "You know Nic, the nicest thing about being here is this chair. Well not really. You guys are all great too." He shook his head, "I wonder what the hell I ever saw in this job in the first place?"

Nicole turned and smiled at him. "The prestige, lovely," she quipped. "And the fact it'll always look good on your resume – the PM's Chief of Staff."

"You're right." Then in a dream-like tone, "Any future boss would have to be a walk in the park compared to this." Looking at his watch, only an hour before the meeting, "Shit. I better phone the kitchen now before her favourite cakes disappear." Picking up the black phone again, he pressed just four buttons. "Hi Mary, this is Jonathon. I need coffee for Hull, her tea and her usual cakes for two please. Meeting is at 10:30. Ok. Nicole or I will be down by 10:15 at the latest. Thanks luv. Have a good day."

Watching their actions, he couldn't help but feel sorry for these guys. What an existence. And this was only Monday. Thankfully he didn't have to put up with this sort of nonsense every day to survive. His life didn't seem so trivial after all.

Burrrrrr ... he intercom shrilled. "Where's that show recording Jonathon?" Grabbing it, he was up and inside her door instantly.

About to hand it to her, "No, put it on now," she demanded. Turning, he opened the DVD player, placing it in and closing the tray. Picking up the combination controller, he handed it to her before leaving the room. "I'll need you later so don't go anywhere." Her blunt words followed him out the door.

"That high-pitched nasally toned drawl of hers gets me," he admitted softly to Nicole while collapsing back in the chair. "The worst Australian accent possible, especially for a woman. Grates on my nerves."

"Understand completely. Tis enough to send shivers down ya spine."

"Agree. Such an embarrassment for us all ... and the pronunciations ... she's providing heaps of material for the comedians these days." They both smiled and turned back to attacking the mounds of folders on their desks.

He'd seen and heard enough here, it was time to check out the lounge area beyond the reception. Choosing a palm frond as his next viewpoint, he observed the floor to ceiling glass walls and door that exposed a long hallway with a row of important looking paintings lining one side. The walk of shame, or death, came to mind. He wondered if most people shuddered in their boots when coming here. After all it didn't seem to be the happiest place he'd ever visited.

A lady in grey walking towards the entrance with a large covered tray in her hand diverted his attention. One of the girls behind the reception desk pressed a switch and the door pushed open with ease. The other young girl was holding open the side door. She entered their enclave. "Hi ladies and gentleman. Had a spare moment, so decided to bring this up myself, and there's a little extra for all of you too."

"Hey Mary that's so thoughtful. Thank you." "You're a treasure." "Thanks." "Oh, yum thanks," each echoed.

"Yes, figured you'd like something sweet to start the week."

"Not wrong." Jonathon said walking towards her to take the tray.

Placing it on the side table near the office door, he picked up the docket and signed it as the girls made idle chit chat. Handing it back to her, "Thanks ever so much Mary, your blood's worth bottling that's for sure. One of us will bring the empties back later. Have a good morning too hey." And she was soon gone.

Even in the reception lounge the wafts of freshly baked cinnamon muffins and chocolate cake filled his nostrils. Rubbing his mitts together, he was just about to check them out when the glass door buzzed open again. Who was this slight, medium height, round-faced, silvery-blonde-haired, man in a dark suit?

"Morning Minister Hull," they all chorused.

"Morning all," he smiled.

"She's expecting you sir." Opening her door, Jonathon picked up the tray and followed him in.

So this was the important visitor. He couldn't miss this. While the door was open he made a dash back in to red robin's office, the aroma of the cakes having already whetted his appetite too.

Amongst the haste and confusion, he couldn't work out which vantage point would be best. The visitor, Minister Hull, had already taken up residence in the rolled armchair he'd used last time. He hovered above the cakes briefly. "What's that?"

The shrillness pierced his ears. "Get rid of it. Now!" exclaimed Moore.

Both men looked at each other, not quite sure what to do first. Swiftly, Hull acted by picking up a nearby folder and rolling it, while Jonathon placed the tray on the coffee table in front of him.

Thump. That narrowly missed his tail, the force of the air tossing him sideways. Instantly realising it was him they were after, he took flight. Frantically he circled the room, trying to get his bearings. From out of nowhere a blast of sticky spray coated his body and wings, stinging his eyes and throat. Oh no …

* * *

Coughing and gagging slightly, Derek sat up, reaching for his water. The cabin lights were low and a few people were already up, including Beth. Smiling. "You ok darling? You were certainly sleeping well."

"Yes. Yes, I'm ok. Not a bad night," he lied. If she only knew, but he'd wait till later, when he felt it was safe to tell her everything. It was too risky at present. "You're bright and bubbly this morning sweetheart," he added.

"Yes, almost as good as sleeping in our own bed. Well, for a plane anyway." Adding, "Our breakfast will be here in about half an hour."

"Thanks lovely. I'll get cleaned up before the queue begins. Be back soon."

It may not have been a long sleep, but he felt refreshed. Not remembering the dream, his mind retreated to the events of earlier in the evening, and the assortment of information he'd uncovered. With everyone awake and possibly looking over his shoulder, he wondered if it would be safe enough to continue opening the files after breakfast.

5. PLANS

Following the delicious breakfast of freshly squeezed orange juice, slices of juicy red watermelon, smoked salmon and scrabbled egg on toast and a freshly brewed coffee, Derek looked around the cabin and decided that he would continue his quest for the *iPad* owner. He still hadn't mentioned anything to Beth. Amongst their idle chatter, it hadn't seemed appropriate. Even now, she was engrossed in one of her woman's magazines while finishing her coffee. Opening up the *iPad* and putting in his earphones, he hoped to create the impression of watching a movie. His attention was once again at the mercy of this machine. Beginning where he'd left off last night, the words filled the screen.

Dynamic economy, shame about the politicians

May 19, 2011 12:00AM

THE Australian economy will be 30 in two more short years.
While it's flexible and dynamic, having been raised on a diet of bold tariff cuts and deregulation, Treasurer Dick Francis and his counterpart Michael Downey are both acting as if they're raising an infant economy that needs massive nurturing.
Unemployment is only 4.5 per cent and our terms of trade are at a 140-year high, but these economic whizz-kids are creating fear, telling us we need to worry about fragility, transformation and patchiness.
The Francis budget, and responses to it from Downey

and the Treasury, reinforce this kid glove approach by justifying the winding back of fiscal stimulus in boom times.

Closing it down, Derek was frustrated. What a waste of space. Old news clippings with more Australian political guff, he didn't even bother to finish reading it. Time was precious. Next.

From: Clare
Sent: Tuesday, May 03, 2011 8:26 PM
To: The Office
Subject: You

You're an idiot, a moron, an IQ less than zero. How DARE you attempt to make light about the Economy. Carbon tax. Boat people. For the good of all? Yeah? You know nothing. You're simply a puppet. A stupid, incompetent, small-minded slug. I'm GLAD Bin Laden is dead, and whatever else it takes to keep us safe is fine by me. Can I suggest you move to Afghanistan now too, and enjoy your authoritarian lifestyle you cretin. At least we'll be safe from your stupidity.

From: alfd
Sent: Wednesday, May 04, 2011 8:20 PM
To: The Office
Subject: No shame

You've always been a class A, red hot, flaming douche bag but now you're that, more so than ever. Have you no shame? Or yet a better question, have you no dignity? You're wrong about EVERYTHING, yet you get out there, day after day jabbering away with load after load of crap! You're truly a certified wing nut, filled with your ideological ideas and nothing more, which is why nothing is working … can't you see that? Can you do us all a favour and go drown yourself? Anyone, even my mother would be better than you right now.

From: Mr Concerned
Sent: Wednesday, June 06, 2011 5:25 PM
To: The Office
Subject: Go sailing

You're a fuckin idiot. Do you realise how pissed we all are about Illegal immigrants taking our jobs, our housing for the needy and elderly, our hospital beds, taking over our suburbs, our daily lives, now telling us what we can and can't do in our own country. Can I suggest you take their boats and turn them back to where they came from? Every other country does and so should we! Can I also suggest you take your loud-mouthed, appeasing ass off on their next boat too? Oh, I'm sorry, That was racist, but I guess I am, I love my country and I want it to remain MY COUNTRY, not what these ungrateful, slimeballs want to make of it because they fucked their own country up so bad. But when it's no longer my good home, because you don't have the balls to stand up to them, just as their people would if we lived in their country, and I have nothing, being surrounded by all their crap and rules, just for you, yes YOU, I will leave a spot right in the middle, and they can have their way with you. But I'm sure they won't even want you. Wake up before it's too late for all of us you idiot!

From: max
Sent: Wednesday, June 24, 2011 10:05 PM
To: The Office
Subject: Congratulations

I know you probably get a lot of hate mail, which made me hesitate to write to you. But I have to for my own satisfaction. You are an incredibly ignorant and stupid person. It is obvious that you have absolutely no idea whatsoever what this country really needs. You see, I have a good, well-paying job and I am only 21. I graduated from Uni last year at the age of 20 with a BA in business and currently work for a successful entrepreneur while also interning for a State Government Department. I have accomplished much already in my young life. But through what you are attempting to do now, I have just been told my internship cannot continue due to your government staffing cutbacks, and my other boss has just lost some huge contracts, so I hold my breath and wait to see if I have a job there too.

You and your new policies will wipe all this out for me and many other hardworking, caring, fellow countrymen and women. So let me ask you frankly; YOU can't be serious with your new proposals? But I know you are. You stand up all godly and righteous, and preach that this is the gospel. Can I suggest you go out and work in the real world. I know it will be difficult for you. I know you had only a few short years … Was it too tough for you? I suspect so. I wonder what you would say to someone like me if we met on the streets? You are a coward, a puppet on a string, hiding behind your henchmen. Thanks for stuffing up my young life so early. Congratulations.

He winced. These were even nastier than the one's he'd seen last night. Swallowing hard, he drew a deep breath and hit the next file.

[28/07/11 5:38:53 AM] Jimjam: Yesterday was crap and this morning is looking no better – even worse. BF is driving me crazy.
[28/07/11 5:39:31 AM] Coco: Hang in, things'll be ok. U used to love it – thrive on it … couldn't gag you!
[28/07/11 5:40:05 AM] Coco: So what's on the menu today?
[28/07/11 5:41:48 AM] Jimjam: Murder – if I have to listen to one more tantrum. That mouth may just drive me over the edge – have no respect anymore. The spiralling downhill popularity bugs BF to death tis affecting us all.
[28/07/11 5:43:50 AM] Coco: He, he – but you wouldn't kill … not possible or worth it. Surely you haven't really thought?
[28/07/11 5:45:27 AM] Jimjam: Oh hell yes. Would be easy,

so darn easy .... slow and painful ... suffer baby ... like we have to. Luv it ... helps me sleep.
[28/07/11 5:46:01 AM] Coco: Ohhhh u devil u. Have to tell me more later, but glad thoughts have brightened ur day – have good one hon. I've gotta get going I have a late meeting. Lol x

A small light flashed in his head, but he was unable to grasp what it was. Re-reading the conversation, he still couldn't put his finger on it. Grabbing a small notepad and pen from his shirt pocket he made a note of the file number: 112807. Looking across at Beth, she was still absorbed in doing her thing. It looked like a sudoku, or crossword in the magazine. She wasn't clingy or needy. Another quality he liked about her. Looking down, ping, the next file opened.

SUCCESSES:

A. Mohandas Gandhi, political and ideological leader, India – shot and killed, during nightly public walk in Birla House grounds. Hindu radical, Nathuram Godse, and co-conspirator Narayan Apte, links to extremist Hindu Mahasabha.
B. John Fitzgerald Kennedy, (JFK), 35th US President – shot and killed, open-top limousine, public parade. Non-conclusive. Conspiracy theory, FBI, Cuba, CIA, USSR, despite numerous investigations, death still shrouded in mystery. Lee Harvey Oswald convicted but maintained innocence until death.
C. Abraham Lincoln, 16th US President – shot in head at theatre performance, by John Wilkes Booth, Confederate spy, angry over Lincoln's support for the freedom of African Americans. Booth was caught and fatally shot 12 days later.
D. Julius Caesar, Roman political and military figure – walking past the Theatre of Pompey, he was stopped by a group of Senators (as many as 60) disillusioned

at his rule, to read a fake bill that allegedly gave power back to the Senate. As Caesar did this, he was stabbed 23 times. Marked the end of the Roman Republic. Out of the bloody aftermath emerged the Roman Empire.

E. Archduke of Austria, Franz Ferdinand, heir to the Austrian throne (and catalyst for beginning of World War I) – he and wife shot riding in an open-top car in Sarajevo by members of The Black Hand, a Serbian group attempting to gain independence for all the states annexed by Austria-Hungary. World War I began two months later, with Austria-Hungary declaring war on Serbia.

F. Malcolm X (Malcolm Little), American black Muslim minister, man behind the Black Power movement of the 1960s and 1970s for freedom of African Americans, had been member of Nation of Islam, changed to Sunni Muslim – shot 16 times while giving a speech to crowd by 3 members of the Nation of Islam.

G. Lee Harvey Oswald, former US marine, who US Govt claimed was responsible for the assassination of President JFK – assassinated two days after President in the basement of the Dallas Police Headquarters by Jack Ruby, a Dallas nightclub owner with links to organised crime. Apparently angry and upset over JFK, and sought revenge.

H. Martin Luther King, behind American Civil Rights Movement to abolish racial discrimination of African Americans – fatally shot while standing on balcony of his second floor motel room by escaped convict James Earl Ray, a white man, opposed to the Movement. Captured two months later in London, extradited to Tennessee and sentenced.

I. Robert F. Kennedy, US Senator, Presidential Candidate for the Democratic Party, and younger brother of JFK – shot 4 times at point-blank range, early morning by Sirhan Sirhan. Motivation unknown,

assume he was a Palestinian terrorist seeking revenge for US support of Israel in the Six Day's War of 1967.
J. John Lennon, founding member of The Beatles, and peace activist – shot 4 times when returning to his New York city hotel by Mark David Chapman. Motivation unclear. Chapman still in prison.
K. Alexander Litvinenko, Russian KGB agent, turned dissident and possible MI6 agent – poisoned by a cup of tea in his hotel room, but fell ill after eating at the London sushi restaurant Itsu. Was receiving evidence about another murder there. Two days later condition deteriorated, rushed to Barnet General Hospital in London. Died three weeks later, suffering acute radiation syndrome spawned from exposure to the radioactive polonium-210. No one has been convicted of the murder; however, suspicions of Russian government involvement.

Here we go again, more famous murders. Scribbling additional notes on his little pad, this time under headings: Chats; Murders; Stats; Political info; Hate letters. Checking it through, that seemed to cover what he'd seen so far. Going back he noted the file numbers under each heading before opening the next one.

Next he was confronted with a list of *YouTube* links. Unsure whether he could view them while in flight, he tried one. 'Safari' began to open. He waited with anticipation. It was slow, but eventually the screen appeared. The internet was available, but for a price, and not one that he really thought was worthwhile to watch public *YouTube* videos, which he was sure would not reveal the owner to him. Oh well, noting the file, he'd check it out while they were stopped in Singapore, after telling Beth of course. The following files contained more Australian political newspaper articles. Glancing at the headings and a few sentences were enough, as they weren't providing any answers for him, only showing how much trouble the Australian Government seemed to be in. He must ask Don, when they get to Sydney, about this.

Moore promises tax cuts in carbon deal

June 26, 2011

TAX cuts and increased family payments will form part of the Government's carbon price compensation package, Prime Minister Carla Moore announced today.
Speaking at Western Australia's Labor Party conference in Perth, Ms Moore outlined her plans for the tax cuts and increased household assistance payments that would be finalised in coming weeks.
"I understand that many people are anxious about the impact of a price on carbon," she said. "I fully understand they expect to hear what it's all about, the details and costs, and I'm going to do that."
Tax cuts and payments would be targeted at "those who need it most", Ms Moore said.
"We will act fairly. We will not let Australians down."
Meanwhile Opposition Leader Adam Scott has pledged income tax cuts if the coalition wins the next election.
"I promise a tax cut without a carbon tax," he told the federal council meeting of the Liberal Party in Canberra today.
"We will fund tax cuts through prudent economies in government spending and improvements in economic productivity."

More needed from Moore government

August 05, 2011 12:00AM

A WORSENING of the economic conditions here and overseas dictates that the federal government must chart a new course on economic policy.
In a severe shock to the global financial system, the

US last week was subject to its first credit rating downgrade in history.
As Prime Minister Carla Moore and Treasurer Dick Francis have rightly indicated, Australia is not immune to adverse international economic events.
Just last week, $100 billion was wiped off the value of Australian shares on the back of the developments in the US.

With only a few more files to go, Derek was anxious to get through them, then formulate what he needed to discuss with Beth.

BPS Report extract:

We are involved in a giant self-inflicted policy wound on Australian equities. Every foreign investor I see believes Australian company management is excellent, but Australian political management is woeful.
As one Chinese investor said to me in Hong Kong last week "Would you buy a stock where the CEO is Carla Moore, CFO is Dick Francis, independent directors are Jones, Johnston, and Oliver, and the executive chairman is now Gerard Green?"
The very best thing that could happen to the Australian equity market is the removal of the incompetent, anti-business, income redistributing, Moore/Independents Government.
If it was a public company all of these people would be in front of a court 'showing cause' as to why they should be in positions to damage the wealth of the corporation and failing on their duties and obligations.

On Carbon Tax:

If 0.7% of the earth's atmosphere is carbon and 97% of that is naturally made and only 1.5 % of that 3%

comes from Australia why in the world are we sitting on our hands, people, and just accepting this Carbon Tax? Wake up Australia, you are being taken for a ride.

Just two more factual reports or opinions ... duly noted. Last one.

AS·SAS·SI·NA·TION (noun)

1. *murder*
2. *killing*
3. *shooting*
4. *elimination*
   of an individual, who is usually a famous celebrity, politician, religious figure, or royal. Usually in cases of assassination there is a clear motive – jealousy, political or religious idealism, contract killing, revenge etc.

Stunned, eyes bulging from behind his glasses and mouth wide open, his thoughts were interrupted by Beth. "You alright darling? You look like you've seen a ghost. What are you doing?"

"Ahh nothing ... I'm fine ... I just had a thought ... Nothing important ... Work stuff." Stumbling, he looked across hoping she'd accepted it. Quickly smiling, he picked up her hand and changed the subject. "You're looking as beautiful as ever sweetheart. You getting excited about seeing Don, Sue and the kids?"

"Oh yes – and that gorgeous warm sunshine. Lots of lazy fun filled days ahead." She beamed. "Have I told you how much I love you lately, and the fact that we're able to enjoy these times, darling? I am so lucky to have you. You know that?"

"Yes sweetheart. And I'm lucky to have you too. You are the sunshine of my life." Moving her hand to his mouth, he kissed the back of it, before squeezing it lightly and replacing it on her lap. "Do you think it's too early to celebrate with a champagne?"

"Oh you devil. You know the way to my heart."

With that he pressed the attendant call button and requested two glasses of champagne. Closing the *iPad* he tucked it in the side pocket. There wasn't much more he could do now, even if he wanted to. Toasting to their love and holiday, the discussion centred on more of what they wanted to do this time, including a wine tasting weekend up at the Hunter Valley and perhaps hiring a houseboat on the Hawkesbury. Something the entire family could enjoy as well. While desperate to discuss the *iPad*, he thought it would be better once they were in the private Club Lounge at Singapore's Changi International Airport.

6. THE DILEMMA

Placing the *iPad* in Beth's handbag before disembarking in Singapore, Derek still wasn't sure what, or how, to tell her of their dilemma. A multitude of ideas and unanswered questions remained. He was anxious to get it sorted.

"What's the rush darling?" she questioned, as Derek tried taking Beth's arm to move her past the line of perfume counters.

"No rush ... I just thought you'd like to get to the Club and freshen up."

"In a minute. I'd like to check my perfume prices. I'll need some more soon, that's all."

"Ok, take your time." He hoped his impatience wasn't showing he really wanted to get to the Lounge and connect to the internet.

Ten minutes later they were finally seated in a cosy back corner with no one in earshot. Grabbing Beth's bag, he removed the *iPad*. He caught her quizzical look out of the corner of his eye, "Sorry darling, I need to do a couple of things on the internet. Do you want to go and freshen up, and then grab us a couple of drinks and some snacks on the way back?"

Still looking at him, she rose and said nothing, but thought his actions extremely strange. While she's perfectly capable, he'd always looked after her when they travelled.

Finally connected, he immediately opened 'Safari'. This time a *Gmail* home page filled the screen. Quickly, he added the word it displayed to his notepad, 'Coco'. Darn, it also required a password. Leaving the home page open, he went to the file of *YouTube* links and began watching the first one: a political skit. The next was similar. All appeared to be scathing attacks about the Australian Prime Minister or other Ministers, with a few speeches in between.

Beth returned just as he was finishing his notes. Jumping up to help her place the items on their little side table, he thanked her and toasted to them and the holiday again. Without taking a mouthful she just looked, waiting for his explanation. When nothing was forthcoming, she blurted, "Well, are you going to tell me what's going on?"

"Um, nothing really…" Before he could get any more words out she attacked, and his mouth was left hanging open in astonishment.

"Oh yes there is! You've never asked me to get our drinks in the Club before. And I've never seen you this edgy either, even when all hell is breaking loose around you. What's going on? What, or who, is more important than me?" She couldn't stop her anger. He was lying and she knew it. Why?

"Well …" He tried to be diplomatic. Oh what the heck. "Well, this is not our *iPad*."

"What?" That wasn't the response she'd expected. "How come? It looks like ours. Are you sure?"

"Yes. Positive. Here, look." He showed her the *Gmail* homepage. "I found out last night when I went to watch a movie. There's no movies or music on this one." He could see she was dying to ask more questions, but he was also determined to get out everything he knew before they'd have to board their flight again. "However, there are a whole stack of files relating to the Australian Government, political news articles, hate mail and …" pausing, he didn't want to scare Beth.

"And what?" she jumped right in.

"Ah, detailed notes on the murders of a variety of important people."

"What? No?" Shaking her head.

Nodding his, he picked up his notebook, "I've made a list of all the files, and their contents."

"You're not joking. You're really saying what I'm thinking you're saying? Surely not?"

"Unfortunately, yes sweetheart. Here, have a look at my notes and check out the files yourself. Tell me what you think. I'm going to freshen up quickly." Looking at their untouched drinks and food, he grabbed his glass, taking a big mouthful.

"Back soon. Have fun!" He was finally relieved.

Staring at the various pages, Beth's mouth gaped. Her eyes were like saucers. This was unbelievable. Surely they had to be wrong. Looking up at Derek as he returned with two more glasses of wine, "I agree. But I truly hope we're both wrong. So what do we do now?" And, as an afterthought, "Do you think this Coco may have ours? This happened at security, didn't it?"

Bending down, Derek kissed her tenderly, "Yes lovely, I'm sure it happened at security, and I'm hoping the owner has ours. In the meantime, I think we should just keep it to ourselves and wait till we're at Don's. When the kids aren't around I'll discuss it with him."

"Good thinking Maxwell Smart," she winked.

"Thank you my lovely 99." And they clinked glasses.

"I'm worried we may not get our *iPad* back if we hand this in to the authorities. They won't really care. This is probably so minor in their daily work. Anyway, Don will know best, I'm sure. Let's just relax for now. I've hardly had any sleep yet." Derek confessed.

Filling her in on the details of the various files and his thoughts, she added her few comments. "So, what do you reckon the password might be?"

Pursing his lips in thought, "Maybe murder?" he tried it. "Politics? ... Assassination? ... Writer? ... Oh I give up. What do you think?"

Hands poised, she quickly typed 'Chanel'.

"Flight QF2 to Sydney is now boarding at Gate 30," screeched the Club intercom just as the email page began loading. Pausing, they looked at each other and the screen; still blank, apart for the loading bar telling them it was only a quarter way through. The more they glared at it the less it seemed to move. So frustrating. Handing the *iPad* to Derek, Beth picked up her handbag. The loading bar had hardly moved when the second announcement came over the intercom. Knowing they had a long walk ahead, they proceeded towards the main doors and their gate. A short way down the hallway they lost the connection. Even though disappointed, Derek was the happiest he'd been since finding the *iPad* wasn't theirs. Turning to Beth, he smiled. "You are the clever one, aren't you?"

"Just a hunch. Maybe looking at all those perfumes before paid off." She flashed him a cheeky grin. Placing the *iPad* back in Beth's bag, they picked up the pace, making the gate in plenty of time for the security checks on liquids, before walking down to their plane.

Settled once again, Derek made a few more notes before picking up his book, but truthfully his mind was still on the *iPad* and its contents. Glancing across, Beth caught his look and winked. Yes, they made a good team in more ways than one.

7. DECISIONS

London, 30 November 2011

Bloody computers. Just like men, great functioning capability but when you need them the most they can't perform, or totally let you down. Unreliable things. At this eleventh hour she just didn't need the added hassles, or expense. Her mind was filling with every despicable word imaginable, and more that probably hadn't even been invented yet.

Gritting her teeth, fingertips firmly behind the laptop lid, she slammed it down with such a force it almost bounced off the desk. Storming over to the window, arms crossed, she looked out at the rain bombarding the glass, causing it to creak and groan from the focus. Teetering on the verge of tears, she couldn't help but think how true – it never rains, but pours.

Pulling herself together, she tried to focus. She'd just lost over six months worth of work, years of research files, plus the material required for her next twenty-four hour deadlines. It was a nightmare. While some stuff was backed up on thumb drives, and there were a few hard copies around, she'd not backed anything up for the past month. She'd been on such a roll she'd just kept churning it out and hadn't worried about anything else. Cursing her own stupidity, she needed to think who could help her here in London. At home in Australia it wouldn't be such a problem.

Frantically tearing open all the cupboards, she finally spied the huge telephone directory tossed in the corner of the hall closet, almost obliterated by the pile of boots and runners. Lifting it with both hands and giving it a good shake, it looked pathetic in its crumpled form, but it was now her only tool for hopefully finding a computer service guy. She flipped through the creased pages – computer repairs/service. Flattening the page, her eyes followed her finger. All had similar names, certainly no creativity. Spying a couple nearby, their ads weren't big or flashy either. Picking up the phone, she dialled the first one.

"Good afternoon, London Notebook Repairs, how can we help you?" a young male chirped in crisp Indian accented English.

"Hi, your ad says you look after Apple products?"

"That's correct, Ma'am."

"Well, my Apple MacBook has just died."

"Can you tell me exactly what happened?"

"Everything's been fine till just a few minutes ago. I went to save and it just froze. I hit shutdown and restart, but absolutely nothing. Totally blank. It's just not rebooting. Could you possibly have a look if I brought it straight round? It's really urgent. I've got heaps of work I need on it ... " Pausing for breath, she realised she was being unreasonable. "Oh, I'm sorry, I know everyone probably says that, but I really do have deadlines. Plus I'm flying out in three days time. I'm just in panic mode right now, as I also don't know anyone in London who could help, or I could even borrow a computer from."

He must have believed her. "I'm open till six this evening. Bring it round and we'll see what we can do. My name's Krishna. You are ... ?"

"Coco. Thanks Krishna, you're a lifesaver! See you soon."

"No promises. I'll look at it when you get here. Goodbye."

Her heart skipped with hope as she gathered all the bits and pieces into her computer bag, including thumb drives, just in case he could backup her stuff. He sounded like a nice guy. Tying a scarf firmly around her neck, and pulling on her coat and gloves, she raced out, slamming the apartment door behind her, only to reopen it a few seconds later to grab her large umbrella.

It was torrential outside. London was displaying its wintery best. She'd been equally as miserable just thirty minutes earlier. Now, charging headlong, her steps had purpose, pinning all her hopes on this Krishna.

Rounding the corner she spied an Apple logo and bright red letters 'London Notebook Repairs' heralding his shop front on the other side. Crossing over and opening the door, it chimed her entrance. There was no receptionist, or if there was they weren't around. Waiting patiently, she began looking at the new computers and other gadgets in the glass display case. Her MacBook was four years old; maybe she should look at upgrading? The new ones were much sleeker and lighter looking. Reasonably priced as well, but an expense she really didn't need at present.

"Hello, can I help you?" A male voice interrupted her thoughts.

"Hi, I'm Coco, I called a little while ago. Are you Krishna?"

"Yes. Hello Coco, call me Kriz. Please can I see your computer?"

Placing the bag on the shop counter, she handed it over. "Please? I hope it's nothing too serious. It's my life."

"As I said before I will see, but I'm not God. Although many clients think I am." Smiling at his own joke, she admired his smooth coffee coloured skin and kind face. "I may be a while. Do you want to come back later?"

"No." She said a little too quickly. "If it's ok, I'd rather wait. Without my computer I really can't do anything."

"Well, take a seat then." As he disappeared into the back room she resumed perusing the various new items, seriously hoping she wouldn't have to buy anything.

Staring out at the depressing weather, she saw some people scurrying for cover, while those too close to the overflowing gutters were being splashed by passing cars. She was glad to be going home in a few days. Why do all her friends think that working overseas is exciting? Living out of a suitcase for weeks, sometimes even months on end, the varying climates, and no real friends or family around isn't all that wonderful. Sure you get used to it, even skilled at packing, and with email, *FaceBook* and *Skype* it's easy to keep in touch – when your computer was working, that is. She really wondered how her bosses used to operate without all this technology at their fingertips. Probably the only drawback work-wise was that it made everything almost instantaneous, so there were no excuses for missing a deadline, or not getting that scoop.

Noticing an Oriental mother drag her child swiftly to the safety of the other side of the footpath, just missing a wave of water from a passing car, it reminded her of her own family, and also how cosmopolitan London had become.

Born in Lebanon, her family had emigrated to Australia when she was five. Naturally she enjoyed the freedom of growing up in such a wonderful country. Surrounded by spirited and independent girlfriends, she'd followed suit, even officially changing her name at seventeen, from Ghaydaa Mazari to Coco Martinez. As far back as she could remember her friends had nicknamed her Coco, her own name being too difficult to pronounce. With her dark hair and fine features they reckoned she looked like Coco Chanel, so it had stuck.

However, she had disappointed her parents on many levels. While still a Muslim, she no longer seriously practiced her faith; then she'd become a journalist straight after leaving school, changed her name, took to wearing strapless tops, short skirts, plus drinking alcohol, even preferring travel and work to marriage. She'd turned down their prearranged proposals, and now at twenty-nine they feared she'd never find a suitable husband, or have a family. Personally, she didn't even care about marriage, or children. But she did love her family, even her two older brothers and their children, despite the fact that none of them fully understood her.

She was good at her job, and enjoyed the variety it brought, thriving on the travel, particularly being able to live in and learn about other countries and cultures. With a multitude of friends around the world, she had several 'home' bases – New York, Los Angeles, Paris, and Canberra, Australia with Jonathon.

Kriz's voice interrupted her thoughts. "Do you want the good news or the bad news?" Turning, he had a supercilious grin across his face, as if half teasing her.

"Naturally the good news."

"Ahh, now that is probably not want you want to hear, but as you chose this first ... the good news is I can fix your computer." Her eyes widened while letting out a sigh of relief. He continued, "But the bad news is I doubt that I can recover all your files."

Her shoulders sagged. Bummer. "Oh well. I do appreciate you looking at it so quickly. What do we need to do now? Will it take long, and how much?"

"You ask some valid questions, but unfortunately I cannot fully answer all yet. I do not have the part here to fix your computer. I will need to make some phone calls. Also the cost. I am not sure, but I think between £400 – £700."

Registering the shocked look that flashed across her face and the gaping mouth, he quickly added, "But it may be less. I really don't know for sure. If you give me your telephone number I can call you when I know for sure?"

"Yes, ok ... that would be good. Thank you." Numbly, she wrote down her name and number. Just what she didn't need. Gosh, from the prices in the display case, she could have a new computer for a bit more than that. She looked up from the paper, "What about one of the new ones over here? What would I be looking at?"

"The new *MacBooks* range from £700 – £1,400." He noted her quizzical look and pursed lips, "Maybe something cheaper would suit? What about the new *iPad2*? They're light, easy to use and much cheaper – half the price at £350. I can transfer any recoverable files, and do a setup for you for no additional cost."

Softly, she bit her index finger in thought, "What do you think is best for me? I really don't know much about these *iPads*."

"Well, they can do just about everything your MacBook does, except the keypad is on the screen. Do you use an *iPhone*?"

"Yes."

"Well it's like a larger version of that. You can synchronise your *iPhone* and *iPad* too."

Her faced brightened for the first time since entering his

shop. Opening the display case he pulled one out and placed it on the countertop. Grabbing a brochure from the display stand, he opened it, pointing out and demonstrating the various details.

Neat, light, compact and fast ... very nice indeed. Clever. Deliberating – but it didn't solve the immediate problem of her lost work, or the added expense, but she could begin working almost immediately.

"When will you know about my computer?"

"Hopefully tomorrow lunchtime at the latest."

Looking at her watch, it was now three-thirty. He closed at six.

"Would you be able to set up the *iPad* with my stuff by tonight?"

"I'm not sure, but I could try for you."

Still debating, either way she probably wouldn't have anything to work with until tomorrow. She may as well wait, rather than waste money she didn't really have, or care to part with, at present.

"Ok. Can you please let me know as soon as possible about my computer and the cost? And can I leave you these thumb drives also? If I decide on the *iPad* could you please load these on to it along with anything from my computer?"

"No problem ma'am. I will call you when I have a cost for you. Have a pleasant afternoon."

"Thank you Kriz ... thank you for looking at it so quickly, I really appreciate it. You have been a huge help. Talk to you tomorrow. Bye." Shaking hands, she walked out still fuzzy minded on what to do, plus the fact she could do nothing more tonight. It was times like this that she missed her friends the most, and now with no computer she couldn't even Skype them. While she could Skype on her *iPhone* it wasn't the same. You had to put the phone to your ear to hear them properly. Not worth the bother unless one happened to call her. She'd moan in silence about her woes. Thankfully there was some nice wine at home that would warm her despondent soul.

Slouched back in the large armchair, halfway though the

second glass of red; the shrill ring of the phone interrupted her melancholy thoughts.

"Hello."

"Good evening. Is this Coco?"

"Yes. Kriz?" Recognising his accent she sat upright, noticing the clock displaying 17:58. Heart pounding strongly in her chest, hopefully he had some good news. Not wanting to jinx it she waited for him.

"I have the price regarding your computer. I can obtain the part by tomorrow afternoon and have it ready for you Friday morning. The total cost will be £650. What would you like me to do?"

Weighing it up, she still wasn't sure. "Do you think it is worthwhile repairing, Kriz? Truthfully please. If you were in my shoes with not a lot of spare cash for this sort of thing, would you fix the old computer or buy a new *iPad*?"

"That's not a fair question. It is difficult. For me I would have both. But I would use both too."

"Well at the moment you know I have nothing, and it's like having had my right hand cut off!"

He laughed, and then stopped abruptly. She wasn't laughing. He sounded more sympathetic now, "I know, I would feel the same way."

She did the mental arithmetic, "Kriz, if I could have both for £750 I would, but at £1,000 I just can't. I don't have that much at present. Can you do me a deal?"

She could hear him tapping his pen against his teeth as he thought. "I do have a demonstration model *iPad2* I could probably work out a deal for you."

Now he had her full attention. "Really? Kriz, if you can do that, and fix my old computer please for the £750, it's a deal."

"Let me get back to you please."

"Ok. Thanks Kriz." And she hung up. Amazed at herself. One minute she was grumbling about having to fork out any money, now she's considering having two computers. Not that she really needed two either, but if she had another one now, she wouldn't be in this predicament. While her *iPhone* was still good for picking up emails and even doing Skype chat, it was much more expensive while away, and work only paid for work use – having to itemise it all on her return, so she tried not to use it for personal use unless absolutely necessary. Besides, the work that needed doing urgently couldn't be done on it anyway. But with an *iPad* she could. Was this the red wine kicking in? Excitement was rising in the pit of her stomach ... the thrill of a new toy.

Smiling contentedly, her hand out-stretched ready to pick up the bucket sized wine glass, the phone's piercing ring almost caused her to knock it over. "Hello."

"Coco, this is Kriz again. I can do that deal for you with the demonstration *iPad2*, as well as get your old computer working again. For £850 including VAT. Do you want me to proceed?"

"Oh yes ... yes please Kriz. You are just fabulous. You've made my night."

"Well if you are not going out, I will have the *iPad* ready in about an hour and I could drop it off to you on my way home if you want?"

"Wow, that's certainly service. You're a real gentleman and a scholar. Thank you ever so much Kriz."

Giving him her credit card details, she couldn't believe her luck. How wonderful. No big company would've done this. She looked at the wine. She'd better not drink anymore; she had work to do – burning the midnight oil again.

Arriving within the hour, Kriz walked her through the various applications and features of her new toy. Excited, she offered him a wine to celebrate. There was something easily likable about this tall, handsome, dark-haired Indian man. She melted when looking into those dark eyes and friendly smile. She felt at ease with him.

Settling on the lounge with their wine they chatted easily about life, work and families. The laughter flowed along with the wine, followed by some serious petting. The feeling was obviously mutual. Throwing caution to the wind, she let the forces of nature prevail. Why not enjoy it while you can, she thought. This wasn't her normal style, but she was only here for a couple more days. It had been a long time since she'd felt like this with anyone and wanted to consume all she could for as long as possible.

Simply divine didn't come anywhere near explaining her fulfilment. He'd met all her expectations and more. Lying back on the bed exhausted, she couldn't wipe the smile from her face, or the joy from her heart. All she could think of was she wanted more of this delicious dessert. Why did she now have to be leaving within forty-eight hours? Needless to say work would have to wait until the morning.

In the clear morning light their passions had not dissipated. Unfortunately, work dictated they must both get on with their daily life, but not before making arrangements for later. She felt a little guilty. She wouldn't normally go to bed with a guy she'd only known a few hours. She could see he was also a slightly uncomfortable when leaving too. She knew in his home country, like hers, this was taboo. But they were in London and here you can try before you buy. It did make life so much easier, and what their families didn't know wouldn't hurt them. About to kiss her, he stopped and blurted, "I would be honoured if I could take you to dinner tonight please?"

"I'd love that. Thank you." She couldn't wipe the smile from her face as she closed the door behind him. One more bite at the cherry. Yum.

After cleaning up, she showered and Skyped JJ. It was six in Australia, hopefully he'd be home from work early. It rang out and she was dejected. Sending a brief text, she knew he'd get it when he logged on.

Wandering around the apartment, her mind was a whirl. What had happened last night? And he wanted to take her to dinner tonight. So perhaps it wasn't just a heat of the moment thing. Nice. He seemed sincere too. Anyway, no big deal, just a couple of days – very enjoyable if the pleasures of last night continued. Interrupting her daydreams, the familiar Skype video calling tone chimed.

"Hey gorgeous what you up to? Just got your message." Relieved to see Jonathon, she almost burst into tears. So much had happened in the past twenty-four hours it was comforting to have him there.

"So fabulous to see you … I'm fine now. Had a few hassles yesterday. My computer died. Lost all my latest work, or most of it. It's being fixed and will be ready tomorrow morning. I've just bought this new *iPad* too."

"You rolling in the money hon?"

"No, the *iPad* is cheap. Plus this wonderful guy did a deal for me and it means I can do some work today and catch up before I leave."

"Great."

"Hey, just wanted to check that my appointment with your boss is confirmed?"

"Yes, Monday at ten. It's all set. Everything is organised and in place. No worries. But we can run through the details and last minute bits and pieces after you arrive."

"I fly out tomorrow evening. You're still ok to pick me up on Sunday morning at nine?"

"Sure thing, sweets. Will be there with bells on. You've no idea how I've missed you. You are the light of my dreary life!"

"Sure, sure. How's other things anyway?"

"No better. If anything it's worse … hopefully not for too much longer though. But we'll discuss everything on Sunday hey? I don't want to bore you with the lay of the land now; you seem to have enough on your own plate. Just go and get yourself organised. Everything is in hand back here. You know the old saying, 'What goes around, comes around.' Well the clock is ticking …"

"Ok, talk then. Thank you so much. Missing ya heaps. Counting the hours till Sunday. Just take care …"

"No worries. All good. Safe travels. Bye."

"Bye."

His reassurance warmed her soul on this bleak London morning. While the new flame was also going to warm the night, she could feel it already. Making a cup of tea, she began reconstructing the details of the work that needed to be emailed before she left. Today had to be work, work, work. Her own little projects which had boosted her income significantly of late would just have to wait, perhaps taking precedence over sleep while flying.

Jubilant from the night's activities and her discussions with Jonathon, knowing everything was now back on track, she just had to prioritise to satisfy her boss. A smile spreading across her face told her this would ensure she could relax and thoroughly enjoy this evening and whatever it would bring with Kriz.

Having already checked the files he'd loaded onto the *iPad* she knew she'd have to virtually start from scratch. Taking out her notes she threw herself headlong into it. Within four hours, satisfied with the results, she emailed it directly to her boss in Australia, and a copy to herself before something happened to make it disappear into cyberspace again. She didn't want a repeat of yesterday.

Checking her 'to do list', she marked that off and then began the next task in preparation for her morning meeting and interview with Jonathon's boss, the new Australian Prime Minister, Carla Moore. She was the first Australian woman Prime Minister, but with just over a year in power her reign was thwarted with massive internal and external problems. Her popularity, if you could even call it that, was plummeting to a record low for any Prime Minister. It was now at twenty-one percent.

Coco had built a reputation for her hard hitting and honest interviewing and reporting style, but even she knew this was not going to be an easy task. Carla was an excellent debater and a hard hitter too. It could be a battle of the strongest female. A gnawing tightened in her stomach. The last time she remembered feeling anything like this was when she was a junior journalist on her first job, hustling with the big boys. At only five foot one in height and just forty-nine kilos she was a lightweight and she'd fought hard to get in front and be heard. Luckily a fast learner in more ways than one – pointy high-heeled shoes are sharp, and are a handy weapon when trying to keep in front.

Just as she was finishing and reviewing the format, her phone rang. "Hi."

"Good afternoon Coco. Has your day been successful?"

"Yes, brilliant and very fruitful thanks Kriz. You and my *iPad* have saved my life."

"Well I have more good news for you too, I hope." She gasped in anticipation. "I have your old computer ready. Can I bring it tonight before dinner?"

"Oh yes please ... that's superb! Just perfect. You are an exceptional man. Thank you so much. You've made my day, my week, in fact my entire stay in London. We'll really have something to celebrate tonight." Her exuberance flowed.

"Good, um, yes, um, I will see you tonight then ... at seven."

Was he nervous? How cute, she thought. "Yes. I can't wait," she oozed as she hung up. She was having fun. He really was something else and she was looking forward to tonight, in more ways than one.

Looking at the clock ... two hours ... plenty of time. Overjoyed at the turn of events, she needed to celebrate now. Opening the fridge she spied half a bottle of white in the door. Perfect. Pouring a splash into the huge glass, she walked over to the window and looked out. What a difference a day can make. She was eternally grateful to Kriz. He was wonderful in everyway. She smiled looking out the window at the busy city.

Already dark, the streetlights highlighted the bustling crowds rushing to buses, trains and nearby bars and restaurants after work. Traffic was bumper to bumper. She wondered why anyone bothered to drive in the city itself. It was much quicker and easier to walk, or use the usually reliable transport system.

Then she remembered back to the dark day of the London bombings just six years earlier and last year's court hearing, she'd worked both of them. Fathoming how these terrorist brains operated intrigued her. Having covered a variety of their activities over the years, including 9/11 and Saddam's capture, she'd made it a point of researching these groups and individuals. What made other people want to kill each other had initially interested her, but it was now becoming an obsession. She'd met people who would kill a person, even a notable one, for very little at all. She shook her head at how astoundingly easy it was for them to do it, and how much was undetectable too. It was a completely different world that she'd fallen into.

While every government worldwide keeps lists of so-called terrorist organisations, or groups, and the people involved, there are thousands more once you start digging, including many one-man bands, or lone wolves as they're more commonly known. These people often commit more violent acts than the groups. While they claim to follow a movement or ideology, they are not under anyone's command, and therefore do whatever they feel is necessary without much thought or logic. In the course of her various investigations during the past few years, she'd actually met some of these people.

Only a few months ago she'd covered the horrific car bomb attack in Oslo, in which eight people had died, and the subsequent shooting at a summer camp thirty-five kilometres west of the city, resulting in sixty-nine young deaths. Unbelievably, all created by just one man. The thought sickened her. Because of her own background, she'd effortlessly managed to secure the confidence of many of these people. Her reporting had always been factual, always managing to keep her emotions aside. Little did these people know that when she was able to do more in-depth interviews, it was normally for her and not her boss. Amazingly they spilled the beans easily, thinking they would gain more notoriety.

Glancing at the wall clock, 18:25. Darn, where had the time gone? She'd wanted to look her best for Kriz, now it would be a rush.

She was still struggling with her unruly dark, shoulder length, curly hair, when the doorbell chimed. Giving herself the once over in the mirror – she'd have to do. Opening the front door, all she could see was the mass of red roses Kriz was holding in front of his face. Smiling broadly, he handed them to her and kissed her cheeks. Stopping him on the third pass, she gave him a proper kiss and whispered in his ear. "Thank you, they're gorgeous – like you."

Walking towards the kitchen, she offered him a drink.

"That would be nice, thank you. Our booking is for seven forty-five, but it is only ten minutes away," he said happily. "Here's your old MacBook too. It's running beautifully, and I loaded the same rescued files back on it, plus what was on your thumb drives. So your *iPad* and computer have the same things – apart from what you did today of course."

"Hey, that's wonderful. I so appreciate all your efforts. You've been a miracle worker," truthfulness oozing from her voice.

Handing him a white wine, she perched herself on the other bar stool, indicating he help himself to the small bowl of fresh olives and sliced spicy sausage on the platter.

"Thank you my knight." She winked, clinking glasses.

"The pleasure is all mine," he smiled, and she knew he honestly meant it.

8. HOMEWARD BOUND

As Coco settled into her premium economy seat, she couldn't help thinking how much she enjoyed flying in the Airbus A380. For such a large aircraft they were so quiet and more spacious than the Boeing 747s. The ease of entry and exit was fabulous with different doors for each class. People from other areas couldn't wander through either. It was a wonderful design and definitely her preference for flights home – if possible.

The waft of dinner had her taste buds juicing, but she knew it wouldn't be as good as last night, or today with Kriz. What a whirlwind the last few days had been. He was intelligent, witty, charming, sexy, and best of all, single. She smiled, had she hit the jackpot this time? He seemed keen to keep in touch and was more than excited at her return in January. This also gave her something extra to look forward to.

The late evening and long lazy morning with him had left her weary, but ever so happy. She was walking on air. Kicking off her shoes and tucking them under the seat, she languished in the memories, deciding she'd catch up on some sleep straight after dinner and work later. After all, this work was her private project. Everything else was sorted.

Several hours later when Coco woke, all was quiet and in relative darkness. Peering around, there were a few flickering lights from the TV screens behind her. How long had she been asleep? She pressed the reading light briefly and checked her watch – nearly seven hours. That was the best sleep she'd had in ages. Stretching, she walked to the toilet and galley. Returning with a wine and snacks, she was still undecided whether to read, write, watch a movie, or go back to sleep after this. Turning the reading light on she opened her computer bag. The new *iPad* was certainly much lighter than her MacBook. She'd packed the latter into her check-in luggage instead.

While folding the blue leather cover back and standing it on her tray table, the screen illuminated. Scanning the symbols, her manicured index finger tapped 'Pages'. Taking a mouthful of wine and glancing back, her finger was poised to open the file. Her mouth dropped in wonder. It was empty. Not possible, she'd been working on the file just twenty-four hours earlier. Fear gripped her mind. Oh no, don't do this please, not now. She couldn't have lost it all again. She frantically opened other folders. Maybe she'd accidently saved it elsewhere. But there were no files anywhere, and she'd had heaps in there. They couldn't just disappear overnight. Why did technology do this to her?

Tapping the movie folder revealed around thirty titles. Picking it up with both hands, she feverishly turned it around, even upside down. Initial shock and surprise gave way to a horrifying reality. This wasn't her *iPad*. She'd never loaded any movies. So, where the hell was hers? What had happened? Moreover, when had someone switched them and why?

Her heart thumped hard against her chest, her eyes widened and mouth dried. Her mind ran wild. Fighting the hysteria building within, she swallowed hard, trying to think what she should do. It was unfathomable why anyone would want to take her new *iPad*. While there wasn't much on it, realization of what was, beamed like a lighthouse through the fog in her mind. Oh no, surely her recent contacts wouldn't have wanted it? Desperation attacked. But what could she do on the plane? Nothing.

Taking a huge gulp of wine and staring at the seatback in front of her, what was it that Kriz had mentioned about setting up a 'thing' for finding your *iPad* if misplaced? Searching amongst the misty memories she couldn't remember. Darn. Taking another gulp she finished the wine, and closed her eyes tightly trying to will back what he'd told her.

9. X = CE

Sydney, 22 November 2011

Tapping away at the computer on the old wooden desk in the corner of his musty bedsit, Vishnu knew this work would be his saviour. Smiling, he knew he would be set for life, well hopefully. Perhaps he'd even be hailed a hero around the world. He could feel it in his bones.

Standing up from the rusting metal chair, he peered through the cracked glass window to the lane below. There was a couple having a quickie against the redbrick graffiti wall beside a sole rubbish skip. They thought this gave them a shield from the hustle and bustle of main street traffic, just a few feet away. Welcome to Sydney's King's Cross. The words of his landlord, echoed in his head.

He glanced around his tiny room. A single, wrought iron frame bed, covered in a thin grey cotton blanket, lay against the yellowing wallpapered wall. The small white chipboard bedside table next to it was stained and covered in cigarette burns, a remnant of previous tenants. An old wooden wardrobe, missing a door, was in the other corner, and the brown rolled-armed lounge chair he'd found in the lane a few weeks earlier completed the picture. This is what he'd called home for the past eighteen months. Inside, it looked no better than many of the poorer houses at home, but the difference was this was Australia, and outside it offered so much more than India for him. He was grateful. Although it had been difficult working several jobs, he knew with hard work and perseverance he would become someone of importance, with a much better lifestyle. He had plans and they were now beginning to blossom.

When he'd first arrived in Australia, his days had begun at four each morning, in the dark, sweeping and hosing the streets around King's Cross. From eight, he'd worked as a storeman for Woolworths supermarket until four in the afternoon, and in the evenings from five to ten he delivered pizzas. They were menial jobs, especially for an honours Science graduate, and a qualified chemist in his own country, but it brought in money that he could send home to his family.

His qualifications had initially meant little here in Australia, mostly because he had minimal experience and was not a citizen, which limited his opportunities. However, having recently become an Australian citizen had changed things. Life was looking up for him and much quicker than it would have back in India. This latest venture had really kick-started his brain cells again and he was enjoying the challenge.

Seven months ago while delivering half a dozen pizzas to a penthouse at Potts Point, the gentleman had asked him about his university studies. Revealing he was a qualified chemist and scientist, and after a few more questions, a sizeable tip and business card had been thrust into his hand. "Call me tomorrow at ten."

Looking at the card on his desk now, Mr Mitchell Sinclair had made him an unbelievable life-changing offer. As Managing Director of ChemThorpe pharmaceutical company, during the lengthy discussions that following afternoon, he'd asked Vishnu to join his fledgling scientific team. While his work permit was being verified and cleared, he'd given Vishnu a folder of reports to read, to familiarise himself with company policies, products and Australian regulations and procedures.

Two weeks later he'd begun working at ChemThorpe. The company was young, the multi-cultural staff vibrant and enthusiastic – a non-threatening melting pot of wisdom and creativity. ChemThorpe was going places, and he was excited to be a part of it.

Vishnu had continued doing his cleaning and pizza jobs and had changed to stacking shelves at Woolworths. They had been very understanding when he'd told them about his new daytime job. His Asian boss suggesting he could come in at varying hours and some weekends to stack shelves instead, keeping the door open for him in case the job didn't work out. It was easy, so he'd continued at Woolworths.

He would often bring ChemThorpe work home too. His mind never stopped. So he was thankful for a fast internet connection and his trusty laptop, his one large outlay after first arriving in Sydney. His MacBook Air was his lifeline to family, friends, the world and now research for work. He couldn't help thinking, even though his current surroundings weren't ideal, this really was the lucky country, especially for him.

Sitting back at the desk he revised his formula notes. He was excited. His current project was a new anti-cancer drug, one he'd began experimenting with years ago in India during his Masters, but not been able to continue with until he'd begun work for ChemThorpe. Mr Sinclair was extremely supportive and had virtually given him an open palette to do his experiments and work unheeded.

The drug he'd been developing worked by stimulating a patient's own immune system to fight the cancer. It was a targeted therapy, and technically not chemotherapy. Acting directly against abnormal proteins in cancer cells, the majority of tests he'd been carrying out in the laboratory had seen almost instant positive results, with little or no side effects. All current chemotherapeutic drugs affect cell division, or a persons DNA synthesis and function in some way. What he was working on didn't interfere directly with the DNA and targeted the molecular abnormalities in certain cancers. His trial results had shown an increased tumor kill rate and reduced toxicity, confirming his instincts – he was on a winner, both for himself and ChemThorpe.

Now preparing the report for his boss's board meeting presentation on Monday, he felt an excitement swelling within his gut – something he'd never before experienced. When coming to Australia he'd been excited, but this – it was something different, a powerful surge of euphoria. If all was approved, the findings would be released to the media and more extensive trials would begin in hospitals on a broader array of cancer patients.

Vishnu wanted to share his joy, but he really had no one to share it with. He couldn't afford the risk of telling anyone outside of work, not even his family in India. At least not until the drug had been registered, discussed, showcased within his profession, and finally approved. But he did know if everything continued to be as successful as proven so far, his future at ChemThorpe, and living permanently in Australia, was secure.

His mobile began vibrating across the old desk, interrupting his dreams. He snatched it, "Hello. This is Vishnu."

"Hi Vish, Paul here. Just wondering what you're up to?"

"Good afternoon Paul. I've just finished my report for Mr Sinclair."

"You're always working! But as you've just finished, perhaps you'd like to join us this afternoon at my place? We're watching the footy and then having a barbecue."

Although Vishnu wasn't into either football, or drinking like these Australian men were, it was nice to be asked. "Thank you Paul – that is very kind of you. What time would you like me to arrive? And what would you like me to bring?"

"Just bring what you'd like to drink mate, and come when you're ready. The game starts at four. See you soon."

"Yes, see you at four. Thank you."

Placing the mobile back on the desk his thoughts turned to Paul, another fellow scientist at ChemThorpe, but very different to himself. Paul was what one thought of as a typical Australian male, twenty-five year-old surfer – tall, over six foot, muscular, tanned, blonde shoulder-length hair and blue eyes. He was either with other similar looking male friends, or had beautiful model-looking girls in short skirts and very high heels hanging off his arm. He was kind though, including Vishnu in many of his outside activities. While Vishnu didn't feel as if he really fitted, he knew it was his own self-consciousness and not what anyone ever said or did. If anything they all tried too much to help him settle into his new home country, over-explaining the Australian way of life and language; often only adding to his confusion. They were great people, but completely the opposite to his upbringing and friends or family back in India. A fact that often made him homesick. Then he thought about his work and the report he'd just completed – he never would have had the opportunity to complete this work in India, especially so early in his career. He was blessed to be here, and for God giving him this chance at a new life.

Smiling, he placed the report papers in the orange 'board meeting' folder and into his old brown leather satchel that he'd brought from India. Handmade by his father, it was very dear to him, something he would always treasure. It had served him well, both during his school and university days, and now for work. Holding it close to his chest, he thought of his family back in India.

Being born in a Brahmin family, Vishnu Sharma had been brought up in strict Hindu traditions. This was attributed to his father's strict enforcing of austerities, and his birth town of Dehradun, a starting point for the many pilgrimages to the Himalayas. His family was small in size, for India that is – only three children, two sons and a daughter. As the third child and second son, normally the family responsibilities would not be his, but of his older brother.

In the beginning this had allowed him to forge a life of his own to a large degree, hence his move to Australia. But this didn't mean he was estranged, or cared any less for his family. He regularly sent money home and as much as possible to help out, often leaving little spare for himself.

While he dearly loved his hometown of Dehradun in the foothills of the Himalayas, it was small. With just ten thousand people it was more of a tourist centre now, for both pleasure and pilgrimage. There were no scientific institutions such as ChemThorpe and only small individual shops where he would have worked more as a sales person, than a true chemist. To be a scientist he would have had to work away in a major town, and only as an assistant for many years, even decades, before being able to take on his own work.

Being the smartest in the family, his father had had high hopes for him. He'd thought Vishnu would never deviate from his religion and would help to support the family. While initially it was a shock, and against his father's religious beliefs when he'd announced that he wanted to leave India to live and work in Australia, his father had finally admitted that he would have better prospects there, and hence his family would also benefit. Especially since his elder brother had married a girl from a lower, and different caste.

His older brother Hemanth, had always been an average student, initially intent on following in his father's footsteps by becoming a teacher. However, during his studies he'd fallen in love with the daughter of a provisional storeowner. Being from another caste he'd kept the affair secret. When he'd failed his final teaching exams his father had found him a job in a nearby hotel as a clerk. It was a favour, as the hotel owner had been one of his students. It was then that Hemanth had disappointed his father and family by marrying his sweetheart. Naturally he'd been welcomed by the in-laws, as their daughter's husband was a good Brahmin boy. By the time his father was ready to accept Hemanth back into the family, he'd become too henpecked. Resigning his clerk's job as revenge, he'd moved away to work in his father-in-law's provisional store. Vishnu knew this upset his father, even though he tried not to show it.

With only one sister, Vishnu also knew a marriage that included a dowry and other related expenses would be costly for his father. While his father had the option of giving Annoua, now 27, to a less reputed family, he wouldn't do it. So, with the savings and some money borrowed from family and friends, his father had made the necessary arrangements for Vishnu to emigrate to Australia. His father's words resounding even now, "We never want to be there, or anything from you. Please just promise me that you will take care of your sister."

Even without telling him, Vishnu knew that his father, Amogh's major worry was for Annoua. With a son now abroad, it was a lesser social crime compared to his elder son marrying a lower caste. But the chances of getting good family alliances for Annoua rested solely in the Australian dollars Vishnu sent home. He knew if he could send a large sum home soon it would allay his father's woes and Annoua would be set.

Naturally, this always weighed heavily on his mind. But now he could see the light at the end of the tunnel and he was fully focused on making it a reality.

If all went as planned with the new drug development, he wanted to sponsor his entire family to come and live in Australia. Although his parents were now in their seventies and said they didn't want to move, he was always hopeful. He knew it would be a much better life for them too. Maybe one day. He hadn't given up.

His father, Amogh, was a well-respected local man and teacher in the town high school, but his income was minimal. As an extremely proud man he'd always provided for them, and expected his children to aspire to the highest possible educational standards, ensuring security in the years ahead. His father often complained to his mother, Lakshmi, that Dehradun was a corrupt town compared to the holy towns of Rishikesh or Haridwar. But again, he never wished to move from the family home he had struggled to build and maintain. It may be small, with minimal décor and fittings, but it had the essentials, and it was theirs. He owned every brick and piece of furniture, and was proud to be able to provide this for his family.

Vishnu knew their home was basic, nothing like Paul's huge rambling four bedroom, four bathroom Australian mansion, with an expansive garden and swimming pool overlooking Manly Beach. Paul's living room alone was the full size of his family's home. But he considered himself lucky to have such a home in India and that his father had worked hard over the years to feed, clothe and keep his family secure and schooled. They were the lucky ones in his town. Many had much less.

With these thoughts, he had a quick shower and dressed in clean jeans and a freshly pressed blue-checked, short-sleeved cotton shirt. Casual enough for Paul's place, but still slightly overdressed, compared to Paul and his mates. No matter what he did, he never felt comfortable dressed in torn, ragged, baggy or crumpled clothing. He didn't have much in the way of clothes but they were neat, presentable and reasonably fashionable, and he cared for them, just like his personal hygiene. All were important to him. He may not currently have the best living surroundings, but it was clean and he'd upgrade once he'd provided enough money for his sisters dowry and marriage.

10. ALPHA, BETA, GAMMA …

"Get a grip! What are ya – a pansy?" roared Rob, egged on by another half dozen statements by the other guys. Vishnu had to smile at how involved they got with the images on the huge plasma TV screen. While the picture and surround sound certainly made it feel like they were at the football stadium, well as close to, he just didn't feel the same enthusiasm as them. Was it because he didn't know much about the game or the teams? Sure he'd played in the streets growing up, but soccer, not rugby and never in an organised club. Anyway, cricket was his favourite sport. Playing for India had been a childhood dream, but those opportunities weren't available in his little mountain town.

"C'mon get ya act together. Stop pussy footin' around!" The barrage continued, and would for as long as their team was losing. Vishnu tried to look suitably annoyed, but truthfully he didn't care. Draining the last mouthful of juice from his glass and looking across at the guys, he stood, heading for the kitchen. "Anyone for a refill?"

"Grab another half dozen blueys Vish, and some crisps please. You'll find plenty on the bench," shouted Paul.

Sure enough there were about a dozen different bags of crisps strewn on the marble bench alongside the kitchen sink. Picking up a few in one hand he opened the fridge door with the other, only to be assaulted by shelf after shelf of beer – red cans, green cans, and the blue cans. He'd never seen so much beer, outside of a hotel that is. Putting his fingers into the plastic carry handle of a six-pack of blue cans, his eyes widened further noticing the tray of huge thickly cut steaks. Now his mouth was watering. They looked delicious. Vishnu couldn't afford meat like this. The barbecue would be well worth waiting for.

"Hooray! About time!" Greeted him on his return to the

lounge room. It wasn't directed at him: finally their team had scored. Placing the beer and crisps on the large square white coffee table in front of the black leather lounge, he smiled as the guys thanked him. Although their mannerisms were rougher than what Vishnu was accustomed to, they were friendly and accepted him open-heartedly. Standing to the side for a short while, he tried to look interested before heading back to pour another juice for himself.

A most unexpected, but delightful sight greeted him back in the kitchen. Sitting on the high bar stools at the breakfast bar were two girls. One was obviously part of Paul's latest entourage; she was all legs, short, tight white shorts, six inch high red strappy shoes, a tight, low-cut red top exposing perfectly formed breasts, long blonde hair falling gracefully over her shoulders, and loads of make-up covering what he imagined was already a beautiful and blemish free face. The other girl was more to his liking, so he couldn't help wondering what she was doing here.

"Heelloo" they cooed.

"Hello, I'm Vishnu." He extended his hand to each of them.

"I'm Vicki," said the blonde.

"Hello, I'm Ranni" said the petit dark-haired one. "We're friends of Paul's. Just here for the barbecue. You enjoying the game?"

Before he could answer, Vicki stood, "I'll be back soon. Forgot something," and she toddled out the back door.

He turned to Ranni, "Can I get you a drink?"

"A water or soft drink please."

"I've got fruit juice, would you like that?"

"That'd be great. Thank you."

Pouring the two juices he tried to remain calm and casual. "Have you known Paul long?"

"Actually, I only met him last night at the local with Vicki. They've been going out for a few weeks now."

Vishnu couldn't help but smile to himself. Turning and handing her a glass, "Cheers to a good barbecue, as they say in Australia."

"I thought you'd be toasting to a winning game?"

"No. I'm not actually into rugby."

She couldn't help thinking what a nice change that made from the majority of men she'd met in the past three years. Just about every man in Australia seemed to follow one form or another of football. "So what do you do then?"

"I'm a scientist. I work with Paul."

"Oh, I had no idea he was a scientist! How interesting. Please tell me more."

"Not much to tell really. We do lots of tests trying to create new drugs to treat a variety of ailments."

"Not on animals I hope?"

Now that was a sticky question. Was she an animal liberationist? His hopes seemed dashed.

"We have to use mice and other animals first. But we are not cruel." He tried to make light of it, "We're not allowed to use humans straight up. Although I know some have suggested people we should use."

Laughing and patting his hand lightly, "It's ok, I do understand. We wouldn't even have make-up if it weren't for these tests. I'm grateful."

He breathed a sigh of relief, "Where do you work?"

"Well I've been working for Myers, on the Lancôme counter for the last year, but week after next I begin working at Parliament House, in Canberra."

"Oh Canberra, that must be a great job?"

"Yes, that's why I was out celebrating last night. End of one and ... to new beginnings." She raised her glass to his again.

"Yes, all the best," but he was unable to hide his disappointment of her leaving town soon.

"Where do your family live?"

"They're here in Sydney. We emigrated from England three years ago. But my dad is Iraqi, and my mum's Moroccan. I've got three younger brothers too; twelve, fifteen and eighteen."

This explained her exquisite colouring and features. The small slender frame, glossy dark shoulder-length straight hair, soft caramel eyes, and smooth, dark, honey coloured skin. He couldn't take his eyes off her perfectly formed mouth as she spoke. He'd love to kiss it, but that wouldn't be right. No girl had ever moved him so much.

"What about your family?"

"I'm here alone, they're all back in India. My mother, father and sister are still at home, and I have an older brother who's married and lives in another town."

"That must be hard for you. You got any other family in Australia?"

"No, but I'm not worried. I've been very lucky since being here, and my job is wonderful. I wouldn't have had this same opportunity in India. But in England things are good, so why did you come to Australia?"

"Believe it or not, it was difficult for my dad in England. Again, I just think they saw Australia as a good country, where they could make more money and provide better opportunities for us kids. I initially hated leaving all my friends though. It was really difficult. We'd lived in Manchester for five years. It's ok now. Although I still miss my friends from time to time. Internet and Skype make it much easier now. Sometimes they envy me, so that makes me feel better, but I really don't know why they think that. It's not that special here really. Sometimes it can be just as racist. Only there's more sunshine and warm weather to take away the heartache." She smiled mockingly.

"Sounds like there is more hurt than just missing friends here?"

"You're so intuitive!"

"Then why go to Canberra – away from your family? Aren't you worried?"

"Nope. I'm actually looking forward to it. To live my life how I want to, like my Australian friends. After all I'm 21 now. Surely you understand? You're free from your family and their stupid traditions now – aren't you?"

Truthfully he'd never really thought about it. He was in Australia to better his work opportunities and life, not to escape his family. Ranni surely wouldn't be impressed if she saw his single room accommodation either, or knew he sent most of his earnings home to his family, especially for his sister's future marriage. This he'd keep to himself, for now at least.

Not knowing what to say next, thankfully Vicki swanned back through the door saving the day, both arms cradling a large bowl of salad, "Can you give us a hand please Vishnu? There's a few more things in my car … that red Beetle in the driveway. Thanks."

Happily he jumped up, and was out the door with Ranni hot on his heels. "I'm sure it won't take both of us."

"You don't know with Vicki, it's either all, or nothing. And judging by the size of that salad, she'll have the 'all', this time."

Sure enough Ranni was right, the car was full of more bowls – corn, potato salad, a cheese platter and a huge chocolate cake. Tonight's barbecue would be a feast.

When all was set on the kitchen table, Vicki poured herself a wine. She seemed quite comfortable in Paul's place, knowing where everything was in the kitchen for starters, even if she didn't look like she could actually cook. Glancing at the impressive spread on the table, she obviously had talents beyond her looks. "Thanks guys, here's to now relaxing and enjoying the party."

The roars and cheers echoing from the lounge room also meant their team had won: a cause for some real partying. The guys began streaming into the kitchen amongst much raucous and backslapping, reliving the last few great shots.

"Vish, you've done well by the looks of it!" joked Paul, as he walked to put his arm around Vicki, giving her a kiss, he complimented her, "You're looking stunning as usual."

"Thank you," she cooed.

"Hey, you've gone overboard with the sides, they look great though. Thanks special lady!" Giving her another well deserved hug and kiss.

"Ok guys, grab a top-up and let's go start the barbie." Paul instructed.

Taking something with them, everyone moved out to the strategically placed tables surrounding the tranquil lagoon-shaped pool and barbecue area. It was paradise to Vishnu; feeling like a private tropical island, complete with stunning panoramic views across Sydney Harbour. It was Paul's parent's house, but he generally had the place to himself, as they spent most of their time in New York.

More girls began arriving. A few Vishnu had previously met, along with some new faces, but no one like Ranni, who was now talking, or was it flirting, with a couple of muscular, rugged guys he didn't know that well.

He walked to the barbecue, "Anything I can do Paul?"

"Nah, just relax and enjoy yourself. I intend to!" he said, reaching out and giving Vicki a big squeeze.

Paul certainly had the life. Underneath, Vishnu was envious. Wouldn't any man be? Just then an arm slipped through his. "So, where were we?"

Looking down into Ranni's beaming smile revived his spirit. "I honestly can't remember. However, I do remember you saying you're moving to Canberra next week."

"Hey, it's only three hours drive away. You can come visit anytime. And I'm sure to be back in Sydney regularly too. I don't have that many friends and most live here at present." He was reassured. She seemed interested in him.

A couple of girls were dancing to the latest music blaring from the outside speakers. "Would you like to dance?"

Ranni just smiled and put her hand in his. He knew he wasn't a star, but he had good rhythm – and so did she he soon discovered. They moved well together. It wasn't long before others were standing around, appreciating their style, applauding when the song finished. He politely held her hand and bowed, which only brought loud uncontrollable laughter and wolf whistles. Making them both collapse in laughter onto a nearby pool lounger. He felt good in her company: very relaxed. It made a nice change, as he was often unsure of himself in these situations.

"Tucker's on," shouted Paul. "Come and help yourselves."

After piling their plates, they sat at the large table where eight others were already seated. Hardly noticing anyone else during the course of the evening, it passed in a blur of conversation, laughter, dancing, and gentle touches. Vishnu even missed the last ferry back to the city. Having to stay the night at Paul's after Ranni had gone home, he made a dash for the early morning ferry so he could get home, changed and back to work on time.

A brilliant sunrise, as radiant as his heart, greeted him on the ride across the harbour. Patting his back pocket, he had Ranni's mobile number, and a date organised for that evening. He wasn't about to let her slip away to Canberra that easily.

11. NEXT STEPS

Tick, tock, tick, tock ... the huge old railway station clock in the hallway echoed its heartbeat through the laboratory walls. Tensions were high amongst the small scientific team at ChemThorpe, particular those who had worked with Vishnu on the new cancer formula, making it difficult to focus on other work this morning. No after weekend banter or conversations, just intense concentration on their computers, notepads, test tubes or microscopes, in some cases all. However, little was being achieved. The only thing growing was anxiety. This was the first big breakthrough for the team. They were all on edge.

Picking up his coffee mug, Vishnu walked slowly to the kitchen for the fifth time in two hours. Normally he'd have just two or three cups all day, but today it was the only way he could steady his nerves. Cupping his hands around the white china mug and breathing in the sweet aromas from the rising steam, he closed his eyes and prayed – again.

The click of the boardroom door opening brought him back to the present. He watched intently; everyone was in deep discussion and appeared happy.

Seeing him from the corner of his eye, Mr Sinclair motioned, "Ah Vishnu, please come and meet the Board."

Placing the mug back on the bench, he beamed while being introduced to the various members. Breathing a deep sigh of relief, he allowed himself the opportunity to accept their praise and congratulations. "Great work Vishnu." "You've got a wonderful future with us." "Thank you." "Keep it up." He felt ten feet tall. Smiling, he knew they'd granted approval to move the testing to the next phase.

Stepping back into the lab, the team surrounded him with more good wishes, hugs and merriment, only interrupted by a champagne cork popping. In the doorway stood Mr Sinclair, a bottle of Moet effusing a stream of bubbles, his secretary Melissa holding a tray of flutes. "Congratulations everyone! Thank you all for your efforts and excellent results. The board and I are very impressed."

Holding the flutes high, there were clinks all round. "Here's to many more successes ahead."

Not used to any alcohol, Vishnu took only a small mouthful. Trying not to make it too obvious, although he was unable to stop the sour expression spreading across his face. It was bittersweet, and tangy in a strange way. Everything inside him was jumping for joy. His broad smile said it all. He felt truly blessed. Underneath though, he now knew that the real work would begin: the human trials, scrutiny from the government bureaucracy and his professional peers.

Mr Sinclair addressed the team again before leaving the room. "While I'd love to say take the rest of the day off; you know I can't. You also know we have much more work ahead of us to get the drug registered and marketable. The best I can do now is a long lunch, but please be back ready for the strategy meeting at two."

Vishnu could hear Paul organising a table for the team at the local bistro. Sadly, neither his mind, nor stomach was concerned with food. Thankfully, he'd also worked on some future strategy plans over the weekend. Grabbing them from his satchel, he glanced through them, refreshing his thoughts. Perhaps he'd be able to relax a little with the others now.

The conversations were mostly work related during the two-hour lunch with his dozen other work colleagues. It helped ease the knots that had been growing in his stomach. A few of the team were older with vast experience, and their advice was reassuring. He certainly was lucky for the opportunity and the knowledgeable team with whom he worked.

Back in the office, all seated around the large boardroom table, Melissa had the laptop, interactive whiteboard and notepads laid ready. The strategic planning took the rest of the afternoon. By the end though, the three key team members comprising Martin, Richard and Vishnu, each knowing exactly how important their roles were, had task lists as long as their arms. While one major hurdle had been successful, there were many more to contend with now.

Usually only around five in five thousand preclinically tested drugs ever progress to trial on humans. Chance usually dictated that only one of these five new drugs would successfully make it to market. However, being a drug for cancer did diminish that rate by about half – still huge and unpredictable odds.

Drug approval in all western countries is strictly controlled by a government regulatory agency, and Australia was no different. First they still had to file an application to begin human testing, showing all the previous experiments and results. This involved providing details of the chemical structure, how it is thought to work in the body, the effects, and how the components of the compound are manufactured. With the enormous success rates they'd experienced in preclinical tests, they were positive this would allow them to fast track the next stage and begin studies directly on cancer patients for whom the drug was intended. This would then show what would become minimum and maximum dosages. These clinical trials usually involved around one hundred to three hundred volunteer patients. If successful, they'd be expanded to larger groups over time. A percentage of these patients would also unknowingly receive an imitation drug in place of the real one, and be observed for their reactions. They all knew this would amount to several more years work and thousands of pages of data analysis before they'd have their new drug application approved, followed by the post-marketing studies. They were only just out of the starting gate, with the first hurdle successfully mounted. The one common denominator that kept driving them all was the fact that there was strong evidence of superiority with this new drug over any established and existing cancer treatments.

12. FRIENDSHIPS

"Congratulations. I'm so happy for you!" gushed Ranni. "I'm so lucky and privileged to know such an intelligent and clever man!"

Her beaming smile and effusive personality radiated across the dining table at Vishnu. He felt honoured to have her seated across from him in his favourite Indian restaurant, Rajah's on Market Street. The chef, Zephi, was from a small town near his, so they had become instant friends. They always looked after him with additional plates. Hearing his good news, they'd sent a complimentary bottle of champagne to the table. Clearly he was going to have to get used to this stuff, but it was an acquired taste for a non-drinker. Taking small irregular sips, he held the glass so it appeared as if he was drinking more. Ranni enjoyed it though, and the staff also enjoyed her presence. They were in for a good evening. Usually he came on his own, or occasionally with a work colleague, particularly if they had been working late. The kitchen was never closed to him. This was the first time he'd brought a date, or female, and he could see the inquisitive, but approving looks from the staff.

Ranni began quizzing him. "So, when are you going to show me where you work and what you actually do?"

"We don't normally show people what we do. Only Mr Sinclair has ever brought people through."

"But surely you can show me when no one else is around? No one would have to know."

"Sorry, there are guards, and you need a special pass and approval."

"Oh, please ask? I'd love to see you in action," she cooed.

"As much as I'd love to show you, you really have nothing to do with my profession, and just being my girlfriend really doesn't count."

Giggling, "Oh, I'm your girlfriend now hey? Well if that's the case, it should count for something!"

He was embarrassed at his gaff, "You know what I meant. Even if you were my wife I'm sure you would not be allowed into the lab. I have never seen Mr Sinclair's family or friends there, only business associates."

It would be wonderful to show Ranni what he did, in fact he'd love to show his whole family, but he knew it would be nigh impossible. "Please understand, Ranni?"

She pouted, "Ok I'll drop it – for now anyway. So, what's on the menu? They haven't brought us one yet."

"I hope you don't mind, the chef is a friend and he's preparing a special meal for us. It is not part of the normal menu. I'm confident you will enjoy it."

Just then, the entree arrived and the table was soon adorned with mixed plates of traditional northern Indian delicacies of fish alu tikkas, and prawn and vegetable pakoras.

Tasting the succulent cubes of marinated fish tikkas she oozed, "Wow, that is divine." Vishnu smiled – a good start.

The main course would be Bhoona Ghosht, a full-flavoured, medium to hot lamb curry prepared from an old family recipe, and a plate of thali in-season vegetables, raita, and alu ghobi accompaniments. For dessert, Zephi had agreed to bake his luscious orange cake soaked in an orange sauce and served with kulfi, a homemade ice cream.

All went as planned. Ranni loved everything and was such delightful company, even joking with the staff, fully winning their approval. Only one other couple remained when Zephi came from the kitchen, joining Vishnu and Ranni for coffee.

No prompting was required for Ranni to steep him in compliments. "Your cooking is fabulous. I enjoyed everything – so much better than anything I've seen on Masterchef. And that dessert was to die for. I'd ask for the recipe, but I'm not much of a cook really, so I doubt I'd ever do it justice."

Both men were grinning from ear to ear. Vishnu couldn't be more pleased with his first date with Ranni. Zephi was only too happy to be an accomplice as he commented to her, "Thank you for the exceptional compliments mademoiselle, perhaps you can send it in writing to my boss?"

"I certainly can – just give me his email or address and I'd happily send him your glowing report." Vishnu had no doubt she would too – she was fairly forthright – and strikingly beautiful too. Zephi winked at his friend in approval.

On the way home Vishnu wondered how he could wangle his gruelling work schedules in order to see more of Ranni before she left for Canberra. It would be difficult. Sunday and Monday were his only nights off from the pizza deliveries. The jobs being casual employment meant there was no payment for time not worked. On the off chance he blurted, "Don't suppose you'd like to spend a night delivering pizzas with me?" Immediately feeling stupid, he couldn't even look at her as he babbled on. "I'm sorry, I work every other night now – and I'd really like to see you again before you leave that's all." Feeling as if he was digging himself in further, he stopped.

"That'd be cool! S'pose you also have one of those funny cars and uniforms to match hey?"

"Ahh … yes actually, I do. But truly – you'd like to come along?"

"Hell yeah! When?"

"Will tomorrow night be ok? I start at five and work till ten. I will call you after I've started and pick you up along the way – around six, six-thirty?"

"Neat. I'll be ready and waiting."

And she would. He already knew if Ranni said she'd do something she would and full-heartedly. His heart was racing. He wanted to wrap his arms around her and pick her up. But his cultural upbringing bridled his limbs stiffly to his sides. Taking a deep breath in a vain attempt to steady his nerves, he smiled politely, "Good. I'll see you tomorrow. Have a good evening."

About to turn so she could go inside, he was nearly bowled over when she jumped up, wrapping herself around him. "I've had an awesome evening, thank you. You're such an amazing guy. Thank you, thank you, thank you!"

Reactively he placed his arms under her bottom to steady them both. Laughing with her, "You are an amazing woman Ranni. No one has ever reacted this way with me." Catching the quizzical look in her eyes, "I am flattered."

"Good. And so you should be!" Giving him a quick peck on the cheek and another tight squeeze she released her legs and arms, landing flatfooted on the footpath. "Thank you Vish, you're the bestest. See ya tomorrow night."

In a flash she was at the door, blowing him kisses before closing it quietly. The smile in his heart now beamed across his face as he walked back to the train station. If this was love, he was definitely in love with it, and her. What a night.

Looking at the clock at work the next day Vishnu was willing it to be four-thirty, but as usual when you want anything in a hurry, time just drags. Never before had he been so eager to get to the pizza shop. He just hoped it wouldn't be too busy and he'd be able to devote more of the evening to Ranni. She was fascinating, funny and astoundingly beautiful. He was grateful she also enjoyed his company. Shy and reserved even amongst other males, he was even more self-conscious amongst females, especially Australian women. They were so confident and straightforward. Not at all what he was accustomed to. To him, Ranni was different – easy to be with, even though she spoke her mind, it was in a gentle way. Comforting. Reassuring. No vindictiveness. Smiling, he couldn't wait to experience more of her tonight. Just then a jarring thought crossed his mind – knowing his father would never approve of their liaison. He pushed it away just as quickly – he'd jump that hurdle later. If it ever gets that far – after all she is off to Canberra at the end of the week, perhaps never to be seen again. Not if he could help it. But who knows?

Already packed and ready, he bolted out the door right on four-thirty, leaving his work mates gaping in amazement. Vishnu rarely left early, let alone in such a rush. But he was well and truly out of sight before anyone thought to say anything.

At the back of the pizza shop in the staff locker room, he

quickly changed into his dark blue work shirt embossed with the Dominos logo. Thankfully he didn't have to wear the silly little hats that the other shop staff had to. Again he surprised his work colleagues here. It was only quarter to five and he was already standing, keys in hand to take out the next order. No one questioned him, just handing him the boxes, address details and receipt.

Once on the road, he dialled Ranni's number. Picking it up on the first ring her voice resounded, "Hiya sweet one. How's your day been?"

Taken back slightly, he should've expected as much from her. "Hello Ranni, I'm very well, thank you. How was your day?"

"Great. Been organising and packing things for my move."

His heart sank at the thought of her moving. "Yes. Of course." Breathing deeply, "I called now because I am delivering in your area. I am sorry, I know it is early, but thought perhaps if it's not too inconvenient I could pick you up soon? That is if you are ready?"

"Yes, perfectly fine. I'm ready now. So whenever it suits you."

He liked the fact she seemed very organised, another plus he thought. "Wonderful news. I will see you in fifteen minutes then. Thank you."

"See ya then. Bye." And he was left with a bleeping in his ear.

Jumping back in the car after handing over the pizzas he was doubly happy, and not just because the next stop was Ranni's, these people had just tipped him $20. A great start to the evening.

Rounding the street corner he could see her already standing by the gate. In tight blue jeans and a white halter-top highlighting her tan skin, she looked stunning. Opening the car door from inside for her, she grabbed the doorframe throwing her brown shoulder bag on the floor. She flopped on the passenger seat while laughing out loud, "So cute – the car that is!" He knew what she meant and joined in.

"At least I don't have to wear one of the silly hats that they wear in the shop."

She pecked him on the cheek, "No truly – I love it – you look so cute too! A man of many talents and many disguises." Swinging her feet in, she closed the door "Anyway, how was your day?"

"Good, thank you. And so much better now for seeing you. I also just received a big tip on the first job, so it should be an outstanding night all round. But I will not be counting my roosters."

"Chickens."

"Oh yes, chickens – sorry. And you had a good day also – yes?"

"Yes, I'm virtually organised."

His heart dropped, he didn't want to talk or even think about her going away. Not tonight anyway.

As they headed back to the shop for the next orders, she placed her hand on his leg and smiled sweetly. Blood rushed to his head causing his foot to suddenly hit the brake, bolting them both forward. He felt stupid. Apologising and steadying himself, they finally settled into a relaxed exchange of conversation throughout the night. This was certainly much better than his normal delivery nights. They probably also knew more about each other than any other couple on a second date, or even third if you wanted to count the first meeting at Paul's. No other woman had ever made him feel so alive. It was extremely difficult dropping her off shortly before his shift ended. He couldn't help wondering if he really would see her again once she'd moved. He hoped so. As far as he was concerned he'd do everything in his power to stay in her life.

Luckily for him, Ranni was happy sharing two more nights delivering pizzas, enabling them to cement an even stronger friendship. While it wasn't easy to say goodbye at the end of the week, he was definitely confident about visiting her once she'd settled in Canberra.

13. FIND DELETE

Waking in time for breakfast, Coco hadn't realised just how tired she had been. Then reality hit, the *iPad* staring her in the face wasn't hers. As hungry as she was the churning in her stomach negated the pangs. Focusing on what she could do was foremost in her mind. With a big fat zero still weighing heavily, the surrounding pleasant aromas aroused her own need for decent food, so when asked, she couldn't resist, "The oriental breakfast please."

Breakfast not only looked delicious, it also tasted exquisite. The exotic flavour of the prawn and minted meatballs in a soft noodle soup was heavenly, satisfying her in no time. Next the steward was tempting her with champagne. "Why not? Thank you." After all it couldn't make things any worse than they already were. Nothing would be resolved in the next hour that was for sure.

Pausing thoughtfully, she held the first mouthful on her tongue. Kriz mentioned a special feature within the *iPad* that would help find it. There was also something about accessing the files remotely. Swallowing the champagne, she scolded herself again – remember stupid! If she needed her MacBook that was no good, it was in her checked luggage in the aircraft hold. Darn.

Looking around the cabin she couldn't immediately spy anyone else with an *iPad*. Fishing around in her handbag she pulled out the *iPhone*. Checking the time difference, she'd ring Kriz after landing in Singapore. It was her only option.

Before she'd finished the champagne, the steward was there with the bottle to refill it. Smiling at him, she said, "Well it's wine time somewhere. That's my excuse anyway. Thank you."

"There's never any need for an excuse. Plus onboard it's always wine time. Enjoy." She liked his philosophy.

While the champagne may have mellowed her outwardly, inwardly she was still as tight as a leopard ready to pounce. Once inside the airport she found a space against the walkway wall, and quickly tapped Kriz's contact. It wasn't long before it rang. Almost instantaneously she heard a familiar warm voice, "Hello."

"Oh Kriz, it's Coco. Something terrible's happened. My *iPad* ... well it's not my *iPad*, oh ..." she blurted.

"Hey, slow down gorgeous. Take a breath. Firstly, where are you?"

"In Singapore. We've just landed."

"And you are there for only a short while, correct?"

"Yes, but ..."

"Now, is there something wrong with your *iPad*?"

"Yes. I mean no. It's not my *iPad*. It looks just like mine, but it's not mine." This time he let her go – at least she seemed more logical. "I don't know whose I've got and I don't know where mine is, or who's got it, and why someone would want it."

As she came up for air, he jumped in. "When did you lose it?"

"I don't know. I didn't even know that I had the wrong *iPad* until half way through my flight when I pulled it out to do some work. What can I do? I know you said something about finding it when it's lost, but I can't remember what it was. Oh, I'm such an idiot."

"No you're not. Now, just calm down. Have you got a pen and paper with you? Because what you have to do is use your *iPhone* after we've finished talking. So you don't panic about it, I want you to write everything down. Alright?" He was very patient and soothing with her.

"Yeah ok. Just hang on while I get it out." Scrabbling in the large bag and squatting on the floor, her back against the wall, "Ok I'm ready."

"Right. There is a program called 'Find My *iPad*', I set up your details in your *iPhone*, and Mac. Remember I asked for your Apple ID and password?"

Sighing heavily, "Yeah I remember now, but please tell me

what else I have to do and how ... I just can't remember at the moment."

"Well you have to enter your mac.com email address and verify it. Then go back to your 'MobileMe' screen and switch to 'Find My *iPad*'. When the 'Find My *iPad*' message appears, tap 'Allow'. Now you should be able to see your *iPad* on a map. You can then either send a message to it, set a passcode lock, or simply delete the files if you want to." Knowing already what she had on her other computer; he thought he should add the last bit, just in case. After all she seemed rather panic stricken. "Is that all clear?"

"Yes, I think so. I hope so," but really she had no idea until she tried it. It was almost like being blind at present. "Oh why me? Why do all these techno problems happen to me?" She was on the verge of tears and he knew it.

"Hang in there, I am sure all will be fine. Once you see where your *iPad* is, then you can send a message and if someone actually has it they can then respond to you so you can arrange to get it back. That's the best part."

"I suppose so. I'm just so peeved that I've paid out all this money and I still can't do my work. I'm such an clux, fancy not knowing that this one wasn't mine ..."

"Hey stop beating yourself up. It is not your fault. Until you find the person who has yours you're not going to know. So stop jumping to conclusions. Just think where you put it down last."

"You're right. Thank you. You're a gem. I'll call you once I'm in Canberra, unless of course I have any more problems."

"I know, I let you out of my sight for a day and you are out of control again." Both laughed, "But seriously, just take care. And I hope you manage to find it soon. Now go try it. And I hope the rest of your flight is happier. Take care my lady."

"Thanks sexy. Talk soon."

Before trying it she picked up her things and trudged off, thinking it best to go directly to the boarding lounge first. Changi airport was miles long and it always took ages to get back through security and all the way to the boarding gate again. They also had another security check at the gate as well. Over kill as far as she was concerned, but unfortunately par for the course in many airports since 9/11 and she was happy to oblige.

On her approach to the gate she heard a boarding call for their flight. Drat. Would she have time to do what Kriz had told her? She was going to have a try. Logging into the WiFi zone took longer than expected, but it was coming up. There were still heaps of people waiting to board. Following his instructions to the letter, everything was falling into place nicely. She couldn't believe her luck. Seeing 'Find My *iPad*' made her smile. How neat is that? What would they think of next? Then the message appeared 'Do You Want to Find Your *iPad*?' Tapping 'Allow', the screen went blank. Waiting patiently for it to reload she watched the boarding line dwindle. Hurry up. Still nothing. Technology sure knew how to frustrate her. Shaking and waving her *iPhone* still produced nothing. Throwing it back in her bag, she had no choice but to join the last few going through final bag security and the boarding gate. Quickly retrieving her *iPhone* as she walked down the gangway, it was still blank. Muttering under her breath, "Stupid bloody thing." The screen showed 'No Connection'. Gritting her teeth again, she forced a smile and a polite hello to the waiting attendants at the door while flashing her boarding pass.

Back in her seat, she looked at the phone again. Blank. So close yet so far. Frustrated didn't come close to what she was feeling right now. Thankfully the steward was beside her offering a glass of water, orange juice, or champagne. She took the champagne and downed it instantly. "We'll be here for at least another ten minutes so there is no need to rush," he remarked.

"Well in that case, can I have another please?" She helped herself while he stood there speechless. This time sipping it sedately, she smiled back sweetly, "Thank you. I needed this."

Personally, all she really wanted was for the plane to be landing in Sydney so she could find her *iPad*. But that wasn't going to happen for almost another eight hours. Pulling the flight magazine from the seat pocket and turning to the back she scanned the movie section. A couple of new Australian releases and the latest Brad Pitt movie caught her eye. That'll kill the time and possibly another sleep – if she could sleep. She was tighter than a coiled spring. Discouraged. Annoyed. Technology had made her entire last week exasperating. She closed her eyes – please go away – make this all just a bad dream.

As the plane touched down on Australian soil she looked over the instructions Kriz had given her. Refreshing her memory for what felt like the hundredth time, she knew it by heart now. The most irritating part was she knew she couldn't use her phone until after passing through passport control and customs – another half an hour. If she did use it she risked losing it, as they'd confiscate it, and that she definitely didn't need right now. She travelled enough to know these laws.

Luckily, her bags were amongst the first out. Plus, having no duty free, wooden souvenirs, or food items to attract any attention, she was quickly waved to the green 'nothing to declare' customs lane. She was through. Checking her watch, with only an hour before her connecting flight to Canberra, she thought it best to recheck her luggage and get the bus across to the domestic terminal first. The last thing she needed was to miss her next flight.

Pushing the trolley to the Qantas counter at the other end of Sydney's International terminal seemed to take forever this morning. At least there was no queue and her bag was rechecked instantly. Proceeding through more security, she then had to await the bus for the domestic terminal. Just as she pulled out the phone, the bus arrived. Pushing it back inside her bag, she showed her boarding pass and sat quietly observing the airport traffic on both the domestic and international sides, as they crossed from one to the other.

Checking the board, her flight was departing from Gate seventeen in twenty-five minutes. Finally time to try and find where her *iPad* was. Taking a seat in a deserted lounge nearby, she quickly went through the steps again. This time when she hit 'Allow', the map came up almost instantaneously. Her eyes widened. Unbelievable. It was indicating central Sydney. Amazing. It was here in Sydney. Looking around quickly she couldn't see anyone in the vicinity using an *iPad*, let alone one with her cover. She didn't have time to wonder. First she needed to protect her information. She couldn't afford for it to get into the wrong hands. She hated doing it, but there was no other choice. She hit 'Delete'. Staring at the screen it confirmed her action. Looking at the nearby monitor she noticed her flight was flashing boarding. No time to feel remorse, picking up her bag she headed towards the queue forming at her gate just as the desk attendant heralded the final boarding announcement.

Within the hour, the plane landed at Canberra. The sun was so welcoming. It was good to be home.

"Hey sexy." Turning, she saw Jonathon. "How was your flight?"

"Memorable to say the least." She fell into his arms, "It's so good to see you JJ. You have no idea." They hugged while waiting for her bag.

As he drove back to the house, she relayed the trials and tribulations of the last week in detail. "And can you believe, after all that I then had to delete my files too?"

Opening the front door, Jonathon announced, "Well, I have a bottle of Veuve on ice that has your name all over it."

"You're a honey. Now I know why I put up with you!"

"Ha. I think you'll find it's the other way round sweetness," he retorted. Pop. "Now here's to new beginnings, and finding your *iPad*."

"Oh that's right – I'd completely forgotten. I've been so wrapped up in my own woes. I'm so sorry," she confessed. Raising her glass to his, "Congratulations on your new job. When do you start?"

"In two days. Nicole got my job and her new replacement starts tomorrow, so while she does a handover I just have to hang around, literally, as I'm no longer part of the inner sanctum."

"Well, I can understand that – after all you are going to the opposition. I thought they'd have thrown you out immediately."

"Nearly, but they couldn't find anyone suitable to step in at such short notice. And I promised not to spill any beans."

"My interview with your fearless leader is still on, isn't it?"

"Nothing's changed there."

"Great, thank you. Well, here's to a new and better life."

"Good to have you home too Coco. I've missed you."

14. ARRIVALS, DEPARTURES

Walking through customs to a myriad of faces in the arrival hall, Derek and Beth just stood and stared. It was Will they heard first. "Nana, Pop!" As he came running towards them arms open wide. He hugged Beth around her waist, burying his head under her breasts and squeezing so tight she almost lost her breath. She loved every minute – it was so welcoming. Lifting his head she planted a big kiss on his forehead.

"What a wonderful welcome." These were the moments she adored the grandchildren the most.

"Hey, what about mine young man?"

"Sure Pop." Releasing Beth he turned, hugging Derek equally as enthusiastically. Derek lifted Will instantly and spun him around once. "You're a feather weight. We're going to have to bulk you up boy."

"I've just turned twelve, but have grown three centimetres in the last three months. Mum's really annoyed because I'm growing out of all my clothes."

The whole family surrounded them now – their son Don, his attractive wife Sue and fifteen-year-old daughter Emma, the spitting image of her mother and definite model material with those tall lanky legs. It was hard to miss them extending from the short white shorts. "Haven't you grown up?" commented Derek. "You're as pretty as a picture, Emma. Bet your dad is fighting the boys off with a stick." Blushing, this was what she hated most about her grandparents. In fact any of her parents friends for that matter.

"Hi Dad. Mum. How was your flight?"

"Just wonderful Don." Beth couldn't wait to tell all, "I love that A380. We had massagers in the seats and they laid completely flat for the bed. I've even got some Qantas pyjamas now too."

"Yes. I have to agree with her, and you know how rare that is," joked Derek. "But it really is a beautiful aircraft. It is the best flight we've ever had over."

Will had taken over the trolley as they ambled to the car park, stopping only briefly to pay the parking ticket. While only 07:30, the day was already sunny and warm, feeling good on their skin.

Seeing their look, Sue piped in, "They're predicting a high of thirty today and up to mid-thirties by the end of week. So I hope you've brought some light clothes and your swimmers?"

"We sure did. We've been looking forward to the warmth. It's so cold and wet at home. Thankfully, not nearly as bad as the last two winters yet," smiled Beth. "In fact James and Julia are talking about spending the week between Christmas and New Year in Spain with the children this year."

"Nice one – I wish we could go to Spain. It'd be better than staying here all summer."

"Enough Emma. You know we're planning a trip ..."

"Yeah, to Norfolk Island ... thrills Ville Dad."

Reaching the car, Will had already opened the backdoor on the Land cruiser and was lifting the bags in.

"So you really do have muscles attached to those skinny bones my boy."

He smiled, "I do two hours at the gym each day Pops. It really helps. Do ya know I'm the captain of the under-thirteen soccer team too?"

"That's my boy – just like your dad. Congratulations."

"Ok, lets get this chariot on the road before the pay card expires, you lot," Don remarked. "You hungry Mum? Dad?"

"Not really darling, the meals were top class. Real silver service. Much more than we needed, but we couldn't say no. This flight was outstanding in every way. No complaints. Naturally a cuppa would be nice when we get home though."

"Easily fixed then." And they were on their way.

Several hours passed before Derek was alone with Don. Walking around the garden he was busily pointing out areas where his father may be interested in helping out while here.

"Son, can I talk with you in confidence?"

Surprised and concerned, Don looked questioningly at him, "Sure Dad. What's up? You and Mum ok?"

"Sure. It's not us. Nothing to do with us ... well not really ... well you see ..." Derek stumbled over his words, he paused to focus. "You know we got a new *iPad* before leaving, and Charlie helped set it up and everything? Well, the *iPad* we have here is not ours." Looking his son directly in the eye he could see a question was forming, so before he could utter a word, "We know because it hasn't got any of our movies, or music on it. It looks exactly like ours, but when trying to find out who the owner might be I found some very disturbing material."

"Like what? Photos?" Don couldn't help thinking it may be porn or something worse.

"No photos ... just lots of hate mail, political information – Australian and some of your Prime Minister I think, and eh ... a lot about killing people. I've made notes of what is where, but better to show you in private. Then we can work out what to do."

"Sure, let me think what'll be best. And what about yours? Have you done anything about finding it?"

"No, not yet. I suppose we need to report it to the police and then the insurance company."

"No. First we'll check where it is," Don said knowingly.

"What do you mean? I have no idea where it is."

"No Dad, the new *iPad* has a special application that helps to find where it is. I'll show you later too. We better go up and have lunch now." Pausing thoughtfully he added, "I'll get Sue to take Mum and the kids out this afternoon while we try and sort all this out."

"Wonderful. I knew you'd be best to talk to first. Your mother and I have been worried sick. She'll thank you later."

Lunch was enjoyed on the back veranda, overlooking the rear nature reserve. Bellbirds ringing their calls and the loud laughter of Kookaburras competed with the lively banter around the table.

"Ok you lot, Mum is taking you and Nana shopping, and

then down the beach," Don announced.

"I don't want to go to the beach," complained Emma. "We've got a pool here and I wanted Sally to come over."

"Well, I don't mind if Sally goes with you, but Pop and I have a few things to do here and we're going to meet you later at Coogee Pub for an early dinner while listening to the band."

"Oh, ok … if we have to. Can I call her now?"

"Sure. When do you want to leave, Sue?"

"Within the hour, no later if possible," Sue responded.

"Ok Emma?"

"Thanks, Dad," she smiled and bounced off to get ready.

He turned to Sue, "We'll clean up, sweetheart. You get organised." Gently kissing her on the cheek, he whispered in her ear. "See you later. And thanks."

"Just hope it's nothing too serious."

"Me too."

Derek had already cleared the table and was running the water to wash the dishes.

"Hey Dad, we have a dishwasher for all that."

Opening it, Don began stacking the plates, scraping any food scraps into the bin beside it while Derek watched. "I forgot. Must be jetlagged."

"Just wait until they all go and then get the *iPad* out. Otherwise I'm sure the kids will want to play with it." Don turned the kettle on, "How about another cuppa?"

Retreating back to the veranda, Don chatted about his work, the children's schooling, sports and other local comings and goings until everyone left.

Retrieving the *iPad* Derek placed it on the table in front of his eldest son. As the head computer programmer for IBM there wasn't much Don didn't know about computers these days.

Don picked it up, "Much lighter than the first one. I also like the leather cover. It's very classy."

"Yes, your Mum and I thought so too. We didn't think many people would have the leather cover either. Turns out we were wrong. Ours looks exactly like this. I didn't realise until I went to see what movies Charlie had loaded for us. Your Mum was asleep by that stage, so I had no one to talk to about what I'd found."

Opening the cover and speaking to it like another human, Don said, "Let's see what you have to tell us."

Derek just stared at his son. Fumbling in his shirt pocket he pulled out the small pad, opening it to where he'd made his notes. "Here – this is an outline of what was in the various folders." He handed it to Don.

"Dad, there's nothing on here. Not a thing."

"That can't be possible." He jumped up to look over Don's shoulder. "Your mother saw it too. I showed her in Singapore, at the Club Lounge."

Sure enough the screen was blank. Not a single folder or application.

"My guess is that the owner has wiped it clean," announced Don.

"How? It's not possible."

"Dad, today just about anything is possible. Particularly with Apple and Cloud technology."

"Alright you're the expert, and while I don't understand, I trust you. So what do you suggest we do now?"

"Well … no good going to the police with just your notes. They're not going to believe us. They've got bigger things to worry about. And I guess they'll just put the *iPad* in their lost property, never to be seen again." With his thumb under his chin and tapping his index finger against his nose, it reminded Derek of Rodin's sculpture *'The Thinker'* and he burst into laughter.

"What's funny?" asked Don.

"You looking so intent."

"Well, do you want my help or not?"

Just then, Derek's mobile rang, and he pulled it out of his trouser pocket. "Hello, yes …" His voice trailed off as he walked down to the other end of the veranda. When he returned Don questioned him about his *iPhone*. "Can I have a look please Dad?"

After asking a his father one or two questions and touching a few tabs, the next minute he showed it to his father, "Your *iPad* is in Canberra. In Manuka to be precise."

Derek was dumbfounded. "How did you do that?"

"Don't worry Dad, but your *iPad* is in Australia – just over three hours drive from here. You're lucky. My guess is the person was on your flight. Do you think it could have been swapped when you boarded? Did you put it down on someone else's seat?"

"No, it was in your Mum's bag. She gave it to me after we were seated." Then he remembered, "There was a problem at security. The *iPad* went through separate to our other things. After we'd already gone through, it had to go through again. Someone behind us must have had the same one. I think we must have taken theirs … At least they are in Australia not the other end of the earth." Sheepishly, he looked at Don, "What do we do now?"

"Well we can send a message to your *iPad*. Give them your details, and that you've obviously got theirs. Then wait for them contact us."

"You can do that? Yes, I know, yes …" waving his hands. "Just do whatever you think is necessary and explain it to me later, please."

Making a note of the approximate coordinates, Don then proceeded typing out the message. "Right let's get organised to meet the others for drinks and dinner. If we can leave in about twenty minutes we'll get to relax and enjoy the live jazz band before having dinner. I think you'll enjoy The Moneymakers. They're a six piece local group with an excellent brass section."

Driving to the Coogee Bay Hotel, Don tried to explain as best as possible, in very simple terms, the new technologies that allowed him to find the *iPad*, although he was sure his father's mind was still just as foggy afterwards.

15. THE INTERVIEW

Dwarfed, even insignificant, is how Coco felt being escorted down the highly polished marble floored hallway flanked by massive overpowering colonnades – the hallowed halls of the country's powerhouse. It was unnerving. Why did they have to have gigantic monumental buildings in which to decide the country's way forward, or even backwards in many cases. Did it really help the politicians make more informed choices? She doubted it. Perhaps it made them feel more powerful.

Butterflies began fluttering. This was ridiculous, she was normally so composed, very little phased her these days. But it had been quite a while since she'd visited Australia's Parliament House and Coco had forgotten how intimidating the building could make you feel – not just the politicians who occupied it.

Still feeling slightly jetlagged, as well as upset from all the distractions of her technical equipment failures of late, she wished this interview could have taken place later this week, but truthfully she was lucky it was happening at all. Thousands of journalists and organisations requested interviews of the Prime Minister. Most were declined and had to be satisfied with the scheduled press conferences and media releases, or interviewing other ministers and backbenchers to satisfy their needs. So today she was determined to put all her own woeful life and problems behind her, and focus on the important job at hand – an up close and personal interview with Carla Moore.

Whispering, "shoo butterflies" as they entered the Prime Ministerial suite of offices, and adorning a smile in anticipation of a successful interview – Coco was ready.

Her escort pointed to the large brown leather lounge in the reception area, "Please take a seat, Prime Minister Moore will be about ten minutes. Something has just cropped up."

"Thank you." Relieved, Coco sat, using the extra breathing

space to go through her notes and questions. Rebuilding her confidence.

"Hey hon, how you feeling this morning?"

She looked up to see Jonathon leaning over the reception desk. "A bit jetlagged, but pretty good considering." She walked over. "What's happening? Not that I mind a little breather, as long as I still have time for my full interview."

"Nothing overly major, so you should be all right." He talked over his shoulder, "Hey girls, come meet Coco. You remember Nicole?"

They shook hands over the reception counter. "From a long time ago – congratulations on your promotion."

"We'll see about that. But thanks," Nicole smirked.

"And this is the new girl from Sydney, Ranni."

"Pleased to meet you Ranni. I hope you enjoy your time here."

"It's only been a couple of hours, but I can already say with certainty – it's different." Being polite, she quickly added, "In an interesting way of course. I'm very lucky and looking forward to the challenges ahead."

Burrrr. Jonathon smiled. "Ah, the master calls. Probably ready for you."

Entering the inner sanctum, Coco's eyes widened at the expanse of mahogany Hansard-filled shelves lining the walls and the huge desk confronting her. It was both impressive and daunting. The entire scene even overpowered the tall, but thinish frame of the Prime Minister. No wonder she chose bright clothing, like the large black and lime green jacket with dots the size of tennis balls that she was now wearing. Or was it perhaps to divert attention from her sharp pointy nose and brilliant red hair? Coco was now intrigued to know what she had worn for the photo shoot held last week that would accompany her article.

Carla Moore was all smiles. Gushing with kindness, throwing her off guard. Not quite what she'd been expecting from all the stories circulating.

After introductions and arranging her recorder and pad of

questions and notes, they were ready to start. She checked as she spoke into the recorder, "Interview with Australian Prime Minister Carla Moore in her Parliamentary office, Canberra, ten December twenty-eleven." Everything looked fine to go.

"Good morning Prime Minister Moore. Thank you for your time," she began.

"Good morning, Coco. It's my pleasure."

"I realise this is a little late, but congratulations on becoming the first female Australian Prime Minister in history. You've been in the most powerful seat in the country for just over twelve months now, how does it feel?"

Appearing coy the Prime Minister uttered, "I'm truly humbled and honoured in being voted not just by my colleagues, but also the nation, the Australian people, to be their Prime Minister. I'm utterly committed in leading this country I truly love. I'm proud to be of service to the people."

"As you're also an immigrant – do you think Australia should have more migrants?"

"Yes I'm a migrant, like many other Australians today and I proudly call Australia my home. Migrant skills bring a lot to our country and I fully support skilled migration in Australia. However unlike the previous Hull government I don't support the idea of a big Australia through an uncontrolled migration intake. I don't believe Australia should hurtle down the track towards a big population. Migrants, the right migrants can have a lot to offer, especially in our regional areas. That's where we need growth. From the age of five, after arriving from the United Kingdom, I was extremely lucky to grow up in the great state of South Australia. My parents worked hard and they taught me these values, as well as respect and doing your bit for the community. It's these values that guide me as Prime Minister today. I also believe in rewarding the people who live by these same values and rules. I think Australia is a nation full of hard working people … from our troops at home and abroad, our farmers, labourers, shopkeepers, bankers, office workers, teachers, miners, mothers and more. I've seen it in action during the last year. When this nation pulls together we can do great things. Leading a government and nation with this spirit is even more inspiring for me."

It sounded like typical political grandstanding. Of course, she was here to push her agenda, but Coco wasn't buying it. "Would you consider the last year to have been the most difficult and challenging period of your life?"

She was clearly thinking even though the fixed smile remained. "It's been different ... Interesting ... A very testing period. I often wish I had a crystal ball, but even then there's things you can't foresee. There's definitely been some trying circumstances during my first year as Prime Minister. Particularly with a variety of natural disasters, rebuilding many parts of the nation, the election results, global financial crisis, asylum seekers, climate change, carbon tax and of course setting goals and getting on with governing ... getting the nation back on track – focused, moving Australia forward. It's a tough job, but I'm certainly capable of doing it and feel comfortable doing it. I feel I manage the stresses and strains of it better than most."

It didn't take her long to get that political swing back. Though noticing how she glossed over the election results, Coco made a note to come back to that later. "Since you've become leader a lot of people are saying that the light on the hill has dimmed, inferring that the Labor party no longer stands for anything. How would you respond?"

Carla Moore smiled through clenched teeth, "That's a load of rubbish. My party, the Australian Labor Party, stands for the fair distribution of opportunity, and that is what is driving this government. It's what drove the recent budget reforms and the reforms in education. I still think of education as central to my economic agenda, along with the health agenda. All this is driving our perspective about managing our economy and resources boom. And, of course, we've always been a political party prepared to confront the challenges of the future and we're doing just that with climate change now. My Labor Party is moving Australia forward."

Coco wasn't going to get any further pushing that barrow

so she simply returned the plastered smile and moved on. "Eighteen months ago when you replaced Keith Hull you said it was because the government had lost its way. Can you honestly say your government has now found its way?"

Coco registered Moore's glare as it bore through her. But Moore remained controlled and answered concisely, " Since becoming Prime Minister, I've designed a clear plan that my government will be working to and implementing over the remaining two years. We've already done much of this work. Hull's government had lost its way on three issues. One, the minerals resource rent tax. We're now working through this and draft legislation is almost ready for delivery. Two, was asylum seekers. Here we're currently negotiating a transfer agreement. And three, was tackling carbon pricing and climate change. Here my government is already on a very clear path to delivering a carbon price by the first of July next year. So, yes my government is moving ahead on some very important issues."

Coco could clearly sense the building tension though. Hoping to break her she continued, "Since your election the polls have been going down, with the Labor primary vote now the lowest it's ever been, in the low twenties. Doesn't this concern you? And what do you intend doing?"

Matter-of-factly Moore stuck her pointy nose in the air, "I'm not surprised or concerned at all. We've got lots happening at the moment. We're living in difficult times. I know much of our reform agendas are not high in the popularity stakes, but it is work that we must do and my government is determined to do this for the Australian people. Like the carbon pricing ... we're delivering it in a bitterly partisan environment as a result of the political tactics of the opposition. Actually I anticipated it would be just like this. I knew it wouldn't be easy as we pursue this huge reform agenda that Australians are anxious about. Even though the Clean Energy Bill has just been passed in both Houses, we've still got many months of very hard work ahead of us, but ultimately I think the proof for all Australians will be when they live the experience themselves after the first of July next year."

Coco seized the opportunity, " On carbon pricing, do you realise there's a lot of anger amongst the people because five days before the August twenty-one election last year you said – and I quote: 'There will be no carbon tax under the Government I lead …' which you also repeated in the newspaper the day before the election. You said, 'I rule out a carbon tax.' Then because of the hung parliament at the election – the first hung parliament in seventy years, I might add – your government required the support of the Independents and Greens to govern. It must have been a nerve-racking time for you? Now people are saying you sold your soul to these groups in order to form a minority government and this is why you have to support and implement a carbon tax. Surely you can't deny that?"

As Carla pursed her thin lips and squinted, it made her sharp nose more pronounced, reminding Coco of a magpie about to pounce. "I'm sorry but that's not correct." The words hung heavily between them, but Moore breathed deeply and continued in a strong controlling manner. "I have not, and would not do anything I didn't fully believe in myself. Or believe was good for our country. During the last election campaign I talked constantly about how climate change was real, it was caused by human activity, that we needed to cut down on carbon pollution and that the best way of doing that was to price carbon through a market-based mechanism, and that's what I pursued once elected, and what we are actively implementing now."

Coco was on a roll and feeling triumphant. "Well how do you explain this then? In 2009, you said in a national interview, and I quote again: 'I think when you go to an election and you give a promise to the Australian people, you should do everything in your power to honour that promise.' Your Deputy Prime Minister and Treasurer, Dick Francis also said this during the election, 'No, it's not possible that we're bringing in a carbon tax. That is a hysterically inaccurate claim being made by the Coalition.' Surely you're aware that the people are now calling you 'Car-liar'? They are saying we have a liar running the country. How does it make you feel?"

Carla Moore still maintained her composure, even though Coco could feel the daggers being sent her way. "I think you're over exaggerating this. I understand since having announced the carbon price mechanism, we've had many saying they don't like it, or it won't work. However, I believe I have been patient and methodical in explaining to the Australian people that this is the right thing to do. I know our people work incredibly hard. I believe Australians agree that climate change is real and it's the right thing to do to have a clean energy future for this country along with all of the jobs that go with it. I don't want Australia left behind or losing those jobs in the future. That's why I'm pleased the Bill is now passed and we can begin the real work. The money raised by pricing carbon will go to assist households with the cost of living. But at this stage we're still determining the price and what households will get in assistance with the cost of living. At the heart of it, acting on climate change and a cleaner-energy future is important. I won't see this nation left behind. So that's what I'm going to deliver."

Clearly Moore also wasn't going to admit being a liar, and Coco knew the PM also wouldn't give her any pricing details, that directive would surely come from the Greens and Independents with the balance of power, and the real people behind this. "You mentioned being left behind. Who's leaving us behind? America? Europe?"

"Today more than thirty countries and ten American States now have emissions trading schemes. The world is moving along this line. Now I don't believe Australia has to be out in front of the world, but I also don't believe we can afford to be left behind. We are rated amongst one of the biggest emitters of carbon pollution per head of population in the world. To put it simply, if we don't change as the world moves we could get stuck with an old-fashioned, high-carbon-pollution economy and not have the jobs for our future generations. During the election campaign I said climate change is real. I said we needed to address it. And that's exactly what we're doing now for Australia."

Taking a different angle, Coco asked, "With a third of your term down, how would you rate your government's performance so far? Are you happy with everyone's performance, including your own?"

Moore smiled; Coco could see this was coming from her heart. "I have a philosophy that every day I've got to do what I do, better. I've lived by this rule in every position I've ever held all my working life. When I was a lawyer, I used to get up every day and go to work and say, 'How can I be a better solicitor than I was yesterday?' I take the same view as I come into this office every day. To me, it's about striving to do better, each and every day. My message to myself, my message to the team is, we've got a lot of hard work to do and every day we should strive to be better than yesterday. That's the view I take on life and certainly in this job. Naturally, I also learn every day. One should never stop learning. I like to think I've also learnt from every prime minister I've watched during my adult life. They've shaped and changed this job and I've learned from them. But to me, whatever we do in life we've got to always aim to do it better, and I hope I do, and I hope my government does too."

"Your office gets a huge amount of mail each day, both hard copy and electronically. While many are requests, some are of praise and others complaints, but I believe your office holds the record for receiving the most, what can really only be labelled as 'hate mail'… much more than any other Australian government party or any other prime minister to date. Does this worry you?"

Clearly annoyed, Moore took a deep breath and looked sideways before almost spraying the answer. "That's preposterous. I don't know where you've got your facts from Coco, but I'm sure you're incorrect. In this position, as much as we'd like to please all of the people all of the time, it is simply not possible. Someone will always be upset with what we do, what we implement, what budget we bring down. Every government and prime minister before me has not been able to have only happy and contented followers. Australia is a democracy and everyone is allowed to voice his or her opinion and I am not about to say that they can't. Whether it's good or bad everyone's entitled to his or her own opinion. That's what makes living in Australia so special."

"I know it's never happened in Australia, apart from the disappearance of Prime Minister Gerard Green during the sixties Cold War days ... but now with sentiments running so high in many areas, do you ever worry about your own safety? Do you worry that someone may try to kill you?"

Moore attempted to laugh it off. "Coco, this is Australia, not America or the Middle East. Even when world or religious leaders have visited, they feel safer here than anywhere else in the world. Naturally, we still have to take the necessary security precautions, but I have a good team around me and to tell you the truth I've never really felt unsafe or in danger in any way."

"Being in the public eye, many issues from your past are now being dragged up. Of major concern to Australians is that you were once a member of the Communist Party and you have a criminal history... for helping your boyfriend steal over a million dollars from the Australian Workers Union in 1995. No previous prime minister has ever had such a chequered past. What do you have to say to the Australian people in regards to these statements?"

Carla bit her lip. Taking a long breath, she was clearly struggling to stay calm. Coco was pleased, she'd hit another nerve and it was obviously peeving Moore off. "These matters happened a long time ago. Firstly, we all make mistakes when growing up and especially in trying to work out where we want to go in life, with the people we associate and the group we align ourselves with. I made one of those mistakes at university when joining the Communist Party. I was young and naïve. But again we all have choices and it is a choice I made at that time, and then decided it wasn't for me. As for the other incident, I worked for Gallagher and Simpson solicitors at the time, and part of my job was representing the Australian Workers Union. I setup the bank accounts that were later used incorrectly by others, which I knew nothing of. I was in a relationship, which I also ended. I am by no means the first person to find out that someone close turns out to be different to what you had believed them to be. It's an ordinary human error. I assisted fully with the police and was never formally charged with any wrongdoing. However I was falsely accused in the newspapers at the time and that was very distressing."

Smiling politely, Coco focused on a more personal angle now. "Thinking about the future, how would you like Australia to be in say ten years' time?"

Carla leaned back, relaxing into her large brown leather chair, swivelling it gently from side to side before she spoke. "In ten years, I'd like to see that as a nation we'd be extremely confident and clear about our future. At the moment I feel there's hesitancy in the nation's psyche about our ability to deal with major change and facing up to the challenges of the future. So I hope we can overcome that. I'd also like to see a country where we could genuinely say to each other that there was fair access to opportunity regardless of birth or location. Australians are confident, creative people. We don't need to recoil before challenges like climate change, we're up to tackling this, and we will. I want to lead the way for our next generation of activists and idealists for the future of our nation."

"I'd like to continue on another future note ... in September, three days after moving into The Lodge, you turned fifty. You've also never been married. But Greg Peterson your partner and hairdresser lives with you in The Lodge. Firstly, do you think this is a good image to be setting for younger Australians – that it's ok to live with your partner and not marry? And isn't it hypocritical for you to live with someone but also ban homosexual unions?"

Moore became serious and thoughtful, "Marriage is a sacred union and although I am not a religious person I believe in the current Marriage Act. It recognises that marriage is between a man and a woman and that marriage has a special status. In today's world, and particularly in Australia, people are able to manage their relationships how they wish. I'm not telling other people if they can or cannot live with each other or to take their relationship further. I don't expect people to judge me in that arena either. It is my personal choice. Greg and I are happy just as we are at present. We've been together for five years and have progressed. While I have dated a few other men during my life, it is very difficult to sustain a lasting relationship in my chosen career, and more so now. All my life I've been very career focused. Hence we want to be sure. Greg has also been married before and has children. I don't want our relationship to be another statistic. I want to be sure. And although we've never had a fight, taking small steps like living together tests us as a couple. Just like all couples."

This had shown Coco a different side to the PM. She was clearly opening up, so Coco expanded. "No Prime Minister has ever married while in office, and Greg already refers to himself as the 'First Bloke'… perhaps you'll create another first?"

"Maybe, but it is not a first that I'm aiming for now, or in the immediate future. I have a lot of other work … work for the nation to consider first." Carla laughed openly, "Anyway he hasn't asked me to marry him yet. And I'm an old-fashioned girl at heart and believe in being asked by the man."

Coco smiled in agreeance with her last point. Looking at her notes she resumed, "In Australia a new four-part television sitcom has recently aired based on your current relationship with Greg. 'At Home with Carla' has proved very popular, both with television audiences and critics – becoming the most watched Australian scripted comedy series this year. How do you feel about the series, and the fact that it has been nominated for an Australian Academy of Cinema and Television Arts Award for Best Television Comedy Series?"

"Honestly I haven't seen it, so I can't comment. But Australia is a free country. Everyone has freedom to say and do what they feel strongly about. We have some very talented people in Australia in all walks of life. I'm pleased for the producers, actors and scriptwriters and I wish them every success."

"Your communication style has been criticised as being flat and monotonous and is often mocked in cartoons and by comedians, like in the series 'At Home with Carla'. Do you intend to change this, or are you content with your current style?"

Pausing. Moore glared, the daggers returned, squarely aimed at Coco ... "I have no idea what you are implying. Comedians will always find something to mock, especially those in the limelight. I am who I am and I'm satisfied with myself. I'm an Australian of working class Welsh stock and have always spoken this way and succeeded in all I've done. It's never hindered my progress in life."

Coco continued in a lighter tone. "I hear you've added yoga and boxing to your weekly activities since becoming Prime Minister? Is your trainer male or female?"

"I have a female trainer who comes twice a week. Because of the security it's easier if someone comes to me, whereas before I had more options about getting out. I know I can still get out but ... you know how it is. I never would've contemplated having someone come to me before becoming Prime Minister. We alternate between yoga and boxing. I've only boxed with her. She holds the mitts and I just jab at them. It's good fun."

"When you're jabbing away do you envisage releasing anger on one of your adversaries?"

She chuckled. "Nice try Coco. Even if I did, do you think I'd tell you? I look at this training as helping to calm me. I like to think I'm a fairly resilient female and this helps me focus on that resilience and calm to be the best I can in doing this job."

Coco smiled politely, "Well, thank you for your time this morning Prime Minister Moore and I wish you all the best."

Clicking the recorder off, Coco stood and moved towards the huge oak desk to shake hands, but Carla didn't move. Not knowing quite what to do next, she bent and picked up her bag, trying to be casual. "Thank you again Prime Minister Moore, I really appreciate your time. I think it went rather well."

"Depends what you mean by well? You deviated from the questions that had been provided to my staff. I don't like that. You're lucky I still answered." Coco noticed how her entire demeanour had changed – very cold, calculating. "Don't ever do it again or I will not answer your questions or grant you any more private interviews. Do you understand?" The words spitefully sprayed around the room.

"Yes Prime Minister, I understand, but I was just following your line in the hope of extending some of your answers. I'm confident you will be more than happy with the outcome."

"Just make sure I do see a copy and have approved it before anything goes to print. You were granted special privileges, don't abuse them."

"I'm grateful for your time, I know how precious it is. Good morning Prime Minister Moore." With that she couldn't wait to get out of the office. It was beginning to feel like hell was freezing over. Now she knew exactly how Jonathon felt. The atmosphere was enough to bring down the entire Berlin Wall without any help from men or dynamite.

To Coco's amazement Carla did get out of her chair, walking to the door and opening it politely, oozing smiles and cheeriness for the office staff to see. What a back flip. Well nothing surprised her anymore.

"Jonathon please escort Coco out." With that Coco was dismissed.

She turned to the girls. "Any messages?" Ranni handed her a pile. "I will have my lunch now. Have it delivered to my dining room shortly, and no calls please." She promptly closed the door behind her.

As Coco and Jonathon walked back to the front security office, she sympathized with him about his boss, or soon to be former boss. "I see exactly what you mean about the attitude now. She turns on a split hair. I wouldn't have believed it possible if I hadn't experienced it first hand today. Commiserations JJ." Patting him on the shoulder they smiled knowingly at each other.

"Thank you darling lady. Did you get what you wanted though?"

"Oh yes, and more. I've plenty I can build on. She wasn't happy about it. I have been threatened there will be no more if I don't play my cards right."

Reaching security, they took her pass. JJ pecked her on the cheek, "Alright, take care. We'll talk more tonight."

"Thank you so much. Bye."

Racing straight home to JJ's Manuka house, literally five minutes drive in a straight line from Parliament House, Coco couldn't wait to get started while everything was fresh in her head. It was no wonder Carla 'Carliar' Moore was so disliked, and not just because of her policy back-flips. What the Australian people had openly dubbed her was so fitting. Seeing the emotions, looks, light switch personality, masks, and raw essence that this woman had revealed first hand – Coco's mind was spinning, she'd never met anyone like this before.

Her mobile rang, "Yes I've just finished there. It'll be good. Easy. No worries, she'll suspect nothing. Yes, I can assure you of that. Just leave it with me. It'll be sorted … a week to ten days. Tops. Will be in touch."

Taking the cup of green tea to the study and opening her MacBook, she began work.

16. CATCHING UP

"I'm having a great time in Canberra. You'll love it, I'm sure. Loads of things are happening this weekend, please say you'll come down? I so want to share them with you." Ranni's enthusiasm was difficult to ignore. Deep down Vishnu wanted to be at her side too. It had only been five days since she'd left, but one of the longest five days of his life. They'd spoken most nights when she wasn't working late, but even then she'd managed a brief call or text.

"Ok, I will look at it and let you know. Are you sure it is convenient to stay in your house? There is a spare bed?"

"Yes, the sofa has a bed, and it's cool with the others. I've already checked," Ranni gushed excitedly. "Thanks heaps. You're the greatest. I guarantee you won't be disappointed." He wasn't sure just how he'd wangle it, but his heart and mind wanted to be in Canberra with her. Don't they say where's there's a will there's a way?

After swapping with a co-worker and doing a double pizza shift from Friday evening right through to Saturday morning, he was boarding a bus at 0:900 that would arrive in Canberra at noon. Knowing full well he needed sleep, he got comfortable on the back seat of the half empty luxury coach. Never having travelled on a bus like this, he was astonished at the plushness.

Waking when the bus stopped at Goulburn, he looked around to see a huge concrete sheep nearby. Not wanting to venture far, afraid of missing the bus, but curiosity getting the better of him, he asked the driver who was standing nearby having a cigarette. "It's called the Big Merino, but locals call him Rambo. It's a monument to Australia's wool industry. Inside there's a wool exhibition about the two hundred year history, a shop with a variety of merino products and stairs up to the eyes where there's a great view of the surrounding district," explained the driver. "It's all concrete and stands fifteen metres high. Imposing, don't you think?"

Vishnu was awe-struck. "Sure is." Pivoting, his eyes widened, taking in the surrounding landscape of huge ghost gums and savannah scrub stretching to gently undulating hills and vast open grasslands, speckled with white dots. "Are those sheep way out there?" he pointed, asking the driver.

"Yep. This is merino country since the early days of Australia's settlement."

It was remarkable. Such expansive countryside – as far as the eye could see. The huge double lane highway running through the middle of it was virtually empty – for a highway in his mind anyway.

Climbing back on board the coach, he couldn't go back to sleep now, mesmerised by the enormity and ever-changing beauty that passed his eyes. On the approach to Canberra the hills grew sizably, with bluish coloured mountains further behind the few towering manmade monuments he could see, one with a huge flag fluttering in the breeze. That had to be Parliament House where Ranni worked. Very striking.

As the bus pulled into the terminal driveway he could see her beaming face, his waving causing her to jump up and down. Excited in his rush to disembark, he nearly tripped in the aisle, steadying himself just in time. Picking up his backpack and checking himself, he decided a more reserved approach was required. However, he was no sooner off the bus than Ranni's arms were wrapped around him. Not that he really minded.

Ranni was bubbling over with excitement while holding hands on the way to the car. "I can't believe you're here. It's so great. And I know you'll love it. Just wait till you see everything." Her zeal was contagious and he found himself bouncing along with her. He was already glad he'd come, and he hadn't seen or done anything yet.

"How was the trip?"

"Very comfortable. I enjoyed it very much. Such beautiful countryside, Australia is amazing, that's for sure."

Once in her little white Hyundai, she switched to tourist

mode, pointing out all the landmarks Canberra was well known for. "That's the Telstra Tower. We'll go there and see the view later. It's really best at sunset, so pretty. Over there is the National Museum."

They pulled off the Parkway a little further down and she pointed, "This is Lake Burley Griffin. It's a manmade lake, and lots of free activities happen around it. Over there is the National Library, then Questacon – that's an interactive science museum and school kids love it, then the Portrait Gallery and National Art Gallery. Behind it – that long white building is Old Parliament House and above that, like a crown, is the new Parliament House where I work." She was beaming. They got out of the car. "And behind us here is the world famous Australian War Memorial. Pretty neat place, hey?"

Hugging her tightly, he looked into her eyes. "Yes it is very beautiful. But not as much as you."

She kissed him. "You're so sweet. Thank you for coming down." Then laughed. "You know I never thought I'd ever feel this passionate over a load of stuffy old buildings, but ..."

"I have read that they hold many of Australia's treasures. They must be very interesting." He took her hand, "So which do you want to visit while I am here?"

"I hadn't really planned on visiting any this weekend. Everyone reckons you need at least a day for each, sometimes more. But if you really want to, we can do something a bit later. I'd just thought I'd show you around generally first. Then later tonight we've got a friend's party, and tomorrow afternoon we've got music and a picnic in the Botanical Gardens. You'll meet some of my house and work friends too. Sound ok?"

"Wonderful. Whatever you say." He gave her a trusting smile. "I am in your capable hands."

She had a devious twinkle in her eye. "Maybe I need to take you home then."

Restarting the car, she took off up Anzac Avenue towards the War Memorial. It was imposing while at the same time reverent. A beautiful building he thought. Glancing across at

Ranni, even concentrating on her driving she was beautiful too. It warmed him.

As she burst through the door of her shared house in Campbell, "Well this is it. My new home."

"It's very large. Especially for just three people."

"Yes and no. Kathy owns it, and is slowly doing it up. Graham is the other renter. They're fab people. We each have our own bedroom and bathroom, which is so good." She showed him around. "My room is down here. The others are upstairs, plus the computer room. I love this deck off the kitchen and living area. It's great, hey? Means we've all got heaps of space, even when we have friends over."

He looked from the huge sliding glass doors, "The garden is big. Who looks after it?"

"Oh, not us thankfully. A gardener comes every couple of weeks."

He loved her smile and wanted to hold her again, but he didn't trust himself. This was the first time they'd been alone in a house. "How about we sit out on the deck and have a drink."

"Cool. What would you like? Beer, champagne ... ?"

"Just a tea please. No milk or sugar."

"Ok. No worries. Go out and have a good look."

Opening the sliding doors, he wandered out and down three steps to a paved area shaded by a huge leafy tree with purple flowers. Around the base of the tree and along the fence were a variety of small green shrubs and colourful flowering plants. There was a barbecue in the far corner and on the opposite side a love swing. He thought they'd better not sit down there – for now anyway. Within minutes she brought two large steaming white mugs out, placing them on the large glass table, surrounded by eight chairs on the deck.

"Thank you. This is a very lovely place. How did you find it?"

"I was lucky. Kathy is a friend of one of my friends in Sydney. And the last girl was leaving just when I was due to come down. So it worked out perfectly."

Just then, opening the front door, Kathy yelled out, "Hiya Ranni, how's your day been?"

"Good. We're out on the deck. The jug's just boiled too if you want a tea or coffee."

Walking into the kitchen laden with grocery bags was a tall good-looking blonde, he guessed in her late twenties, possibly early thirties. Dumping the bags, she wandered out. "Hi I'm Kathy, you must be Vishnu? Welcome to our humble abode. So pleased you could make it. Now we might get some peace from Ranni."

From her smile he knew she was joking. He stood and shook hands, "I am pleased to meet you and thank you for allowing me to stay."

"You need a hand Kathy?" butted in Ranni.

"No I'll be fine. Just a few things for the picnic tomorrow. You guys relax and enjoy yourselves."

"I'm going to take Vishnu to the War Memorial soon and show him around a bit more. Perhaps give him a closer look at the outside of the 'Ivory Palace' and then up Telstra Tower. We're having dinner up there, so we'll see you at Roger's party at nine-ish, hey?"

"Sounds good. Have a great time and see ya later."

The War Memorial was magnificent. Walking through the main entrance the architecture was bravura. The remembrance wall alone was heart stopping, a mass of red poppies dotted along the three sides bordering the shrine's reflection pool. To think these people lost their lives for the freedom that both he and Ranni now experienced. It was humbling. Pausing, they read some of the names on the way to the Hall of Memory and the Tomb of the Unknown Soldier, before wandering through a few more interesting and informative exhibitions. Walking back to the car park at closing time, he couldn't help thinking it was the quietest time he'd ever spent with Ranni. The entire three hours she was happily absorbing the history and facts, making only the occasional minor reflective comment. Even now she was very passive. He squeezed her hand tightly, "That was wonderful. I very much enjoyed learning that. Thank you for taking me there."

"Yes ... me too. I had no idea about much of that. And to

think we only saw a fraction of it. Thank you. It was lovely having you there to share it too."

She was sparking on all cylinders again. "Ok time to take you up Mt Ainslie just behind us here and you can see the overall layout of Canberra. Do you know it's Australia's only really purpose planned city?"

His eyes were like saucers admiring all the grand buildings and monuments that were strategically placed amongst vast parks or edged by bush land. The circular and geometric road system completed its symmetry. It was like the perfect city had been placed in the middle of nowhere. In fact it had. They were looking directly down on the green copper dome of the War Memorial. Stretched in front was the vastness of Anzac Avenue leading them straight down to Lake Burley Griffin. Lined up on the other side was the National Portrait Gallery, behind it, Old Parliament House and behind that like a crown on the hill directly opposite them was the current Parliament House, it's huge flagpole flying an equally large Australian flag. It was striking. "It's unusually beautiful. I am very surprised. Truly astounded," he stated.

"I know, it's just how I'd felt when Kathy brought me up here earlier in this week. I've never seen a city like this." He could see tears welling in Ranni's eyes. "It kinda makes me even prouder to be Australian now when I see this. And the fact I actually work for the lady who runs our country too. How amazing is that? Who'd ever have thought I'd be doing that? Especially with my background?"

He put his arms around her and held her tight. "Yes it is wonderful. And I apologise for not asking sooner ... how is your new job? Even in your emails and texts you have not told me much."

"Well, apart from the fact it's only been a week, I actually can't say too much." She gave him a sly sideways glance, "You know what I mean, hey?" Now the shoe was on the other foot.

He agreed with her comparison. "I understand. But you will be pleased to know I bought some of my work down to share with you this weekend too."

"Oh fab! I can't wait ..." she bubbled over. "But we've got things planned tonight. Drat."

He was amazed at how little it took to get her excited. It was this spontaneity he loved. "It will wait till tomorrow."

She gave him a loving hug. "Oh, but you know how I hate waiting."

"Can I suggest we keep doing what you've planned for now?"

Reluctantly getting back in the car she instantly changed moods, hurtling down the steep windy road, while he hung on for dear life. Back on the main road she calmed down, driving more sedately. Passing the Defence College and offices she called Russell, they then crossed over the lake and headed straight up to Parliament House. He couldn't help but smile while she drove the circular road around it, prattling on about the building, and pointing out various bits and pieces.

"What's so funny?" probed Ranni.

"I couldn't help thinking ... from this view your building looks like white icing on a green cup cake, topped with a flag instead of a candle."

"You really do have a warped sense of humour after all," she laughed. "Ok, it's nearly time for dinner. Up the top of that tower over there." She pointed to a large hill across the lake and a needle-like structure with a mass of satellite dishes attached.

He was feeling positively cheeky. "As I told you before ... I am in your hands."

"Beware later then," she challenged in return, shooting him a sly glance while turning the car away from her office. Driving across another bridge, he could clearly see the colourful markings of the National Museum, before ascending the steep and winding road up what she referred to as Black Mountain. At several points he knew the outlook from the top had to be magnificent. He wasn't disappointed. It was breathtaking from the car park and also the viewing platform. However, the revolving restaurant allowed him time to take in its full beauty. Especially with the backdrop of the brilliant pinks, reds, oranges and yellows in the strips of wispy clouds streaking the deep azure sky and reflecting in the inky waters of the lake. Just when he thought it couldn't get any better, the buildings and monuments lit up, creating a mass of fairy lights sparkling across the lake and countryside.

The insignificance of the meal didn't even register with Vishnu, only noticing the brilliance of the view both outside and inside the restaurant. He truly was blessed and a very lucky man to be in Canberra with Ranni tonight.

However, the night was still young and she had more planned. She'd said she wanted him to meet her new friends, but he knew she really wanted to show him off. Within minutes they were at a house equally as classy as where she lived. The stunning outdoor garden was festooned with strategically placed candles and torch flares further back in the garden. The music wafting through the air created a magical atmosphere, like nothing he'd ever experienced before. He was captivated.

"Hey Graham, this is Vishnu. Our house guest this weekend."

"Pleased to meet ya man. I hope ya having a great time?" His handshake was strong, belying his slight and lanky frame. Even his smart business-trimmed dark hair was a stark contrast to his pasty white skin, pale blue eyes and studs in his nose, eyebrow, and ear. Add that to the creased, white shirt and faded slashed jeans, Vishnu really didn't know what to make of this guy.

"Good evening Graham. Pleased to meet you ..."

Before he could say anything further, Graham raved on, "Ranni tells me ya a scientist. How cool's that? Ya the first scientist I've ever met. Ya don't look a bit like Einstein though."

"I certainly hope not. But like all people, we are each our own person, no matter what career we choose. May I ask what work you do?"

"I'm a chef actually. Love cookin. I work at Parliament House, like Ranni. We cook for the cafeteria, and also the pollies dining room. It's a living. Could be worse. Anyway enjoy the party mate. See ya Ranni."

Ranni hadn't said a word, until Graham left, just watching Vishnu and smiling. "Sorry about that. He's a little different. I haven't quite figured him out yet, but he seems basically harmless."

He gave her an understanding hug, before they milled around meeting other friends, mostly from Parliament House, but more refined, eloquent, and educated than Graham had came across. Piercing laughter from a large group in the back corner of the garden caught her attention. Purposefully, Ranni made a beeline for them. "Hi Jonathon. I'd like you to meet my boyfriend Vishnu. You know, the scientist I told you about?"

"Yes. Hi Vishnu. Just call me JJ please, everyone does … outside of work anyway."

Ranni quickly explained to Vishnu, "JJ used to look after the PM … her Chief of Staff. But he's now working for the Opposition Leader Adam Scott. Nicole got his job, and I do Nicole's old job in the office." Both men looked at her exhaustedly and smiled.

Unlike Graham, JJ was tall and solidly toned – definitely more the suave political type; cool, calm, collected. No body piercings, just a day's dark stubble neatly shaped around his square jaw line. He was wearing designer jeans and a tailored pale blue cotton Polo shirt that sat snugly around his thighs. The sleeves were neatly rolled up two cuff widths, exposing his muscular and tanned forearms. He oozed confidence both in his appearance and mannerisms.

"Yes, she's a powerhouse … no shrinking violet, our Ranni," JJ commented. "I'm sure the office will never be quite the same any more."

Vishnu nodded. "This I have already seen. But it is a good thing, I think."

"That's enough you pair, I'm standing right here you know." She looked across the circle, "Isn't that Coco?"

"Yes."

Not one for being backward, "Are you two an item?" Ranni asked JJ.

JJ laughed at her naivety. "No. We're just good buddies. Like brother and sister. We went to school together. She stays with me when she's in Canberra. Her work takes her all over the world, so she doesn't really have a permanent base. I'm probably the closest to that."

Ranni blushed a tomato red, "Oh sorry." Pausing briefly, "She's so good looking ... just like a model ..." The guys couldn't help but roll their eyes and smile again at her rambling.

Time passed effortlessly as they mixed and mingled with this group. Vishnu and JJ found an easy understanding in talking about their work and other activities, while Ranni joined a few others nearby. At one stage, Coco joined JJ and Vishnu. "I do a variety of writing for various magazines and papers within the Featherstone Group. It's interesting and diverse, that's for sure. I've also got a few other private projects for sponsors here and overseas that occupy the rest of my days, or nights. So it leaves little time for any life outside of work, I'm afraid."

Although Vishnu didn't mention any of his other jobs, he knew how she felt. That was until he'd met Ranni. Whether he could maintain this pace was another question, especially with his workload increasing at ChemThorpe. It was reassuring to know he wasn't the only slave to work here. Although, Coco's motivation appeared vastly different to his.

Ranni hooked her arm in Vishnu's. "Ok, I know it's after midnight, but if you don't take me home soon I'll turn into a pumpkin. And we've got another full day tomorrow. So come on Prince Charming."

He was happy to oblige, "Lead the way, my Cinderella."

Back at home she prattled on while setting up the sofa bed, "I doubt whether we'll see Graham tonight now. If he's not home before eleven, we usually don't see him till around mid-morning, so he shouldn't wake you up. And Kathy is already home. She's a late riser at any time, let alone on weekends." She gave him a big hug, "I hope you sleep well."

Pulling her tighter he couldn't resist kissing her fervently. There was no resistance. As difficult as it was, he managed to keep himself in check. He respected Ranni, and visualized her as his wife one day. Reluctantly parting, she moved slowly to her room.

Waking early Ranni peeked out. He looked so peaceful. Dare she? Oh why not. He wouldn't be there tomorrow. Tiptoeing out and lifting the duvet, she gently slid in beside him. He didn't move. Propping her head on one elbow, she admired his warm chocolate skin, dark eyebrows and the mop of straight dark hair hanging across his forehead. His hand protruding onto the pillow was long and slender, with neatly manicured nails. But it was his smooth neck, and the few exposed dark chest hairs that begged to be kissed. Mentally complimenting herself on her find, she hadn't noticed he'd opened one eye.

"Good morning my princess."

She was startled, but pleased, "Good morning Prince Charming." She began kissing his neck and chest.

"As much as I love this, we must not. After all, someone may come in."

"We'll move to my room them," she said, grabbing his arm. He wouldn't budge.

"I would love to, but please not here. Not now." Seeing her pout, he said, "Soon my sweet. You are special."

"Ok." She grabbed the duvet cover and threw it back to get a full look. "You want coffee then?"

He quickly reached for the cover, as he only had boxers on. "That's not fair. And yes, tea thank you."

Jumping over, she straddled his thighs, pinning him down as she ran her hands across his bare chest. "Hmmm ..." She ran her tongue across his virtually hairless chest, licking his nipples, making them stand on end, while he tried to protest. Giving him a devilish grin, "All's fair in love and other things."

"If you are not a good girl, I will not show you my work after."

"I'm always a good girl." She said, playfully kissing his cheek, "So you better keep your promise to me big boy."

He knew when he was beaten, so he lay back with his hands under his head and let her cover him in kisses. Wrapping his arms around her when she least expected it, he returned her kisses and then pulled away almost as quickly to lift her off the bed. "It is time for tea please. Otherwise I will be too weak for anything more."

"Ha. False promises. We'll see," she said trudging off to the kitchen.

An hour later, while Vishnu was showing her some of his work charts, various formulas and some small samples of the mixtures that went into making the medicine and tablets, Graham walked in. Repeating some of the processes, he noticed Graham's intent interactions. He actually seemed interested, and appeared to understand it. Proving to him that you couldn't judge a person from just one meeting.

The remainder of the day flew by, before he had to catch the bus back to Sydney. He'd particularly enjoyed strolling through the array of native flora at the Australian National Botanical Garden, at the base of Black Mountain, where they had been the previous night for dinner. He and Ranni talked about many things, but he knew this was no longer a fleeting affair. They both felt the same way and wanted to continue their relationship, even from afar. Distance was not going to stop them.

At 13:00 they'd met Kathy and a few others for a picnic lunch at a large grass clearing and stage area within the gardens. Within minutes of arriving, hordes of people also descended, placing small folding chairs and picnic blankets on the ground, and arranging an assortment of foods and drinks. An hour later, the area was fully covered with people, while a six piece jazz group played on the stage. It was electric. Energetic people danced openly in front of the stage, many barefooted, while others relaxed in their chairs happy to toe tap while sipping their drinks. Even Ranni and her girlfriends had dragged him up to dance with them. Protesting minimally, he'd thoroughly enjoyed it. It was these memories and fun times that would stay with him during the bus journey home and all through the coming week. He already missed Ranni, and they'd only just waved goodbye.

17. MEETINGS

While Derek tried to enjoy the time with his grandchildren and family, it was difficult to stop his mind thinking about the *iPad*. It'd been almost a week since Don had sent the message, and there'd been no response. He pulled his son aside, "We still haven't heard a thing … is there anything else we should be doing?"

"Honestly Dad, all I can think of is sending another message and hope they see it. Can I have your phone again please?"

"This time can you also show me slowly as you do it please? I need to learn and understand how it works. Then I'll be able to monitor it myself."

Don went through the various steps several times with his father. Derek was dumbfounded by the technology. It was brilliant. Very clever, to say the least. "How amazing. What will they think of next?"

"Don't ask, Dad … you can now talk to the new *iPhone*; ask it questions or leave it messages and it'll reply back."

Looking at him in disbelief, he knew he wasn't joking. "Well I'll have to have one then, before my brain gives out to Alzheimer's."

"Think that's a way off yet, Dad. But technology is moving fast, that's for sure."

"You know son, I'd really like to see if we can get our *iPad* back, and give the one we have to its rightful owner." Don sent him a sideways glance, but remained silent. Receiving no reaction, Derek continued. "So your mother and I have been thinking. We think we should hire a car and go to Canberra for a few days. You ok with that?"

"I suppose so. I can't really stop you, but are you sure you want to go alone?" Don was genuinely concerned; "You may be exposing yourselves to danger. What if that *iPad* does actually belong to a murderer or terrorist like you suspected?"

"Well ..." Derek, being a fraction more thoughtful, said "Perhaps they'll just be grateful to have their own back. Besides who's going to harm a couple of doddering old souls like your Mum and I? Surely we look pretty harmless – don't we?"

Shaking his head, Don could only smirk in reply. "Are you sure you wouldn't like me to come with you, just in case?"

"We're not children. I'm sorry ..." he said, catching himself in time. "While that's kind of you, I know you're very busy. Besides we can just tell the family we've decided to see Canberra while we're here this time. That way no one else will worry."

Although he hadn't really been fighting hard, Don gave up, knowing his father had already made up his mind. "Fair enough. So when were you thinking of going?"

"Actually, I have Avis dropping off a car a little later."

Astounded, Don nearly choked, "So you've already organised everything? You're just telling me?"

"Yes, I suppose. Your mother's packed a few things. We've got the car for a week and thought once we've got the *iPad* back we'd do some sightseeing. Maybe even drive up to the Snowy Mountains and Thredbo. It's only a couple more hours further on, and we've never been there."

"Please make sure you call me every day and let me know where you are, and what's happening?" Derek was stunned, he sounded just like him when Don had left to come to Australia.

"We've booked accommodation for the next few days. I'll give you the details later." Derek reassured his son.

"Just take care Dad. If you're not sure, go to the police and seek their help. And I mean about anything. If the slightest thing doesn't feel right, don't stick your neck out ... just go to the police," adding, "and call me too ... just in case."

"Of course, of course. I may be getting old ... but I'm no fool." Thoughtfully, he added "Plus I'd never put your mother at risk."

Later that afternoon, Derek and Beth checked into The Carrington Suites. Placing their bags inside the apartment, they looked at each other, then hugged and shared a knowing smile;

both were adrenalin pumped, like teenagers again on a grand hunt. Not a fraction tired after the four-hour drive, they decided to go straight to Manuka shops for a few groceries and breakfast items.

While seated at a coffee shop, Derek decided to check the 'Find *iPad*' feature on his *iPhone,* just as Don had shown him. Excitedly he said, "Oh my. Look honey ... look ... our *iPad* is near here. According to this it's just up the road there."

His hand was shaking the phone so much Beth couldn't get a clear look. She almost snatched it from him. "Give it to me. Oh ... oh yes. Wow ..."

"Let's walk up and see if we can identify the place?"

"Not before my coffee and cake." She glared at him matter-of-factly.

"Of course darling. I meant after our coffee." Like hell, he thought, but he wasn't about to dig a hole for himself.

While Derek twitched and fiddled, Beth found it easy to relax and enjoy every mouthful. After all, this is how women get their energy to work hard all day, and as much as she also wanted to find the *iPad*, she knew she needed her strength. Though secretly she was enjoying watching Derek squirm.

After what seemed an eternity to Derek, he still managed to maintain a loving smile for his wife, as they set off up the street in the direction of the blue dot on his *iPhone*. He was surprised at how the dot redefined its position the closer they got to the target. After a couple of blocks it indicated a modest white low-set brick house opposite them. "How wonderful is that?" He exclaimed, smiling at Beth and pointing, "It's indicating it's in that house there."

"What should we do now?" he mumbled. "It doesn't look like any untoward folk inhabit the place, it's too neat. But I don't feel we should just head up and knock on their door either."

Beth, felt even more hesitant, "Perhaps we should just watch it for a while ... you know, like a stake out."

Smiling lovingly at her reference, he looked around to see if there was a suitable place to park the car for the 'stake out'.

"Honey, was our apartment facing the main road?"

"Yes. Why?"

"Look there." Derek pointed to their hotel building a mere one hundred metres away up the road. "I think we may be able to look from the comfort of our own suite."

She laughed with him, "Just like in the movies." She pecked him on the cheek. Taking her hand, they strolled happily back to the shops to retrieve the car and shopping. This was beginning to be fun.

Delighted that they had a clear view of the house and driveway, Derek set up a chair and small table beside the sliding patio door. Placing his binoculars, small notebook and pen, plus a drink coaster on the table, he relaxed in the black leather half circular armchair. It was firm and comfortable, but thankfully not for sleeping in.

Beth happily put the shopping away in the small kitchenette, "Would you like another coffee or tea, sweetheart?"

"A tea would be lovely, thank you darling."

She prattled on while making it. "I can't believe we're actually right across the road from where our *iPad* is. What are the odds of that? I know you think I'm crazy, but I firmly believe that someone is looking after us."

"No, you're not crazy," he said, looking over at her lovingly. "But I do know I'm crazy for you."

She cheekily waved her forefinger at him, "Sorry no hanky panky ... you're on duty."

As she brought him the tea, a car pulled into the driveway of the house. Grabbing his binoculars, Derek almost knocked the cup from her hand. "Sorry darling ... there's action at the station."

Beth gave a running commentary of her observations. "He looks smart ... not how I imagined our suspect. He's carrying a briefcase ... maybe he's making the payoff?"

"Shhh."

"He can't hear me."

Irritated, Derek snapped back, "Just let me concentrate."

Derek observed the tall, dark-haired male wearing an elegantly cut dark business suit walking purposefully from the grey BMW towards the front door. Beth could be right. They'd just have to see what happened next, or how long he stays. However, when he inserted a key into the front door it was obvious he lived there.

Sighing, Beth turned to Derek, a questioning look on her face, "What now?"

"He could be the owner, or even a tenant. Just have to wait and see if there are others, or visitors."

As he was almost nodding off, the front porch light came on. Sitting bolt upright, Derek put the binoculars to his eyes again. Although it was twilight, he could clearly observe the same male in casual attire as he linked arms with a tanned, dark-haired woman. Was it his wife, or girlfriend? She looked like a model.

"Beth, get your bag, we're going out. Quickly. I'll meet you outside," Derek ordered. Without even waiting for her response, he was out the door and down the stairs. The couple were walking in the direction of the shops, probably for dinner he guessed. Walking slowly along the street, he was able to keep them in sight, quickening the pace once Beth had caught up. Pointing them out, he knew Beth would make a mental note of them both.

Reaching the main intersection, they looked up and down both sides of the street. In the last minute they'd lost them. They had to be in one of the dozen restaurants or bars at that end of the street. Most had large glass windows, or were totally open to the street, with additional tables and chairs along the footpath. Walking slowly hand in hand, Derek said, "Let's go down this side and up the other. Keep your eyes glued."

"She was wearing white pants and a red off the shoulder top. He had dark jeans and a nicely fitted light-blue shirt on, with his sleeves rolled up slightly." Looking at Beth in wonderment, he loved her for this, but it baffled him how she knew these things in such detail.

Making out as if they were deciding where to eat, they looked purposefully into each establishment. Reaching the pedestrian crossing half way down the street, they'd had no luck. Crossing over they headed up the other side doing the same thing. Reaching the intersection again they looked at each other. How could they have missed them?

"There was only that one place we couldn't see into. They must be in there," said Beth.

He had to agree with her. "Right then, you ready to check it out?" Nodding they went back.

Pushing the heavy timber door open exposed a dimly lit timber bar with piano music coming from somewhere over the back. Looking around, there was barely room to move. People were shoulder to shoulder and at least six deep along the bar. Instantly they knew this was going to be like looking for a needle in a haystack. Like a bloodhound, Derek wasn't giving up now; he was close, he could smell it.

Gripping Beth's hand even tighter and eyes vigilant, they edged their way towards the back of the long, narrow room. Momentarily unable to move, Derek glanced up at the bottle-lined shelves behind the bar. Stunned, he bent speaking directly into Beth's ear. "Look up there. Can you believe it?"

Her eyes widened, then narrowed as she glanced at the opposite side to ascertain how far down the couple were sitting on high chairs, backs against the wall. "Down there," indicating as she shouted above the noise. He pulled her back, "Perhaps we should stay around here. We can see them in the mirror. They'll have to go past us to leave."

"I knew I didn't marry you just for your good looks." Kissing his cheek, she said, "I'll have a white wine thank you darling. I think it will be a long wait."

By the time he'd returned with their drinks and a bowl of nuts, a few people had moved and Beth had secured the perfect viewing area – two high stools around a small round table. "Cheers my darling, here's to a good day's sleuthing, partner."

Sitting back they discussed options for approaching the couple, after all they looked fairly harmless, even normal. Relaxing, Beth's toes were tapping, "I can see why it's so popular here, and it's got that old fashioned cosy English pub-style atmosphere and pleasant music."

It was almost two hours later before the couple made a move. With fewer people around, they now had good visuals of both, and whether foolish or not, they'd decided Derek would speak to them. In spite of this, he changed his mind as they walked past with another couple. Leaving their drinks, Derek and Beth followed closely behind. Nearly 23:00, the place was a hive of activity for a Wednesday evening, with masses of people milling around the street and spilling from other bars and restaurants.

Derek's heart skipped when the couple bid farewell to the others at the intersection and began heading home. Beth increased her pace too. They caught up to them just as they were turning into the driveway of the house. "Excuse me, I'm sorry to bother you," blurted Derek. "But we think we dropped our car keys around here earlier this evening … you haven't seen them by any chance?"

Turning to each other, and almost in unison, "Sorry. I haven't seen any keys around." Jonathon took the lead, "Where's your car?"

"Over in those apartments. We're staying there. It's a rental car, but I didn't want to call the office yet, in the hope we'll find them. We've just been retracing our steps."

"Hold on and I'll just get a torch to help you." He touched Coco on the shoulder, "You may as well go inside and get organised. I can help these people." With that she followed him inside.

Derek looked at Beth, about to say that the girl looked like a Coco, when JJ returned. Switching the torch on, he introduced himself, "Hi, I'm Jonathon. You're?"

"I'm Derek. This is my wife, Beth. Thank you. This is so kind of you."

"From England by the sounds of that accent. Your first time to Canberra?"

"Yes to both." Derek was impressed with Jonathon's pleasant manner and perceptiveness. The couple seemed really nice, surely they couldn't be … he didn't want to think about it.

As they were all looking intently around the flash-lit area, Derek cleared his throat "Umm ... I have a question for you Jonathon. We lost our new *iPad* recently and ahh ..."

Jonathon paused, looking directly at this man. He didn't look that old, or incompetent, but he couldn't help wondering what he was going to come up with next ... lost car keys, now an *iPad*. Maybe older people get like this. Deep down he hoped he never got this way. Standing motionless, he waited for Derek to continue.

"Umm ... well the thing is telling us that it's in your house ... the *iPad*, that is." It was out.

What did this guy just say? Did he really say his lost *iPad* was in his house? Jonathon shook his head, "I have no idea what you're talking about. I don't even own an *iPad*."

"You see the *iPad* has this feature ..." Derek blurted the details about the 'Find' feature and how they lost it. Mentioning they'd flown out last week.

Suddenly the penny dropped. "Ah it's not me you want to talk to, it's Coco. She's just come from London, and the *iPad* ... of course, she lost her *iPad* too." Turning to go inside, "What about your car keys?"

Embarrassed, Derek confessed, "Err ... that was just an excuse to talk to you. I have my car keys right here. But thank you for being so helpful and understanding ... even now."

He shook his head. This guy was unbelievable. "Hopefully I can catch Coco before she goes to bed then."

He opened the front door, "Coco, you decent? I've brought the lovely couple back."

"No worries, just checking my emails. You find the keys ok then?" She strolled through the study doorway into the living room. Extending her hand, "Hi I'm Coco. You've come back to celebrate?" She was used to JJ's open hospitality, so before he could say anything, she thought she'd offer for a change. "What would you like to drink, red, white or champagne? Don't tell me tea or coffee," she smiled, "I don't know how to make that at this time of night."

Without thinking, Beth was in like a shot. "I'd love a white wine, or champagne if you're opening it, thank you dear."

The men just looked at each other. Eventually JJ spoke, "Before we open the champagne, Derek here has a question for you I think, hon."

Puzzled, they all stood waiting for Derek. "Well ... Jonathon here tells me you have a new *iPad* ... we have one too ... but we somehow lost it recently ..."

Leaning back against the breakfast bar, Coco didn't allow him to finish. "Oh my ... You've traced your *iPad* here. So you must have mine? These things are amazing."

"I know, tell me about it. When my son showed me, I couldn't fathom it. It truly is a lifesaver." Talking over each, eventually JJ saved the day, "Ok, so this really does call for a celebratory drink. While I get organised why don't you two exchange your *iPads* and then we can continue the how's, whys and wherefores over a champagne."

Derek dashed across the road to the apartment, while Coco trawled through her pile of books and work folders on the study floor, confident that's where she'd left it last. Sure enough, it was on the bottom of the last pile. Since deleting her files, she'd not given it, or her *iPad* another thought. She had too many other pressing issues and deadlines to contend with this week to bother.

Once each *iPad* was back with its rightful owner, they continued their stories till the champagne was empty.

Derek explained how it had possibly happened, "I think it must have been our fault. I can't believe it's that easy to pick up the wrong *iPad* going through security."

"I know I'll be marking mine in some special way and checking it before I travel next," voiced Coco without going into details. "I was frantic not being able to work on the flight."

Derek also thought it inappropriate to mention what he'd seen of her 'work', or anything about his suspicions, after all she was a journalist, and her files could be for any sort of project or story.

As they were saying goodnight on the doorstep, Jonathon's mobile rang, "Excuse me a minute." Listening intently, goosebumps exploded over his body. He looked visibly upset. "You're kidding? No you're not. I ... I don't believe it." Hanging up he stood ashen faced for a minute before Coco's voice broke the silence, "You ok? What's wrong? You look like you've seen a ghost."

"It's Carla ..." Seeing Derek and Beth still there in the doorway, "I mean the Prime Minister ... she's just been taken to hospital. She collapsed at the Lodge tonight." He made his apologies, "Can you please excuse me? I have work to do now. It's been lovely meeting you both and I'm glad all has worked out ok. Enjoy the rest of your stay in Canberra and Australia. Good night." Coco was left to say the final farewells and close the door.

18. ACTIONS

Questions hung heavily on Derek and Beth's minds as they strolled solemnly back to the apartment in silence. Safely inside, the tight-lipped floodgates opened. "Oh my ... you don't think? Surely, not ... she seems so nice. They're both so lovely really." Beth couldn't stop shaking her head.

"Perhaps I should have mentioned something. I just thought it inappropriate to say I'd looked through all her files."

"No, you handled yourself really well darling. I was very proud of you tonight. Anyway, she never asked about her *iPad*, so you weren't obliged to say anything."

"Do you reckon though?" He took a deep breath, "That perhaps it's something to do with ... um ... the Prime Minister being ... err ... sick now?" His stomach was churning with the thought.

"Who knows? If I were to trust my womanly instincts from tonight's meeting, it would be an unequivocal 'no way'. But because we know more, I can't give you that answer darling. Even I'm not sure."

"I'm having the same feelings sweetheart." Giving her a big hug, he added, "Thank you for your support tonight. At least the outcome was successful in obtaining our *iPad*. If we hadn't come down, we may never have got it back. I find it strange that she didn't have the time to care, or the interest in finding hers, or us though ..." He paused in reflection, "In the light of what's happened, I think we deserve our own little nightcap celebration." He reached behind the couch, pulling up a bottle, "You want a Baileys sweetheart? I was saving it for a special toast."

"You are a darling," and she kissed him.

Filling two tumblers with ice, he poured the thick milky coffee-coloured liquid over them causing loud crackling and squeaking. Handing Beth hers, "Something sweet for my sweetest partner."

"You always know how to melt my heart." She grinned from ear to ear. "Yes, to us my darling lover. I'm a very lucky lady indeed to have you."

Settling in, they recalled the evening's events and conversations with Jonathon and Coco, reviewing what each thought. Then together, they enjoyed playing with their *iPad* before retiring to bed. It had been a long, but rewarding day.

Waking at first light, Derek tiptoed to the lounge. Looking out at Jonathon's house he noticed the BMW was gone, and a light was on in the study. He couldn't stop his mind from regurgitating the files he'd read on Coco's *iPad* and the fact that the Prime Minister was now in hospital – from what though? Perhaps it was minor ... nothing to do with what he'd seen. Maybe it was just his over imaginative mind, from watching too many television detective series. Jonathon's concern and reactions certainly made it appear far more than a minor aliment. It seemed genuine too, for his former employer. Thinking about Coco's bodily response, she'd strangely shown little interest. Puzzling, considering she'd mentioned having just interviewed the Prime Minister for an in-depth magazine article.

He made a coffee. It was nearly 06:00. Flicking the television on, it was the lead story. Sitting on the edge of the couch, he leant forward, listening intently ... *'Prime Minister Carla Moore was taken to hospital overnight after collapsing at The Lodge. Doctors report she's in a stable condition, but will remain under observation today.'* That was it? Derek was disappointed, it was almost like no one really cared. He couldn't imagine the BBC doing a report as flimsy as that. It would've been an hour-long monologue for sure.

Thankfully, he wasn't completely disillusioned with the Australian media. Following the news and subsequent advertisements, there were several interviews with political commentators, the Deputy Prime Minister, and opposition politicians to fill the next half hour. All seemed intent on saying how hard she'd been working, and the strain of the last year was simply too much for a woman. While these comments were all coming from males, Derek couldn't agree, especially from what he'd just seen from the file footage in some stories. This Carla Moore appeared rather capable, confident and forthright, knowing her mind. Then again, he was no political analyst.

Rising to make another coffee, Derek saw Beth in the hallway. "Want a coffee sweetheart?"

"Hmmm, sounds good. Thank you." She joined him in the kitchen. "What's happening?"

"Nothing much just saying ... listen yourself." The news headlines were read once again.

She took a sip from her coffee. "Do you think its just exhaustion, as they're claiming?"

"Who knows, but from what I've seen on TV this morning, she doesn't appear that fragile to me."

"Wonder what's really wrong with her then?"

Further listening to the Morning Show and various commentators didn't dissuade them. Just as they were trying to decide what to do next, Derek's mobile rang.

"Yes. Yes, we're fine ... I'm sorry things got rather hectic yesterday, and I forgot to call you ... Yes, we got our *iPad* back ... Yes, met the people last night ... very nice couple ... not at all strange ... Yes, we're watching that on TV now ... not good at all ... No, I don't think so, but I'm no detective ... We were just talking about what we'd do today ... No, I won't forget to call you later ... Stop worrying, we're perfectly fine ... Thanks, love to everyone, goodbye."

"That was Don I presume? You forgot to call him last night?"

"Yes, I'm in trouble. He was also concerned about the Prime Minister being in hospital. Wondered whether it was linked."

"Well, I certainly hope not. Anyway, where were we? Yes, what to do today ..." She handed him the visitor guidebook, "You choose. I'm easy. Everything looks interesting. I'm going to have a shower and get ready."

Flicking through the small booklet he noted there was certainly plenty to do. Marking a couple by turning the page corner, he then dashed to get showered and dressed too. On showing Beth his choices, they chose the art gallery.

* * *

Knowing Vishnu began his days early, Ranni didn't hesitate in calling at the wee hour of three-thirty. "Hi, so glad you're there, is terrible here, distressing ..." she was breathless.

"Hey slow down ... what's wrong? You at home? No one's there are they?"

"No, no one is here ... I'm home and ok, but it's the PM, she's not. She was quite sick yesterday, and overnight they took her to hospital. It's panic stations everywhere. I'm off to work in a tick. Just wanted to let you know. Don't worry if you can't get me. Ok?"

"Perhaps it will be better if I don't come down this weekend."

"Oh no, please come down. I couldn't bear not seeing you."

"You may be too busy, that's all."

"I honestly don't know what's happening. I'm so new to all this. We can't work twenty-four seven; that I'm sure of. So please still come down? I'll need you, that I do know."

"Just for you wonderful one. Please email, or call me though once you know what's happening ... ok? I must go now too. You take special care. Love you."

"Ditto. Talk later."

Picking up a newspaper on his way to work, Vishnu scanned the front page. It certainly didn't sound as dramatic as Ranni had just made out. Not thinking anymore about it, he shoved the paper in his satchel and concentrated on the job at hand. Though it was undoubtedly the hottest topic on everyone's lips, headlines on every newspaper, on every television screen, every radio – everywhere he went someone, or something was referring to the Prime Minister's health. Even when he arrived at the lab, everyone seemed to have his or her own take on why she was sick. Personally, Vishnu didn't really care. Everyone gets sick from time to time. He assumed she had a virus of some kind, and would be back at the helm in a couple of days. At least then it wouldn't interfere with his weekend with Ranni.

Totally absorbed in his own planning and testing work, the buzz from his phone startled him. Now nearly four in the afternoon, it had been over twelve hours since he'd heard from Ranni. He checked her message: *'Not good. She is getting worse. Be on the news soon.'*

Announcing the latest to the lab staff, they decided to adjourn to the boardroom and check it out on the big screen TV. *'The Prime Ministers office has just released a statement that in the interim, while Carla Moore remains in hospital under observation, the Deputy Prime Minister Dick Francis will be deputized as caretaker Prime Minister. The public should not worry. This is a precautionary measure to ensure the continued smooth running of government, and Ms Moore will resume her role when well enough.'*

While the mass of journalists fired questions at Dick Francis and the Labor Party President Matt Drury, nothing new emerged about the Prime Minister's health. As Vishnu walked back to the lab to pick up his things and go to the pizza shop, he sent off a short sms, *'Please call me later when you can talk. LOL V x'*

Calling almost three hours later, Ranni was still agitated. "It's frantic that's all. It's all so new for Nic and I. We're not being told the whole story. Now we've got Francis in the office and his key staffers. It's crazy."

"What's actually wrong with the Prime Minister? Has she got a virus or what? Or do you believe she really is exhausted?"

"I don't really know. She was actually sick after lunch yesterday. You know, vomiting. She said she had a headache too ..." Pausing to think, her speech slowed, "Then she left early, as there were no important meetings ... so unlike her ... now she's in hospital and everyone's panicking, verging on hysteria. Personally, I reckon there's more – we're just not being told."

Vishnu could do little to assist, apart from offering long distant hugs, and announcing he'd be there within thirty-six hours.

Back at her house, Ranni was subjected to the same questioning from Kathy and Graham and was only able to offer the same answers and opinions. Graham persisted, "Did she look green? Could she walk properly? Did someone have to help her?"

"I have no idea Graham, I don't get that close and truthfully I think those questions are irrelevant," she said rather annoyed at his persistence. "I'm exhausted. I'm going to bed. I can see another long day ahead."

* * *

After a full day, Derek and Beth were now enjoying a late afternoon lunch in the Sculpture Garden restaurant in the grounds of the art gallery. "What a magnificent setting," enthused Beth. "Look at the mist sprays amongst the trees on the other side of the pond ... it's magical."

"I agree sweetheart." But Derek added in a warning tone, "Don't get any ideas for our little backyard. Hear me?" Returning his smile, Derek knew instinctively he wasn't totally safe.

After several pleasant hours viewing the expansive Aboriginal art display, and the special post Impressionist 'Masterpieces from Paris' exhibition at the National Art Gallery, only these images filled their minds and conversations during lunch.

Overhearing a couple at a nearby table discussing the Prime Minister's condition, Beth relayed it. "That couple say the Prime Minister is not being released from hospital today, and the Deputy Prime Minister has been appointed interim caretaker."

It took a few moments for Derek to register what she was talking about. Then the earlier dramas and concerns came flooding back. "Oh my. That doesn't sound good then."

Returning to the apartment they called Don to formally 'check in', as Derek termed it. Don was also concerned about the Prime Minister's health. Even though the media were not confirming it, she had to be incapable in some way for the Deputy to be installed in her place. "Have you still got those notes Dad? And no one but Mum and I know about them? Good. Well hang on to them. Guard them closely … Because I agree, something doesn't feel right … Just don't do anything stupid."

"We'll be fine, son. Stop worrying please." He cut him short. "I have to go, your mother has dinner ready. We'll call tomorrow. Good night." There was no way he was going to elaborate to Don what they'd just decided to do, knowing it would worry him far too much.

Looking across at Jonathon's house, "Ready hon? Let's go."

After ringing the doorbell, he wasn't surprised when Jonathon opened the door looking rather frazzled. They'd just watched him drive in after a forty-hour stint at work. JJ was surprised at seeing the couple again, "Oh hello, you haven't lost any car keys, or another *iPad* have you?" he smiled, trying to be friendly.

"No, thankfully. We've got some questions for you and Coco if that's alright?"

"I can't speak for her, she's not here, and as for me, only if it's brief as I really need some sleep I'm sorry… just a tad busy at present. I think you understand."

As he wasn't opening the door any further, and he hadn't invited them in, he obviously thought the doorstep was the place. "Ummm … can we come in please? I just think it will be more pleasant."

Sighing reluctantly, he opened the door further, "Ok … but only for a few minutes."

An hour later Jonathon opened the door again. Walking back to the apartment Beth couldn't keep quiet, "He seemed as stunned us. Truthfully, I think he knows nothing. He didn't want to believe your theory either. You could see the doubt setting in."

"I know hon. I just hope we've done the right thing." But Derek was deeply troubled. "What if he calls Coco and she is what we think, and then she disappears. What are we going to do then? I just wish she'd been there too, so we could've got all the answers."

"What do you want to do now then? Some dinner and a drink at a restaurant perhaps?"

"No, at home … the apartment please. I need to watch to see if she comes home now … or if he goes out again. I won't be able to rest till we can talk to her too."

While Beth made a salmon salad, Derek kept watch. Picking at the food, he couldn't stop himself from pacing around the area in front of the large sliding door. He knew instinctively there would be action – just when, was the question.

Within the hour a late-model black sedan pulled into the driveway behind Jonathon's car. Coco and another man of sizeable proportions in a dark business suit got out and walked briskly round to the back of the house. Derek was puzzled why they went to the back. Up till now he'd only seen people use the front door. Ten minutes later they re-emerged with Jonathon in tow, both were carrying small bags. They were making an escape. Snatching his binoculars from the side table, he zoomed in on the number plate. Scribbling it down, it seemed unusual, D10227, not what he was used to seeing in Australia, or at home in the UK.

Having already forewarned Beth, they raced out the door and to the car in the hope of following. However, as he'd already assumed, he was too late, the car was nowhere in sight. Still heading in the general direction of its departure, he was hoping to catch up somewhere.

In the meantime Beth dialled 000, the emergency number, and was now conveying the basic information, car registration and description to the police. While she felt scepticism in the officers voice, he hadn't told her she was mad or hung up yet. Trying not to prattle on too much had obviously helped, as he'd asked them to stop looking for the car, their patrol people would do that. "Ma'am, we'd also appreciate it if you and your husband can please come straight into the AFP – Australian Federal Police Headquarters on London Circuit and talk further with an officer?" Beth agreed. "Then please ask for Sergeant Harrison at the counter. Thank you Ma'am."

She keyed the address he'd given her into the GPS for Derek. Within ten minutes they pulled into the car park next to the building. Greeting them, Sergeant Harrison was large in every sense of the word. At least six foot three tall, Beth couldn't take her eyes off his huge girth. He looked like he was about to give birth to quads. His jovial nature helped break their nervousness. Showing them into a private room to the left of the main counter, she wondered how they were all going to fit. It was so small that when he pulled the table out so he could get behind it both her and Derek were almost squashed against the other wall. Nothing like cosiness, she thought.

Sergeant Harrison began by taking their names and other personal information. Then the questioning and stories began in earnest. "Please, if you can go back to the beginning, and tell me the events as they happened?"

Derek began, with only the odd interjections from Beth and the brief clarification from his notes. Harrison said nothing until the end, although his occasional facial expressions indicated perhaps he didn't fully believe them. "That's a very interesting theory you have Mr and Mrs Rosengold. Can you please wait here while I confer with the Chief? Thank you."

Another marathon effort for Harrison's departure meant one of them was best to leave the room, allowing for his easier manoeuvrability around the table. Hoping Harrison wouldn't mind, Derek moved one of their chairs to the other side, so he and Beth sat watching the door instead.

When Harrison returned with a tall, wiry, crew cut, plainclothes detective, Derek and Beth looked surprised, wondering how they were all going to fit in the shoebox of a room. With the door closed, Commander Harry Cross sat, while Sergeant Harrison stood at the end of the table.

Having gone through everything for the third time in the last two hours was beginning to grate on Derek's nerves. He felt like telling them all to get stuffed, but knew it wouldn't solve anything. The fact that it may land him a charge, or a night in jail, also didn't appeal. If they thought he was a nut case, they could possibly even send him off for a short visit to a psychiatric unit. He was sure the police could do anything if they really wanted to; that's how television portrayed it anyway, and he didn't want to test the system.

Taking a deep breath and steadily removing the small notebook from his shirt pocket, he slowly described how their *iPad* was mistakenly exchanged at Heathrow. Then what he'd discovered on Coco's *iPad* while hoping to learn the identity of the owner. Pointing one by one to the list on his notebook, he reiterated the contents. Deliberately pausing while he put his notebook away again before continuing, he examined the expressionless faces of both men.

Feeling dejected, he tried to temper his words, "I'm sorry gentlemen, but I feel I'm wasting my time and yours. It appears you don't believe a word I've said. There's little point in continuing with the actual events, or my theory regarding your Prime Minister." Placing both hands on the table he began to push himself up.

Commander Cross waved his hands, indicating for Derek to stay. "No, no please sit Mr Rosengold. I want ... I need you to continue."

Sitting down, Derek leaned back in the chair looking from one man to the other; they both nodded. He resumed with their coming to Canberra two days ago, meeting Coco and Jonathon, getting their *iPad* back, and his take on what may have happened to the Prime Minister after their discussions with Jonathon a few hours earlier, and the resultant activity at the house.

"Because of this, you now think someone has attempted to murder the Prime Minister ... that these people are the ones trying to kill her? Is that correct, Mr Rosengold?

"Yes."

"Why?"

Derek's blood pressure was rising again, he felt like saying *'because I've got half a brain and can add up ... plus I've seen it on all those bleeding detective series.'* Knowing that wouldn't gain him any kudos, he took a deep breath and steadied his reply. "Mostly because of both Jonathon's and Coco's actions, or reactions to the various events. I feel they know something, or are involved in some way. I know it seems strange, but it's more than just a hunch. It's a deep gut feeling. I'm sorry I can't explain it any further ... that's your job. You're the experts in this field."

"According to the media reports the Prime Minister isn't that ill."

"And when have the media ever been totally honest? For that matter when have politicians ever been totally honest either?" Derek questioned.

This caused both men to smile. "Well put. We can't argue with that analogy Mr Rosengold." Clearing his throat, Commander Cross continued, "We have the details, names, address and car registration. We also have your contact details if we need you again." Standing, he reached to shake Derek's hand. "Thank you so much for coming in this evening Mr and Mrs Rosengold; we'll take it from here. Sergeant Harrison will show you out. Good night. "

Standing in the car park staring blankly at his wife and the surroundings, Derek wasn't quite sure what to do next. Everything that had occupied his mind since first opening the wrong *iPad* was gone. Offloaded. But he had nothing to show for it – no result. There was a void.

Beth grabbed his hand, "I'd like another Baileys please darling. I think I've earned it ... and you too."

"I agree. It was hard work trying to get that through to them. Now I can see how the police earned their nickname."

"You're not calling them thick are you darling?" Both laughed as they drove back to the apartment.

Standing by the balcony door swirling his Baileys with a flick of his wrist, Derek couldn't stop looking at the total darkness surrounding Jonathon's house; the BMW still in the driveway. Coming up behind him Beth slipped her free arm around his waist, "Cheers, Detective Rosengold."

"You're sweet hon, but I can't help thinking there's more to this. It's really bugging me. Something isn't quite right."

"I know my Mr Perfect. But stop worrying. We've given it to the experts; it's no longer our concern. We have our *iPad* back. So let's forget it and get on with our holiday?"

His mobile rang. "Oh … I forgot to call Don again." By the time he'd explained everything in detail again, he was well and truly exhausted. "Don agrees with you … we should forget it now and just get on with our holiday. We still have another night here, so you decide what you want to do tomorrow sweetheart."

19. QUESTIONS

Media updates on the Prime Minister's condition seemed static. Vishnu hung out for Ranni's updates. Not that they included much more information, but he suspected it was slightly more credible.

Arriving on the early morning bus, he was surprised to see her sparking on all cylinders, especially as she'd also worked through the night. Throwing her arms around his neck and smothering him in kisses, it took a few minutes for her to come up for air. "I'm so, so happy you're here. You've no idea how horrendous these last few days have been. Apart from the huge learning curve for me, it's amazing seeing the country's power machine in full throttle."

"Please tell me the latest information then," he pleaded.

"Oh, not much more. Apparently she keeps drifting in and out of consciousness and doesn't even know who she is." Quickly adding, "Don't repeat that; it's not in the news. Only we know. The doctors are not sure what it is. They've done scans, but it doesn't appear that she's had a stroke or anything. No tumours either. It's weird. She's not eating, or able to keep food down, so they've got her on an intravenous drip."

Taking him straight home and into her room, she said. "I'm sorry but I need some sleep and I'm sure you do too, but you won't get any out there. Plus I know I'll sleep better in your arms." Looking at him cheekily, she pulled him closer, "I promise not to grape you," she jokingly whispered in his ear.

He was beginning to understand her Australian humour, but as she undressed he retorted, "I think if you want me not to 'grape' you, then you should keep yourself covered, in case my hands or body sleep walk without my brain controlling it."

Loving his cute humour, she couldn't help teasing him a little more by rubbing her body against his. "I may just like your sleep walking body intertwined in mine."

"You are impossible my lady." Stripping down to his t-shirt and boxers, he jumped into bed beside her. Managing to control his passions was difficult; she was delightful and he wanted more. They both did, but instinctively he knew this wasn't the right time either. Before long they were sound asleep, spooned together with the cotton sheet lightly covering their legs.

A loud banging at the bedroom door woke her three hours later. "Ranni, sorry, but I need to talk to you urgently."

Shock made her jump up. Peeking out the bedroom door she asked, "What's up?" Then waking properly and realizing it was Jonathon, "Oh my god, is she ok? Has something happened? No one's called me. How did you get in? Wait I'm not dressed …"

"No change with Carla that I know of. I just need to talk to you. I'm sorry to burst in like this. Kathy let me in."

"Ok, I'll be out in a sec."

Leaving Vishnu in a deep sleep, she pulled on her gym pants and top, running her fingers through her tussled hair as she walked out. "Coffee?" Before he could answer she'd flicked the jug on. Rubbing the sleep from her eyes, she continued, "Sorry, just got to bed a few hours ago … haven't had much sleep these last few days."

"Yes, I know. I'll try not to keep you up long." Not quite knowing where to begin he stammered a little, "Look Ranni, I'll be perfectly honest. I need some information, off the record."

She looked at him curiously. What could she know that he didn't? "Shoot."

Stuck again, "Ah … how is Carla? Truthfully?" Adding, "I worked for her a long time and I'm worried. Even I know what's happening is not normal. So I bet she's not just overworked and physically exhausted."

Erring on the side of caution, she wasn't about to tell him what she'd just told Vishnu. "I honestly don't know any more than you. I'm the newbie remember. You'd know now with

Francis in there I'm told virtually zilch. Have you asked Nic?"

"Yes, she said basically the same; which I find hard to believe. That's why I came to you. While I'll admit to despising Carla in the end …" Ranni shot him an unbelieving look, "Yes, I know it's rather strong, but I have to be honest. I did feel that way towards the end. Surely you understand where I'm coming from … you've read that 'hate' mail … and seen the way she switches faces?" She nodded in agreement. "Anyway I do care about her – and for her. I don't want to see anything happen to her. Especially not like this."

Unsure of his last statement, Ranni decided against saying any more. And what did he mean 'not like this'. "Sorry, I can't help you further. Now I really need some sleep – do you mind?" Showing him to the door, "I'll let you know if I hear anything, ok?"

"Thanks Ranni, I'd really appreciate that. Sorry for the intrusion. Bye."

Returning to her bedroom, Vishnu hadn't moved. The devil in her wanted to jump on him. Instead, she happily crawled sedately back next to him, and within minutes was in dreamland again, his body oozing the warmth and serenity she needed.

Surfacing by mid afternoon, Ranni staggered to the kitchen making more coffee and a tea for him. Taking it back to her bedroom ensured some privacy. She was fed up with answering questions she couldn't fully discuss. Although the house sounded quiet, she wasn't sure if Graham or Kathy were upstairs, and she wasn't going to check either.

However, a few minutes later when the doorbell kept ringing she plodded out. Two stocky looking men in dark suits and wraparound sunglasses stood at the door. It reminded her of the movie *Men in Black*. Noticing another similar looking guy behind the driver's wheel of the black sedan in the driveway, she immediately became suspicious. Beginning to push the door shut, one of the men stepped forward putting his foot and half his body firmly in the way. He quickly flashed a badge, "Police. Can we come in please?" With little choice she opened the door, but locked it firmly behind them. She felt uneasy on passing her bedroom door, "Darling, can you come out and join me with these gentlemen, please?"

Surprised at her formality, Vishnu was dressed and out by her side in seconds. Holding out his hand to the policemen, "Hello, I'm Vishnu. You are?"

Neither shook his hand, or gave their names, they just flashed their badges, while the burly one said, "Police … You had a visitor earlier. What exactly was the nature of his visit?"

Vishnu looked blankly from Ranni to the two men standing, arms folded defiantly in the middle of the living room – their presence dominating the room. "He's a work colleague. What's it got to do with you?" Ranni replied rebelliously.

"Don't get smart with us lady, or you'll be sorry."

"Excuse me," interjected Vishnu. "You are in our house with no explanation, or even an introduction of who you are." Stepping forward, his mobile in his hand, he said forcefully, "I'm afraid I must ask you to leave, or I will call the real police and complain."

"There's no need to do that. We're only interested in the previous visitor."

Ranni flopped on the couch. "What's the big deal? I'm sorry, I'm just not in the mood for stupid games right now."

"Well ma'am, your former work colleague is a suspect in a possible attempted murder."

Shaking her head in disbelief, "What? No way! Whose murder? He wouldn't hurt a fly …" Remembering his words, she stopped immediately.

"If you can just tell us what you two discussed, we will decide the rest."

"Nothing much, he just wanted to know how the Prime Minister's health was. Until two weeks ago he'd worked with her for years."

"And?"

"And what?"

"What did you tell him?"

"Nothing. Nothing more than what he already knows. Exactly what we're giving to the media. That's all I know."

"Come on lady, we know you work for the PM too, and you do know more than what's in the news. Just tell us what you told him, and what he told you."

"Nothing. Honestly, nothing more than I've already said. He works for the Opposition Leader now. I cannot talk to him, or anyone else for that matter, about any of my work. Not even you. And I won't. I like my job too much."

"You do know lady that we can arrest you for obstructing the course of justice ... you don't want that do you?"

"No. But I'm telling you the honest truth. All he wanted to know was if I knew anymore about Carla's health other than what's in the media and what is being said at work. I told him as a newbie, which I am – a whole two weeks now – I get told nothing out of the ordinary. And it's true."

They looked at Vishnu, "Can you verify this?"

"No. I didn't even know we had a visitor earlier. I'm down from Sydney for the weekend, and have just worked a twenty-four hour shift myself. I was asleep in there and heard nothing." He looked over at Ranni, "I presume they are talking about Jonathon?"

"Yes."

"You're the Indian scientist with ChemThorpe?"

"Yes ..." His mouth dropped in surprise.

"You men seem to know much more than us." Ranni was unable to keep the sarcasm from her voice. "Are you satisfied now?" Arms crossed, she just glared, their behaviour abominable.

"Thank you for your time." The burly one handed her a business card, "If you remember anything else, or he returns, please call us immediately."

Jumping up, she stormed past them towards the door, opening it in a flurry, "For the umpteenth time, I've told you everything I know. I have nothing more to say to you, or anyone." Stopping herself short of saying 'and good-riddance', she took her anger out on the door, slamming it so hard behind them, the glass panels either side vibrated.

"I can't believe the audacity of those two. I've got a good mind to report them." She was fuming. Vishnu could almost see the smoke pouring from her ears – and rightfully so, he thought. Wrapping his arms tightly around her, he pulled her close. Before he could say anything she began sobbing heavily. Tightening his grip he rocked her gently in silence.

Ten minutes later she was all spent. Nuzzled into his chest she heaved a sigh of relief. Pulling a tissue from her sleeve, she wiped her eyes and cheeks before blowing her nose long and hard. A few more sniffles and she was breathing sufficiently clearly. Lifting her head she looked into his deep dark eyes, they seemed to lay a blanket of comfort over her. No words were spoken. None were necessary. The gentle strength in his arms and eyes said it all.

"Would you like a drink?" he asked quietly.

"Yes, I think I need something alcoholic please."

Manoeuvring her to the couch, he said, "Get yourself comfortable. I'll get it."

Handing her a large wine glass, half filled with a crisp light white he'd found open in the fridge door, he settled beside her. "To my wonderful lady, the light of my life. It'll be ok soon."

Coyly, she smiled in return, "You are precious … To you my rock – thank you." She kissed him before taking a sedate mouthful. This was not the Ranni he knew, something was rattling her cage, making her a frightened kitten instead of his tiger. Keeping these thoughts to himself he just continued cuddling, stroking and rubbing her neck and head soothingly in silence. She was lapping up every ounce. He knew when she was ready she'd confide in him, until then he was prepared to wait.

* * *

"How many times do I have to tell you I haven't done anything? I haven't tried to kill the Prime Minister and I haven't employed, or trained anyone else to do it either." Coco's words spewed forth in angst, as she paced up and down the small dimly lit room. Throwing her hands in the air, "You won't be happy till I say I've done it, will you?"

Leaning back in the old office chair and putting his hands behind his head, Federal Agent Boyce spoke passively. "Please sit down. Just relax and tell me your version of the events then."

She couldn't relax. She'd been at Police Headquarters for nearly twenty-four hours, with little or no sleep. The holding cell they kept taking her back to was putrid, with drunks urinating themselves while sleeping off their inebriated state, or street people that hadn't showered in goodness knows how long. She had no idea what had happened to Jonathon, or the driver who had also been arrested when their car had been stopped near Lake George, about thirty minutes out of Canberra on the way to Sydney.

"How about you tell us why you were on your way to Sydney then?"

"I've told you we weren't going to Sydney. It doesn't matter what I tell you, you don't believe me, so I no longer care."

Always one for telling the truth, she'd told him that originally, but he'd dismissed it. Unless she was prepared to tell him that she'd conspired to assassinate the Prime Minister, he wasn't going to accept anything else.

Referring to the stack of papers in front of him, Boyce said, "According to an analysis of your computer files, you stored and deleted files containing some rather incriminating information, that could put you away for a lifetime." Almost pleading with her, "Look, the Prime Minister is sick, gravely ill in fact, but she's still alive at this stage. However, unless you tell us what was actually given to her, doctors are fighting a losing battle, in which case you could soon be facing a murder charge and more. So I suggest you start talking now. We may even be able to do a deal."

"Deal, or no deal, I don't have the answers you want." She was desperate to add, *'you imbecile',* but knew it wouldn't help. "Hey, I wish I did, but I don't. When will you get it?" Pausing briefly, she watched as he sat back with a supercilious smirk across his face. Her hand was itching to slap him. "Surely Jonathon and the driver have collaborated my story?"

"Not at all. Actually, they've left you high and dry young lady."

Her eyes bored into his soul. She didn't, couldn't and wouldn't believe that. "You're lying. Look, how many times do I have to tell you, those files were for a book I'm writing about assassins, terrorist groups and individual mercenaries. If your computer guy is so smart he'll see the interviews there too. Why the hell would I have in-depth interviews if I'm doing the killing?"

"I don't know. Why don't you tell me?"

"I did tell you. But you don't believe me."

"Tell me again then?"

She sighed heavily, "I've been able to get close to many of these terrorist leaders, gaining the confidence of those in prisons or detention centres. I've got them to open up, tell their story. It's taken several years. Now I'm working with ASIO in the hope we can identify and infiltrate some of these more dangerous ones, and stop the attacks before they happen. Surely you've spoken to the people at ASIO by now too? You do know who they are don't you? Australia's Security Intelligence Organisation?"

"It's being investigated, along with all your other stories."

Slumping down on her chair, she didn't know what else to say. She was exhausted, both physically and mentally. All she could do was pray for the truth to prevail – and soon.

* * *

If he hadn't been there, seen it with his own eyes, experienced it first-hand, Jonathon wouldn't have believed this sort of thing happened in Australia. Naturally you hear of it in third world and 'shadier' dictatorship countries, but here in Australia … he couldn't grasp the reality of the situation. Growing up, he'd done some wild things with his mates, but never anything that would've landed them in any serious trouble. Now here he was handcuffed to this straight-backed metal chair in the middle of a stark room. A lone light hanging directly above him made it difficult to define the man standing to his left amongst the shadows of the wall, the harshness of his voice echoing in the room's emptiness. Terrified for his life, he was finding it awkward to focus on the inane questioning.

"How many times do I have to tell you, I don't know anything except what's already been reported in the media. I work for the opposition now. We are only told what is absolutely necessary. And I have no idea what Coco was up to either."

"But she lives in your house."

"She stays with me when she's in Canberra, which isn't often. We're not married, or even lovers."

"Friends often discuss more than a married couple ... surely she confides in you?"

"Not really."

"But she has confided in you?"

"Minor things. Her lovers sometimes an ..." About to say work, he quickly decided that wouldn't be a good idea.

"And what?"

"Nothing actually ... just personal stuff. We grew up together, so we're more like brother and sister."

"Gawd, that's hard to believe. I've got a sister and we don't even talk. How about you tell me the truth?"

"I am. I can't tell you any more unless I lie." Anxious, tired and frustrated, Jonathon sat tight-lipped. He was stunned that these guys reckoned they were detectives. They were working on the same theory as the elderly couple – that someone was trying to kill the Prime Minister. Namely, Coco assisted by him. He thought he knew her well, but was now beginning to have serious doubts, wondering exactly if and what Coco was actually involved in.

When he'd phoned her after the Rosengold's visit, she'd returned his call asking if he'd accompany her to a farm about forty-five minutes from Canberra for the night, she'd explain the files then. Without any real thought he'd agreed. If he was called back to work urgently it wasn't too far away. Then she'd turned up with a driver and insisted he leave his car behind.

Gus, the driver, was from the Department of Defence she'd said, with no further explanation; she'd elaborate at the farmhouse.

Needless to say they didn't get there. Midway along the highway beside Lake George they'd been stopped by an unmarked car. Without warning, or elucidation, they'd been frisked, handcuffed and taken back to Canberra by these burly men in dark suits. Taking Coco first, he and Gus followed separately when two other cars had arrived fifteen minutes later. He had no idea what had happened to Coco or the driver. He'd been taken through a heavy steel door into a large concrete building that appeared windowless, and in partial darkness. Photographed and fingerprinted, they'd then shoved him into this room for questioning; actually more like interrogation for seven hours now – if the large wall clock was correct.

Not knowing whether his boss knew of his whereabouts or not was also panicking him. The detectives had taken everything, his overnight bag, laptop, mobile, wallet, and whatever was in his coat pockets, including various work notes and business cards.

After more of the same questions and his answering: "I've already told you that," the detective walked out of the room, returning ten minutes later, unlocking his handcuffs and saying, "You're free to go. Just don't leave town." Just like that.

While he wanted answers, he wasn't going to tempt fate. He just wanted out. Fortunately a car took him home immediately. Exchanging nothing with the driver, not even a thank you, he couldn't wait to get in the door and the safety of his own home. After a much needed shower, he'd slept solidly for ten hours.

On waking, he was surprised there were no missed calls or messages on his phone. Quickly calling work, he found everything was under control and he wasn't expected in till later that night. Fully revived, he began making notes about the line of questioning the detective had taken. It intrigued him. He wanted answers.

Coco's room was just as she'd left it a day earlier. Trying her number, it went straight to messagebank. He wasn't going to leave a message; the number would indicate it was him. If she was around, he knew she'd return the call when she could. Downing his coffee and pulling his jeans and polo on and ran his fingers through his hair. As he felt the two-day stubble, he looked in the mirror ... he'd do. He wasn't meeting the Queen or anyone of importance, and time was precious.

A few minutes later his hand was poised over the apartment button. Should he or shouldn't he? Hesitating for a minute, his mind was made up when a woman walked into the foyer. Within seconds she said, "Hi JJ, come on up."

He was floored. How could she be expecting him? The door opened as soon as he exited the lift. "Hey lovely, how have you been? I've missed you."

"You're sweet Nic." Air-kissing her cheeks, "Truthfully I feel like crap."

And in her honest opinion he looked it too, but she wasn't going to agree with him. "Yes, life's pretty horrendous at the moment hey? You do look like you need a drink though ... coffee, or something harder?" Before he could answer, "I've just opened the champagne for an early lunch, brunch actually. I feel I deserve it after this week. Want to join me?"

"Ok, you twisted my arm."

After a few minutes of small talk about his new job, he managed to swing the conversation around to the Carla's health, and what was really bugging him. "Hey, I know you can't say, but off the record and as friends, we both know there's more than what's in the public domain. Rumours are flying left, right and centre that someone's trying to kill her. What're your thoughts?"

"Really? Oh, do tell me more, 'cause I haven't heard them." She grinned cheekily at him, "Do you really think someone's actually carried out one of those millions of threats we have to sift through daily?" Laughing out loud, "That'll really give the cops something juicy to follow up."

Sitting back casually, he added, "Well who knows? You're right, the cops will be busy with the bag loads of 'love' letters that's for sure." He wasn't laughing along with her and looked worried, "Honestly, you don't really think someone has tried to kill her do you?"

"Don't be silly, we'd never be that fortunate. No apparently it's just a virus that's gone to her lungs, like a phenomena thingy." At times like this Nicole enjoyed playing the dumb female role. And she knew she did it well.

He'd worked with Nic for too long and knew he wasn't getting anywhere, "Well, I have heaps to catch up on in my few hours off, so I better get cracking. Good to see you are doing so well, and I hope Carla's on the mend soon. Keep me informed hey?"

"Sure will. You just take care too. See ya."

Walking back to his house, he was annoyed with himself. It was like getting blood from a stone, but he wasn't about to give up just yet. Jumping in the car he tore over to Ranni's house, receiving the cold shoulder from her too.

Leaving Ranni's house, he was disgruntled. Feeling in his pocket, yep, good, and off he charged. Looking in the rear-view mirror, he was sure he'd seen that same car across from his house earlier. Zipping up a few side streets, yes, they were following him. Tearing around a few more corners, he quickly turned into a private underground car park of a mate's apartment block. Luckily, he had a swipe for the security gates in his car, and was safely inside before they passed. From here he could see the side street through the breezeblock wall, and watched the dark sedan drive up and down. Each time, he knew they were doing wider sweeps. When it got to twenty minutes apart he took a chance, making his escape.

Once inside Parliament House and the safety of his office, he knew he could do what he needed there in privacy. Even though he wasn't due at work yet, he was positive no one would question him.

* * *

Being pulled over in any situation was not on his agenda. Gus was a specially trained and accomplished personal driver for the Defence Chiefs. He'd been awarded for his service throughout his career. He knew what he'd been assigned to do this night, never dreaming that it would involve being arrested and handcuffed by a specialist division of the Federal Police. Fortunately for him, he knew one of the detectives who'd arrived in one of the other cars. Once they'd taken Jonathon away they uncuffed him and sat with the car doors open talking in the roadside car park.

"Yes, I'm working for the head of ASIO now ... I don't know either of those two really, especially him. I've picked her up and taken her home several times in the last week. But it's the first time I've seen him. She never talks." He was a little cagey, "I'm not sure who she sees in the office either. But the instructions come from the top – my boss. Tonight I'd just been told to take her out to a safe farmhouse we have out this way ... just for the night. If you need clarification, call this number." Handing over his boss's card while they finished their cigarettes.

"Thanks mate. Appreciate the honesty, saves us heaps. When you get back, by all means tell your boss what we've told you. If he's got any problems tell him to ring me." He handed Gus his card. "We'll have to catch up for a drink, or game of pool like the old days soon too, hey?"

"Yeah, haven't played for ages. Anyway be in touch. Thanks. Good luck."

Heading straight back to ASIO Headquarters, Gus parked the car in the secure Russell lot. Swiping his pass activated the lift to his boss's office.

"Come in Gus. Please shut the door behind you and take a seat. I'll be with you in a minute." A distinguished gentleman of five foot eleven, Mr Wallace Davison was commonly referred to as the chief spy catcher. For three years he'd been Director General of Security with ASIO. His organisation was Australia's equivalent to the British MI5, and its duty was to protect Australia and its people against acts of foreign interference, politically motivated violence, attacks on defence systems, espionage, sabotage and terrorism. However, ASIO officers were unarmed, with no police powers to arrest. If this was necessary they worked in conjunction with the AFP. It was hard to believe that prior to heading ASIO, this quietly spoken grey-headed man had been Australia's top spymaster with ASIS, Australia's overseas Security Intelligence Service. He'd spent a lifetime in the spy industry. To look at him you'd never have suspected it.

"Right. Sorry to have kept you waiting. Tell me the details please Gus?"

Gus spared nothing, beginning with his taking Coco home to get her things and picking up Jonathon, to his conversation with his AFP mate. "Here's his card sir. He'll tell you it straight from their side. I'm sorry there wasn't much I could do."

"That's fine Gus, you did the right thing. Thank you for the contact, I'll look into it. You go home and don't worry about it anymore. I'm sorry you got involved. Good night."

"Night sir."

While he'd love to know more, after all his years in the Service he knew both Chatham House Rules, and the need to know basis, and how to switch off afterwards. On the way home, he stopped at the local bottle shop and bought a six can pack of Melbourne Bitter. Across the road was a video rental shop; not being football season a movie was the next best thing.

20. ANSWERS

Jonathon felt persecuted; even though he knew he'd hadn't done anything wrong. Not unless you counted his evil thoughts and death wishes for Carla Moore towards the end of his employment. Maybe karma was catching up with him.

Turning on his office computer and logging on, a gnawing thought ate away in his mind ... what if the police were checking this computer too? Surely they couldn't get through the government's super secure firewall? Presuming they could, should he proceed? Debating with himself, he rose and walked to the staff kitchen for coffee. Someone had just made a pot, and the delicious aroma was wafting up the hallway bringing out half the office staff.

"Hey, thought you weren't in till the graveyard shift?" said one of his colleagues.

"Yeah, just a few things I wanted to follow up on. I'll be back on deck later."

"Great. I'm pleased to know your dress standards aren't slipping just because it's Saturday." Another mate chirped in.

"Hey, any more on Carla?" he threw the question to them both.

"Well the rumour mill is ripe – reckoning assassination attempt. Apparently the police are holding someone on suspicion. Of course we haven't been able to confirm it yet. But we're working on it."

"So what's the 'rumour' theory on how they tried to kill her? Obviously not physical." Smirking, JJ couldn't help himself.

"Poison, but again all rumours. Doctors have done umpteen tests, but are unable to confirm the substance."

Sufficiently hyped from both the coffee and news, and referring to his notes, he typed a few keywords into Google ... Russian spy; poison.

Transfixed, his eyes bulged without even opening any individual pages. The short descriptions were enough to give him goosebumps. Everyone was right ... the police, the old couple. It could happen. It had happened to Litvinenko. Working for both MI6 and Russia, he was a double agent asking for double trouble that found him in 2006 in London. Not only was he a double agent, he'd also accused the Russian Prime Minister of being a paedophile. This guy sure had a death wish ...

He glanced more closely at the fifth item down on the BBC News site:

Sophistication behind spy's poisoning
28 Nov 2006 – The **poisoning** of the former **Russian spy** Alexander Litvinenko would have required considerable scientific know-how, according to experts.

This puzzled him. How could Coco be involved? She wasn't a scientific genius in any way. She had many attributes, but scientific know-how and expertise wasn't one of them. He didn't think she'd been doing any additional studies on the side either. However, she had a range of weird and wonderful friends, but he didn't know any scientists among them. Then his brain began flashing alert. Oh my god ...

Opening a couple of the links, he wanted to know more before he confronted her. Reading from the UK Daily Mail online from 21 November 2006:

Mr Litvinenko can barely lift his head, so weak are his neck muscles. He has difficulty speaking and can only talk in short, painful bursts.
He now faces a bone marrow transplant because his body is producing so few white blood cells which maintain his immune system.
Any infection could kill him and he has a "50-50" chance of survival.

This had to be it, or something similar. The sums made sense. What didn't make sense was why would Coco be involved? Printing out a few of the articles, he threw them into a folder. About to go to his car, he had second thoughts. Pulling out his phone, he hit a number. Ringing for almost a minute, he was about to hang up. "City morgue, duty stiff speaking."

He was taken aback … "Ah … pardon?"

"Just joking, it's Ranni, who's this?"

"Oh Ranni, great, it's JJ …" From her heavy sigh her knew there was change in her attitude, "Please don't hang up. Please hear me out. Listen, firstly where are you?"

"Home with Vishnu. Why?"

"Good, even better. Look, I mean, I have something really important I need to discuss with you and Vishnu because of his expertise. But I'm in an awkward position and think it may be dangerous if I come to you."

"Too bloody right!" She was unable to hold her anger any longer. "Two thug D's showed up here after you'd been around earlier. Whatever you're into, I don't want to be a part of it … sorry." About to hang up, his quick talking stopped her.

After a few minutes, she relented, "Ok, we'll meet you in the car park."

She told Vishnu the outline while she tossed a few things in her handbag and wrapped the lanyard of the pass around her wrist. "He wants to talk with you too. Ok?"

Nodding his head, he picked up his wallet from the bedside table and headed to her car. Checking up and down the street, she couldn't see any unusual cars, but kept checking her rear-view mirror all the way to work. Signing Vishnu in at security, she drove to her designated spot. JJ was waiting beside the back wall. Before she could open the door he was beside the car, "Did anyone follow you?"

"Not that I noticed. So, what's all this spy stuff? And what's it got to do with us?"

"Can I sit in the car with you? I just think it'll be better than going upstairs."

Reluctantly she unlocked the back door and twisted around

to face him. Sitting in the middle, he started by telling her about what had happened with the old couple, then Coco, the police, and what he'd just found. Laying the pages he'd printed from the web on the console between the front seats, he closely watched Vishnu's expression. "You know, don't you?" confronting him directly.

"Yes, of course I know how this would work. But who would do such a thing to your Prime Minister? She is not a spy, and from what I have seen she is not a bad, or even corrupt person."

"No, but she's not the most popular person in Australia at the moment either. Tell him Ranni."

All eyes were on Ranni, waiting for her answer. "Yes it's true. She gets bags and bags of hate mail everyday. I actually have to sort it, just in case there is anything 'real' in it. It goes to security then, and they analyse it further." Seeing the look on Vishnu's face, she continued, "And no, I haven't come across any that have said they were going to kill her … not like this. This article describes some of her symptoms though." She looked from Vishnu to JJ, "Surely it's not possible?"

Vishnu confirmed, "It is very possible, and undetectable with the scans we use," commented Vishnu. "While Polonium-210 contains radiation, it doesn't emit gamma rays, but alpha particles. Hospital scanners detect only gamma rays, because it's normally only these that do damage. Alpha emitting substances can cause significant damage only if ingested or inhaled, acting on living cells … like a short-range weapon. If this is the case with your Prime Minister, it is not good I'm afraid."

Picking up one of the sheets she read, "It says here that Litvinenko lived more than three weeks before dying. But they only diagnosed it correctly and began treatment just hours before he died." She looked up at both men, "Carla's only been sick for three days, four max. We need to tell someone. Now." About to jump out the car, JJ grabbed her arm.

"Wait a minute … I agree we need to tell someone, but let's work out who's best. I'm sorry I'm hesitant, but it's more from what's just happened to me. I'm worried if we tell the wrong people nothing will be done. We have no idea who's behind all this ... Hell; the cops have been trying to pin it on Coco and I. I have no idea where she is right now either. And frankly I'm verging on paranoia."

Seeing his reasoning, they began making notes on the back of one of the sheets.

* * *

Picking up the phone, he dialled the number on the card. "Federal Agent Rodgers, this is Wallace Davison from ASIO. I believe you spoke with my driver earlier ... Yes Gus, that's correct. Look before we go any further, I propose we discuss this face-to-face and preferably in my office. If it is suitable to you, I will wait here now?" Giving him the necessary instructions, he hung up.

Within twenty minutes Federal Agent Rodgers and Commander Cross were sitting across from Davison in his ASIO Headquarters office at Russell. Listening intently, Davison had encouraged them to say their piece first, nodding or cupping his hand around his chin and mouth from time to time. Analysing their body language within minutes, he'd assessed their characters. Before answering any of their questions he turned the tables, asking a couple of his own. After stringing them along for a few harmless minutes, he thought he'd better put them firmly in the picture.

"That's an interesting theory Commander Cross, but I must inform you it is not correct. Coco is in fact telling the truth. Through her in-depth interviews with some of these terrorists she has uncovered sensitive and vital information for Australia's security and safety. Obviously, I'm not at liberty to disclose the actual information. What I can assure you is that Coco is not an assassin or terrorist herself. Nor is she in cahoots with any such organisation, or individual."

Stunned, the men sat there, "But her computer was analysed and shows incriminating documented information."

"Yes, I know exactly what it shows. I've seen it. I have also seen more on her notes, and listened to tape recordings that I know you don't have. While there is talk of various ways of killing, or mass destruction, none of it relates to our Prime Minister. If it did, I would have been the first to call you." He paused briefly to ensure they fully understood before continuing, "Can I ask when you'll be releasing Coco please? And when you do, can you please have her brought here immediately. I'll arrange for our driver to take her home afterwards. I'm sure you understand the sensitive nature of our work and the need for debriefing. Also, Chatham House Rules apply ... nothing leaves this room please gentlemen?" Standing, he shook their hands and walked to the door. "Thank you for your time and understanding. Good night."

True to their word, Coco was delivered to his office within half an hour.

He was shocked at her appearance, "I'm so sorry this has happened to you Coco. Are you ok?"

Managing a smile, she said, "Nothing a good shower, a glass of wine and some sleep won't fix. But this is something I never thought would've ever happened to me, not in Australia anyway."

"Well I can help you with the first two things. Do you want to shower here first? Then you can relax while we go through things. I have a wine chilling."

"That would be heaven, Wal, thank you." She picked up her overnight bag and he showed her to his private ensuite. "You're a gem. Thank you."

Fifteen minutes later she looked like a new Coco. Feeling refreshed, she slumped into one of his large armchairs, next to where he'd placed a white wine for her.

Cupping her hands around the large cold wine glass, she relived the events for him. An hour later, shaking her head she said, "Honestly, I don't think I could've handled much more. While I had nothing more to tell them, it was scary. Exhausting. I now know if anything was to happen when I'm overseas within any of those groups, I wouldn't last a minute. I'm sure they'd be much more ruthless than our guys."

"I have faith in you young lady, you are much stronger than even you think. Again, I'm sorry this has happened to you. I have no concrete answers yet, but we are working with the AFP team to get them. In the meantime, I want you to go home and rest. I'll have one of the drivers take you shortly. I'll be in touch."

She was putting on a brave front for him, "Stop worrying. I know it's not your fault. And yes, I'll be fine." But underneath she was severely shaken and about to crumble.

While thankful to be home, there were no lights on. Worried, Coco hoped JJ was home and in bed. Tiptoeing to his room, she peeked in. The bed was unmade, but there was no sign of him. She heaved a sigh of relief on noticing his overnight bag against the wall: at least he'd been released. Perhaps he was at work, although a suit was hanging on the wardrobe door. This usually meant it was ready for the morning. He was always organised.

Looking at her watch, it wasn't that late. Just gone nine-thirty. Although tired, there was no way she could rest properly until she knew where he was. Picking up her phone, she hit his name. "Hey ... you ok? Where are you?"

"Hey, hon where are you? And more importantly are you ok?"

"At home, I'm ok, just worried about you ..."

"I'm at work."

"But your suit is on the door ..."

"I've been doing personal stuff. Listen, stay up I'll be there shortly. I have some news I'm sure you'll be interested in. Sit tight."

He arrived home within fifteen minutes. On seeing Ranni and Vishnu, Coco sighed disappointedly. She'd wanted to talk to JJ alone. He hadn't mentioned bringing anyone back.

"You remember Ranni who took Nicole's job, and her partner Vishnu?" Gauging from her forced polite smile she remembered them, but wasn't happy they were here, so he quickly got to the point of why they were with him.

She relaxed after hearing their assumptions. "So what are you proposing to do now?" She wanted to hear their plans, before she told them her side.

Ranni took the lead. "We decided that going to the police was pointless, especially after what's just happened to you and JJ. So, we thought of telling both Francis, as my interim boss, and JJ's boss, Scott ... but together. We were just working out their schedules when you called. You're quite welcome to be with us too. We can get you a visitor pass."

"I think I may have a better, more powerful solution for you," she replied. "First, I have to tell you a few things from my side, but it mustn't leave this room otherwise other people's lives, including my own, and possibly yours, will be in danger."

They looked at each other bewildered; so she was hiding something. What?

After giving them the big picture overview version of her work, the findings, and her consequence involvement with ASIO, who were now carrying out their own investigations, she sat back, taking in their expressions.

Shaking his head, JJ gave her a cheeky wink, "And I thought I knew all about you. Aren't you the sly one?" He hesitated briefly, "When the old couple told me what they'd seen on your *iPad*, and their speculation about Carla's illness, I thought they were nuts. But after what happened, I now know they're quite smart to have even come up with those assumptions. So, what's your big plan?"

"I think we should tell Davison at ASIO first. After all, he has people looking into it further. And we know we can trust him. Plus, at his level he'll be able to pull both political heads and the AFP head in. If nothing happens after that, it won't be our fault."

"Brilliant," echoed Ranni and JJ, while Vishnu nodded. She was more than just a pretty face.

Immediately, she hit Wallace's contact on her phone. "Sorry to bother you sir, are you still at work? Good ... my friends are here, and more information has just come to hand ... I think it best we hand it over to you ... Four of us ... Yes, no problem ... See you soon. Thank you."

"He's sending a car for us immediately. Make sure you've got all your papers and information with you."

Coco introduced everyone as they sat on the four chairs that Davison had lined up in front of his desk. Jonathon pulled out the files he'd been amassing, and began his presentation. When appropriate, he asked both Ranni to speak about Carla's current condition, and then Vishnu for his scientific input. Coco concluded with her proposal for him to tell the powers that be, and the way forward. Although she knew he didn't need her to tell him the recommended course of action.

"You're all incredible ... I may have to offer you jobs. And yes, I see why you've chosen me as the messenger ... very ingenious." He paused in deep thought. "It may take a little while to organise everyone, so I'll get the driver to take you home for now. I may need you all to be on hand though, just in case any further clarification is necessary. I will give you a call, so stay nearby. Thank you all."

Once he'd seen them out, Wallace instantly began scribbling notes back at his desk. It would be another long night. At times like this he was glad he had no family to contend with. Work was his life and he had no regrets.

Arriving back at JJ's, they decided champagne was in order. The last few days had been long and out of the ordinary in more ways than one. With an unbelievable outcome in sight, it was cause for celebration. It had been a superb collaborative effort. Just as they were making a toast the doorbell rang.

This time JJ was happy to see the old couple. "Please come in. We have news that we must also thank you for." Introducing the Rosengold's, he handed them champagne and made another toast first, before bringing them up-to-date.

21. SOLUTIONS

Several hours later, the large boardroom at ASIO headquarters was buzzing with bodies and whispered conversations. Sipping at their cups of tea or coffee, anticipation was running high. Gathered around the enormous oak and granite inlay table were; the caretaker Prime Minister Dick Francis, Opposition Leader Adam Scott, and AFP Commissioner Ian Michaels, each with their Chief of Staff and media advisers, along with ASIO Deputy Director-General Tony Johnston. Hush prevailed as Davison walked into the specially designed secure and soundproofed room. His secretary was the only female in the room, and took a seat to his right at the top of the table: her computer and notebook in place.

"Thank you for gathering so quickly gentlemen. I won't beat around the bush. In the last twenty-four hours major developments have come to light. While I've been liaising with some of you or your staff, I now feel that you all should know the circumstances and facts at hand. We also need to make some urgent decisions that I am confident will ensure a successful outcome."

Everyone was silent, waiting for the news. "My deputy Tony Johnston has been consulting with Prime Minister Moore's doctors. I'll let him fill you in on her condition."

"I obtained this report from Dr Kelly, at Mother of Mary Private Hospital, just two hours ago. Prime Minister Moore is resting comfortably in a private suite, however her condition has not improved since she was admitted just over three days ago. She is still suffering from acute stomach cramps, and has diarrhoea and vomiting if given anything orally. She is now on intravenous drip. She is physically weak, and her vitals are slowly dropping. She continues to drift in and out of consciousness. An MRI scan was clear. Other viral tests have returned negative as well. With no confirmed diagnosis, varying treatments have been administered, to no avail. In the meantime she continues to be monitored regularly." Resuming his seat, Davison continued.

"While there is no improvement in Prime Minister Moore's condition, I did receive some enlightening news earlier this evening." Continuing for a good ten minutes he expanded on the lead up events, and his meeting with Commander Cross and Rodgers from the AFP, as well as Coco and her friends about the supposition. Summing up, he handed out an A4 sheet with bullet points about the proposal. Each man carefully studied the notes. Nodding ensued.

Responding first was Dick Francis. "Has Dr Kelly been informed yet?"

"No sir. This is primarily why I called the meeting tonight. This is purely an assumption at this stage. Even though highly educated and scientifically backed, it has only come about because of other incidents not specifically related to the Prime Minister Moore's health. Also, we have to remember we have no evidence to even suggest Prime Minister Moore may have been poisoned. So, my question to you this evening gentlemen is ... do we suggest the doctors look at this theory further or not?"

Humming murmurs between the chiefs and advisers filled the air. Before they concluded, Davison gave them another option. "Do any of you wish to hear further scientific data from an expert?"

Looks and nods resulted in a resounding yes.

Minutes later Davison returned. Introducing Vishnu to the group, he listed his credentials, including his budding new cancer treatment work. Humbled and slightly embarrassed, he was not used to addressing such important people. Thankfully Ranni had been stoking his fire in the other office, so fuelled with confidence he began.

"You have already seen our hypothesis. This is based on the autopsy findings from Alexander Litvinenko's murder through poisoning. The symptoms he had, and what the Prime Minister now appears to be suffering, appear very similar. This is why I am suggesting she has possibly been poisoned by the highly toxic radionuclide polonium-210. Only a small quantity, just fifty nanograms will eventually kill if ingested. In Litvinenko's case he had around ten micrograms of the poison in his system when he died. This showed up in the autopsy. That was over two hundred times the lethal dose. Traces were later found in his teacup."

Waiting for a minute to see if there were any questions, no one moved. All eyes were fixed on him, awaiting his next word. It was nerve racking, but this was work he knew about, so he continued confidently, "Polonium works fairly quickly. Depending on the dose, vomiting can occur either instantly, or up to three hours later. Unlike normal radiation exposure, polonium emits only alpha particles, not gamma rays, and is therefore unable to be detected by hospital scanners and normal testing. While small amounts of polonium can be found in soil and leaves, only when it is ingested, or inhaled, does it begin destroying living cells. Polonium is found in tobacco leaves and comes from the phosphate fertilizers in the soil. This is why heavy and long-term smokers suffer lung cancer. Obviously, I am not trying to tell you how to do your jobs … and I fully understand that no polonium testing has yet been done regarding the Prime Minister. However, as it is early days, and her condition is currently unaltered, perhaps only slightly worse since her admission, I think it would be best to begin treating the Prime Minister immediately. The treatment she needs to be given for this is the same as a cancer patient. Hopefully she will respond well. In the meantime, if this is not the case it will not overly harm her. I believe she was physically quite fit. This will help. While the doctors are treating her, testing needs to be carried out. When and if any poison is identified, then further specific treatment can be given if required. But if a patient is left to suffer untreated, the toxin will only get a stronger hold."

Davison asked if they had any questions for Vishnu. Dick Francis introduced himself, "What you've just presented is quite alarming in this day and age, especially in Australia. We are no longer involved in cold war activities, or with Russian spies. So why would someone be trying to kill Ms Moore?"

"I have no idea sir. And I am sorry, but I am not skilled in how the criminal mind works. I am sure those of you closest to her may have theories. My only concern is assisting in her recovery and future well-being, if I can."

"Tony Johnston, Deputy Director ASIO. Can you enlighten us on how someone may have obtained polonium – if that's what's been used – and how would we recognise it?"

"Polonium was discovered in 1898 by Marie Curie in France, and she named it after her birthplace, Poland. It's found naturally in pitchblende. She was looking for the radioactivity in pitchblende at the time, and that was it. She needed tons of pitchblende to obtain a minuscule amount of polonium. It can now be produced in a nuclear reactor. One milligram of polonium emits as much alpha radiation as five grams of radium, and is ten times more toxic than hydrocyanic acid. Polonium is a solid, and silver in colour, but gives off a blue glow. Today, polonium is used in thermoelectric power in space satellites, as a neutron trigger for nuclear weapons, to reduce static charges in industrial applications such as textile mills, and in making photographic plates, and is on brushes for removing dust from films. Mixed or alloyed with beryllium, polonium can be used as a portable neutron source. Polonium also dissolves readily in dilute acids. As you can see, only a small amount is needed to poison someone. It is widely available, but only if you know what you're looking for and where to look. Does that help?"

"Definitely. Thank you."

Davison looked around the table and everyone seemed satisfied with the answers. "If there are no more questions for Vishnu, we'll move on?" Silence. They shook hands. "Thank you Vishnu, this information is extremely helpful. Good night."

After speaking softly to his secretary, he then addressed the others, "Marion has a complete record of tonight's meeting. Only minutes of the basic facts will be distributed. If detailed information is required please come through me. Now, continuing with the main point … do we all agree that we ask

Dr Kelly and his team to look at this theory further, and as Vishnu has suggested, ask him to begin a cancer treatment on the Prime Minister while we carry out further investigations into the possible causes?"

A resounding approval filled the room.

"One more question gentlemen and we can wrap this up. Who do we appoint to talk to Dr Kelly?"

Dick Francis looked at his opponent Tony Scott, then to Wallace Davison. "Your deputy is already working closely with Dr Kelly and his team. I think he and you should continue talking with them. If necessary, take that scientist Vishnu too; he knows his stuff. They may also have some other ideas. We want the best possible treatment for Ms Moore and as soon as possible. I propose we also prepare a formal letter signed by this group to give you the authority to insist on the treatment if you feel it is required. As Vishnu said, we don't want to delay this matter any longer than necessary."

"Thank you for the vote of confidence gentlemen, and thank you for coming out at such short notice. Good night."

After showing everyone out, Tony returned to Davison's office. Vishnu, Ranni, Coco and Jonathon were also seated on the settee in conversation with his boss. "Sorry I didn't realise there were others here."

"Come in Tony. You know Coco and now Vishnu. You also would have seen Jonathon in the meeting. He was Carla Moore's Chief of Staff until recently, but now works for Adam Scott. This is Ranni who works for Carla now."

Jonathon made his apologies, "I have to go now anyway, I've work to do. I just wanted to say thanks to you and Vishnu sir. It's a pleasure working with such professionals. Goodnight." He ran out to catch up with his boss. He loved his job, there was always something interesting happening.

Davison finished making tentative arrangements with Vishnu regarding the meeting with Dr Kelly. Then Vishnu, along with Coco and Ranni, was pleased to go home to bed. It had been a long and emotionally packed day. He had to admit life with Ranni certainly wasn't boring. Even Coco was relieved to be in one piece, and to know that some good was now being achieved. Although still hyped, she was hoping that after a long shower she'd sleep well.

Now alone, Wallace and Tony spoke further about the meeting, including other plans and details that had wider implications for Australia's security. While ensuring the PM's recovery was important, the bigger question was, if someone had indeed attempted to kill her through poisoning, then it was vitally important to catch the person, or persons as soon as possible. Investigating this was taking priority. But with little solid evidence at hand, it was going to be a difficult task.

The next day Dr Kelly joined Johnston and Vishnu in Davison's office, with Marion again recording the proceedings. Dr Kelly began by confirming there was no improvement in the Prime Minister's condition.

Davison got straight to the point. After explaining the previous evening's meeting, he noticed the doctor's face light up and asked, "So you would consider this theory, even though we have no evidence to substantiate it yet?"

Dr Kelly nodded enthusiastically. "Of course. In this day and age anything is possible – unfortunately."

"Have you got the required equipment and facilities to begin treating the Prime Minister immediately? Or if there's anything you need, please don't hesitate to tell us, so we can arrange it for you."

"Thank you Mr Davison, that is very kind of you. Naturally I'd have to check, but I think all should be in order for now. I will let you know otherwise." Dr Kelly turned to Vishnu. "I have heard rumours … excellent ones … on your new drug too. Can you tell me a bit more about it please?"

Although coy, it was difficult to hide the pride he felt about his new drug. "It has no official or commercial name yet, but at ChemThorpe we call it CTCE, which simply stands for ChemThorpe Cancer Eradication. As you know all current chemotherapeutic drugs affect the patients DNA synthesis and function in some way. But CTCE doesn't appear to do this. It is constructed to stimulate a patient's own immune system to fight the cancer by targeting the molecular abnormalities in certain cancers. My trial results have shown increased tumor kill rates with reduced toxicity. It is a targeted therapy, and technically not chemotherapy. Acting directly against abnormal proteins in cancer cells, the majority of tests in our laboratory have produced almost instant positive results, with little or no side effects."

"That's remarkable. I had heard as much. It will be a huge advancement. A real positive for cancer patients. I don't suppose … it … you'd think we could use it on the Prime Minister perhaps?"

"Oh no … I mean I do not think so. It's not ready yet. We're only preparing it for human trials now, but it has not been approved for this yet. We have at least another couple of months work to prepare the obligatory paperwork alone. As you know doctor, this will take ages yet. We still have to provide copies of all our previous preclinical tests and the results, plus the other necessary forms and approvals. Then minimum and maximum dosages for human consumption need to be calculated and suitable patients sourced. My list goes on." Vishnu hesitated, "I do not have the power to say such a thing." Pausing again, he looked at the others, "and to try it first on such a high profile person … I would be extremely nervous. Would I be jailed, or the company sued if she was to die?"

They had to laugh, even though it was no laughing matter. None of them had actually thought of her dying from the treatment. They'd been preoccupied with her dying because of no suitable treatment.

"Honestly, you would have to talk with my boss, Mr Sinclair. He would have to then get approval from the various authorities if he could do it. I am just the simple scientist."

"Believe me Vishnu, you are much more than just a simple scientist."

Looking at Davison and Johnston, Dr Kelly proceeded, "Well gentlemen, I would like to request that you ask Mr Sinclair at ChemThorpe, and the TGA, and whatever committees we will need for the approval to use this new drug.

Immediately. I feel confident it will be much more effective, and have less side effects for the Prime Minister than traditional chemotherapy."

Davison hadn't bargained on him requesting something that wasn't legally available at present. He'd meant equipment, drugs, medicines, or even people that were available and perhaps in another location. But it was too late to back-pedal now.

"I'll see what can be done, however please don't delay treatment on the Prime Minister because of this. If that happens my head, and maybe even yours, will be sought. We have binding orders." Lifting the signed paper from his desk, he waved it around. He'd had no need to show, or even mention it to Dr Kelly until now. At the same time he didn't want to disclose it fully either.

"Perhaps we have to tell the powers that be that I know this CTCE will be the best course and the least harmful." Turning to Vishnu, "You'd agree with me?"

Vishnu wasn't sure whether to answer or not. Of course he had confidence in his drug, but they were talking about using it on the Prime Minister of Australia. She didn't even have cancer yet. Sure, if she had been poisoned as they'd suspected, it would develop and fast, but she'd more than likely die before she'd actually test positive for cancer. Naturally he wasn't going to reveal this either.

"Well?" questioned Dr Kelly impatiently.

"I'm sorry sir, naturally I would like to agree with you, but I would be biased. Wouldn't I?"

"Back me. I need your help here."

Seeing Vishnu's discomfort, Davison intervened. "Look, I fully understand where you are coming from Dr Kelly, and believe me I will do my utmost for you … and Ms Moore. Leave it with me. Tony and I will begin our work. Thank you both for your time this morning. I will be in contact as soon as I have news … one way or the other, Doctor."

After Marion had shown them out he picked up his direct line to Parliament House. "Prime Minister Francis, it's Wallace Davison. I've just spoken with Dr Kelly…"

Ten minutes later. "Yes. The Therapeutic Goods Administration ... I understand. Thank you sir." He replaced the red phone.

He walked into Tony's office. "I've handballed that request to Francis to sort out. He'll talk with the TGA and stress it's only this one-off situation and nothing else. When you're ready come back to my office and we'll pick up where we left off last night. Grab a coffee if you like." Before the words came out of Tony's mouth, "Yes I'd love one too. Thanks." Smiling, Wallace left the room feeling pleased with the course of events.

* * *

AFP Commissioner Ian Michaels addressed Commander Cross's team of four on the outcome of his previous evening's meeting. "As you can see, we can't discount that someone has tried to kill her. While we haven't got a lot to go on, you know where to start and what to do. Naturally, I don't need to tell you how important it is to find the probable cause of her illness as soon as possible. This will assist the medical team with her treatment, instead of the current guesswork. Then, catching those responsible. I'm saying those; because I can't imagine an individual being able to orchestrate this alone ... well ... unless ... you know where I'm coming from ... Just do what you do best. Make us proud. Thank you gentlemen."

He turned quietly to his left. "Cross, have you got a minute?" After the others had left, he said, "Shut the door please."

This was sensitive, but it had to be approached. Clearing his throat, "I had a private discussion with Wallace Davison at ASIO last night too. He was less than impressed with our handling of the investigations of the journalist and the Opposition Leader's Chief of Staff."

Cross began to defend himself but was cut-off. "Let me finish first. You can then give me your side." Nodding, he knew his boss was fair.

"I know she didn't say too much to assist in her defence.

I'm aware of the computer files too." He paused, "What I'm not clear on is why the force, especially since you were only acting from the Rosengold's information? That is correct isn't it? You had no other information from elsewhere at the time. Or did you?"

There was no backing out of this. After gathering his thoughts, he replied, "No, I had nothing else." He registered the look on his boss's face. "But I had gone through the information thoroughly many times before sending the guys for their car. Knowing they were obviously leaving town, and with what I had in hand, we needed to bring them back for questioning immediately. The lack of cooperation also added to our frustrations. Two and two were not adding up."

The questions still hung heavily over the Commissioner's face. Knowing this one had got out of hand, Cross couldn't deny it. He bit his lip. "I know we screwed up this time. We wanted answers – and fast. We weren't getting them. You know it's not the way my team, or I, work normally." He stopped short of saying sorry, because underneath he wasn't. The only thing he was sorry for was that Coco and Jonathon had higher connections than him.

Breathing in deeply, Michael knew Cross and his team had acted improperly and should be reprimanded. However, it was the first time anything like this had come to his attention. The parties concerned were not talking of wanting an apology or pressing grievance charges – not yet, anyway. Pensively, he warned, "Just see it doesn't happen again. I don't forget easily. Now get out there and make sure the results are exemplary. Recoup your reputation."

Knowing he'd been lucky, Cross stood, "We will. Thank you sir." Then he left.

Back in his own office, Cross wrapped his fingers around the huge steaming mug of coffee. As he breathed in the aromas, it helped settle his angst. Watching his team file into the office, he knew them well. They were good operators. Federal Agent Rodgers, his long time deputy, stood silently at the whiteboard waiting for Federal Agents Matthew Green and Sam Boyce to be seated. While Boyce was a long-termer too, his service time wasn't the same as he and Rodgers – both nudging twenty-five years – but Boyce had been part of their team for nearly ten years now. Green was the newest – with them only two years. Having come from a hardcore area of Sydney, his methods and actions were different. Harsher. But he produced results. This was the first time his procedures had been reported as unsatisfactory. Even Cross had to admit he'd thought Green had been excessive with Jonathon. He hadn't discussed it with him yet, but now he'd have to. Later.

Rodgers voice brought him back to the present. "Here's the scheduling for Operation Clambait. Nick Prosser's guys will also be assisting as shown. Before our joint meeting in an hour, is there anything any of you want to include? Any questions?"

Having missed most of what Rodgers had told the others, he studied the A4 sheet of typed text and the schematic on the whiteboard. It looked straightforward enough. People were in place to do checks, interviews and testing. Any necessary warrants were now being sought, just in case they were needed. Sometimes it was the ones you thought who would cooperate that didn't. So in this instance nothing had been taken for granted. Everyone, and every area surrounding the Prime Minister's movements in the days leading up to her illness would be covered. No stone left unturned. Surprise and timing were of the essence. Everything was set to happen simultaneously. Once they began their move the media would be onto it. He knew it. And this they couldn't afford. His gut was telling him it was an inside job, and in all his years as a police officer it had never let him down. The thought made him smile. Then he noticed Rodgers looking at him.

"I didn't think it was that funny ... you with me?" queried Rodgers.

"No ... yes ... you're right ... never mind." Pulling himself together, "Yes, it looks good. As long as the media don't get a whiff, should be solid. Good work – as usual."

* * *

It was 07:00. Everyone was in position. Working in pairs, each had a target. Cross covered The Lodge, Rodgers and some of Nick's men covered several areas within Parliament House. Green and Boyce were each assigned key staff houses. This was the main ring. Then there were a few lesser targets being covered by uniformed officers. There was to be no heavy-handedness, just surprise. They couldn't risk anyone being tipped off, and hiding or disposing of evidence – if they hadn't already. They were guessing the person, or group, wouldn't have yet, especially with the Prime Minister still alive.

At The Lodge, Cross and his team systematically spoke with the Carla Moore's partner, Greg Peterson, as well as all the staff, from groundsmen, security guards including their own AFP guards, to kitchen staff and the domestic help. During a private conversation with Peterson it was evident to Cross how compassionate, sensitive and down-to-earth this man actually was. Not at all what he'd read in the media. Perhaps the Prime Minister wasn't the witch they portrayed either. He'd never been this close to Carla Moore, or anyone around to her. Nor did he know anyone who could, or would honestly make a comment about her, or them personally.

He couldn't disclose to Peterson what they were looking for, or their reason for the searches, but he sensed Peterson knew that it was no simple illness or virus that Carla had. This was the first time a Prime Minister with a non-married partner had inhabited The Lodge, and Cross was finding it difficult referring to her as Prime Minister all the time, and not wife. Peterson on the other hand just spoke of her by her first name, which of course was completely foreign to him at this level.

They were seated in the private study off the main bedroom. "I know you can't tell me details about what you think has happened to Carla, but we're both grateful for all that is being done." The distress was evident in Greg's eyes. "She hardly recognises me now, Commander Cross. We were having next week away together. Her first holiday since taking over … I was going to ask her to marry me … she had no idea. I've got the ring here." Pulling the oak table draw open, he produced a small black velvet box. Opening it, he absent-mindedly swivelled it slowly back and forth so the light sparkled across the single, at least two-carat diamond, platinum set ring. It was impressive. Huge. Cross had never seen anything that big, except on a movie star in those women's magazines.

Greg's eyes became glassy. "Commander please help her … I want my Carla back. I don't care about her work … I just want her by my side. Life is nothing without her here."

While he had no guarantees, Cross assured him they were doing everything possible. Meanwhile, the forensic team collected a range of samples for toxicology testing back in the lab.

At Parliament House, Rodgers team was doing the same, with particular focus on the cafeteria, kitchen and dining rooms, and relevant staff members. It was tedious, but each knew the importance. Their primary concern was obtaining as many samples and traces, and interpreting the results as soon as possible.

Six hours later the teams assembled, sharing their experiences and some findings back at headquarters. With no lab results at hand, they reviewed the various statements from staff, ruling out the least likely and constructing a list of possible, or 'maybe' suspects. Unfortunately, no one looked obvious, or appeared to have motive. Not even Jonathon, who admitted to not liking his former boss in the end. In fact, if not liking Carla Moore was the basis for a suspect list, most of the people they interviewed would be on it. The PM wasn't exactly the most popular person around and that included with staff members, colleagues, or the public for that matter. But those who worked with her admired how she handled the business of governing, and that's what kept her in the seat. It was baffling.

Annoyed and frustrated was how Cross felt as he rose to grab another coffee. He could see it on the faces of the men too. What next? They just had to hope that something in the thousands of tests being run would give the results they needed. If only it was as quick as they showed on television crime series, they could wrap it up today. But it could be days yet.

Tests were being run simultaneously in Canberra, Sydney and Melbourne, not just for speed, but also for verification and accuracy.

After sending most of the guys home, he and Rodgers lounged with their feet crossed on either side of Cross's desk, arms folded over their chests, staring at the whiteboard. Looking at his buddy of twenty-odd years, Rodgers had to ask, "What's your reckoning mate?"

"Hmmm ... a tough one." He took his time and a thoughtful sip of black coffee. Then replaced the mug on his desk. "Plenty of people with motive, who'd like to see her gone, but none that have genuine desire, or would benefit in anyway from it. In all my years I never would've thought I'd see anything remotely like this in Australia though. Do you reckon we're becoming more Americanised? Is it racial? Is it because of so many different migrants, or even illegal immigrants on our shores, or what?"

"I know it looks like we're chasing an assassin, or perhaps a terrorist group, but there's been no claims, or even slight murmurings from anyone yet. Maybe it's a lone wolf? From all those we've seen today, no one came across as fitting the mould. Not that they generally have a mould ... you know where I'm coming from. How about you?"

Cross was thoughtful. "Me neither really. Nothing but nice guys ... and girls ... in fact that Greg Peterson seems a really genuine guy. Slightly reserved, but ever so down to earth." He debated whether he'd say more ... not now, Peterson had personally opened up to him, it wouldn't be right. "How would you describe the staff you spoke to at Parliament House? Any ... well ... misfits?"

"Apart from a couple with tattoos, one with a jewelled stud in her nose ... oh, and if you count another with pink hair – said it was something to do with raising money for cancer, not her usual thing ... nothing either. A mixed league-of-nations though. Wouldn't say they were all 'nice' like your mob, but certainly seem dedicated to their jobs. Many have been there with the last three PMs. Counting Moore that is."

Looking sideways at Rodgers, he couldn't resist the dig, "What do you mean 'league-of-nations'? They've all got to be Australian to work at Parliament House, or in government for starters."

"You know what I mean. A high percentage obviously weren't born here."

"Maybe that's another of the PM's new policies, seeing she's not Aussie born either."

"You may have a point mate. Is it beer o'clock time yet?"

Laughing, he looked at his watch "Yep. Reckon we've earned it today."

* * *

His yelling down the phone was so loud in her ear she had to hold it away in order to hear Paddy clearly. His strong Irish accent was difficult at the best of times, but when he was angry it was nigh impossible to understand. One thing Coco didn't normally do was upset her editor. Unfortunately, her life had been anything but normal, or organised of late. Since her interview with Moore she hadn't had time to complete the piece – and what she had compiled for Paddy, he didn't like. Now he also wanted to know why she, of all people, couldn't get the scoop on what was really wrong with Carla Moore. And while the journo in her wanted to triumph, she also knew it could jeopardise the case and foil the entire operation for the AFP – and that she wasn't about to do, even if it meant losing her job. She didn't care. She had morals. Unlike many of her colleagues she didn't have any paid sources on her books, nor did she take bribes from others to uncover unscrupulous information.

Finally, there was silence. Looking at the phone in her hand and about to breathe a sigh of relief, it boomed again, "You there? You hear me? When will I have it on my desk?"

"Early tomorrow morning, I promise, Paddy. Have I ever let you down?" While she hadn't, perhaps she shouldn't have added the last sentence, but it had escaped her lips before she knew it.

"You better have it all there ... and I mean all ... otherwise you won't be working for me any more. That I can guarantee." Paddy slammed the phone down. His heart was thumping and he could feel his rising blood pressure. He was angry for losing his temper. She'd never aggravated him before. She was good, he knew that, but he also hated having his arse kicked from up above too. However, the current events were different, very different. No one had any information on the PM other than what her spin machine was dishing out, and that was precious little. He knew Coco would have inside information. He was positive. He knew how protective she was of her sources. Even after all the years of working together, he didn't know a single one of them. But her stories were accurate and reliable. There'd never been any legal issues with her work. For that he was also grateful.

Sitting back at her desk, Coco stared at the computer screen, her mind churning over a thousand thoughts. A smile lit up her face ... if it was a scoop Paddy was after she'd give him and the public, plenty to think about.

Within a couple of hours she was pleased with the outcome and knew Paddy would be too. She'd titled it, "Annexation or Assassination?" She was sure he'd run it as the front cover of the weekend magazine.

Pressing send, a few minutes later her phone rang, Paddy's voice reverberating, joyfully this time. "I knew you'd come through. You're a genius. I'm running it as the lead for the magazine, and naturally on the paper's banner. You better be ready to do a back-up for Monday's paper too."

Truthfully she was hoping more facts would be available by then, there was no way she could pull off another hat-trick like this. One thing she already knew for sure though, if Carla Moore survived, she would never be granted another private interview. Sometimes you just have to bite the bullet and go with your gut ... that was her philosophy and she was sticking with it.

* * *

"Commander Cross, have you got a minute?" It was Becky from forensics on the phone. "We found something overnight that could be of interest sir."

"I'll be right over, Becky, thanks." Whispering to Rodgers, both men walked out without a word to anyone else.

"Hi sirs, thank you for coming over so quickly. As you know my team took thousands of samples from all the areas required yesterday. In interpreting the results from our various toxicological analyses overnight against the PMs physical symptoms we've narrowed it to a single substance. While only minute traces of Polonium-210 were found yesterday, it came up in three different locations. We've assessed it would be enough to cause the PMs current illness too."

Looking at each other, smiles began spreading across their faces. Even though it definitely wasn't a joyous occasion, with still a great deal of work ahead in ascertaining who was responsible, at least they were heading in the right direction. That little Indian scientist was one smart cookie thought Cross. At least he'd now be able to confirm with the hospital about treatment if nothing else.

He turned to Becky "What three locations?"

"The PMs office, the Parliamentary kitchen and Ranni's house."

Both men's mouths dropped. Surely they hadn't heard her correctly. Almost in unison, they questioned, "Did you say Ranni's house?"

"Yes sirs."

22. UPHEAVAL

On the way back to the office both men were silent, each consumed in their own thoughts, but on the same subject and, of course, the way forward. Would it need the delicate handling they were imagining? Or would it solve itself easily? One thing they knew for sure, they wouldn't be able to use the straightforward procedures of a 'normal case' – if there ever was such a thing. Anyway, nothing had been 'normal' about this case so far, so why should they expect the results to be any different?

Picking up the phone in his office Cross placed a conference call with Wallace Davison at ASIO and caretaker PM Dick Francis, advising them that minute traces of Polonium-210 had been found at Parliament House and to affirm who would take the lead in talking with Dr Kelly. Thankfully, Francis nominated Tony Johnston again, pleasing the others. They each had enough on their own plates to contend with.

Seated patiently on the other side of the desk, Rodgers studied the analysis given to them by Becky. Looking up as Cross hung up the phone, he said, "I reckon we need to do simultaneous searches … when she's at home. We don't need to alert anyone else in the PMs office either, in regards to her."

"What about the boyfriend – scientist – do you think he could be involved too?" Cross had his doubts.

"Looks possible, but we both know not to jump to conclusions."

"You're right. While we need to see what else we may find at her place and also question her further, I think we need to talk to him too," considered Cross. "Can I leave it with you to organise the warrants and teams? How about six tomorrow morning?"

"Perfect. On it." Rodgers left the room.

Slumping back in his high-back chair, Cross swivelled it gently from side to side while a thousand scenarios swirled in his mind. What if? No ... maybe? Or? Reflecting on what Francis had said to him, it looked like they had approval from the TGA to use ChemThorpe's new cancer drug on Carla Moore too, but only under tightly controlled conditions. The drug Vishnu had developed.

Grabbing his favourite silver engraved pen from the black onyx cup, both presents from his children, and turning to a clean page, he began jotting down his thoughts. This had always been his preferred way of sorting and solving issues, work related or not. He expected it to be a long day and night.

※ ※ ※

The Prime Minister's office was buzzing. Ranni was so excited for Vishnu, although he'd been particularly reserved when she'd rung him with the news from the TGA. She understood his concerns. There were risks, but who was to say other methods or drugs would be any better? There were no guarantees with any of them. To date, no one had ever survived a case of Polonium-210 poisoning. As far as she was concerned they had nothing to lose, and everything to gain if Moore survived.

There had also been an extraordinary procession of Labor Party ministers and backbenchers through the office in the last half hour too. She was sure it had nothing to do with the new drug approval. Nicole was also being unusually tight lipped. Unable to help herself and fearing the worst, she asked, "Nic ... I know you're busy, and I hate to intrude ... but is she getting worse or something?"

"No, no ... not all. It's nothing to do with Moore – it's Hull. The shit's really hit the fan!" she blurted. "He's just resigned as Foreign Minister and is on his way home tonight. He held a press conference in Washington DC ... of all places. He's caning the government and says while Moore is gravely ill Francis isn't interested in working with him, and he has no support from anyone. He's airing all his dirty laundry and grievances in public – and overseas of all places. It's appalling. I can assure you it will be even worse when he gets back on Thursday. We'll be inundated ..." Just then all the phones began ringing. "Told you. Don't answer yours yet. I'll give you some words. Just stick to those. It doesn't matter what they ask you, just stick to what I give you."

Watching and listening to Nicole answer her own phone, she was impressed at how collected and passively controlling she was. "Yes, Prime Minister Francis has spoken with him and we will be issuing a statement shortly. Can I please confirm your name and email? Thank you. We will get back to you."

Scribbling the words she'd just used and also handing Ranni the pad, she reiterated, "That's all you say in a firm and steady voice ... ok?"

"No worries." Picking up the next call, Ranni tingled inside with excitement. A few minutes later, two others from the media team were there helping out answering phones, working on the press statement and organising a press conference for 17:00.

Loving the hype, Ranni wondered why the others seemed so stressed, frazzled even to the point of being peeved. To her this was so much more interesting and exciting compared to her daily grind.

Working late into the night, questions were whizzing around the office. No foreign minister had ever resigned before, nor had a minister ever resigned while overseas. What normally would've only made headlines within Australia was now brandished across every international media outlet. Bets were being placed on what Hull would do next. Would he move to the backbench, resign from government altogether, or challenge for the leadership? No one would know until he landed back in Australia at 06:00 Thursday.

※ ※ ※

Answering her phone, Coco announced, "I'm already one step ahead of you Paddy." The smirk eminent in her voice. Preempting the situation, she'd already prepared an additional piece, first to add to her magazine article on the PM, and another for the paper today. "I'm hitting send right now."

"Times like this I love you more than my own daughter," Paddy said gratefully. "Now, I've got Shaun and Julia covering Hull's arrival, I'd like you and Jones to cover the happenings at the House ... ok?"

"No worries boss." This was the adrenalin rush that she craved most about her job.

About to make a coffee, her mobile rang again. Not looking at the number, she grabbed it on the run. "Hey, what now? Sorry, sleeping with the PM is out of the question ..."

Hearing him clear his throat, she instantly knew it wasn't Paddy. Looking at the ID she thought of hanging up, except she heard him say, "So, that's how you get your scoops is it?"

"Ah, no sir ... I'd just been joking with my editor ... I'm so sorry about that." She could feel the heat from the blotches breaking out around her neck.

"Your secret is safe with me Coco. Listen, I just called to let you know the latest with our other situation ...." Davison selectively filled her in about finding the traces of polonium, and that the TGA had approved the use of the new ChemThorpe drug on Carla Moore for this instance only. "No one has been identified with being involved yet, but I know what I've just told you will be released to the general media at six tomorrow morning. It's embargoed till then. Understand?"

"Clearly sir. Much appreciated."

"And aren't you lucky, you didn't have to sleep with me, or the Prime Minister for this." Both laughed. It was going to be a hectic Thursday morning.

* * *

Derek stood frozen in the middle of the living room floor, the TV controller in his hand ... he couldn't believe his ears. "Beth ... Beth!" eventually escaped his mouth. "Beth! Beth!" he screeched again at the top of his voice.

Jumping out of bed, heart in her mouth, she raced up the hallway. His calls were bloodcurdling. On reaching the room she was relieved to find he wasn't sprawled on the floor, or in any pain. "What? What's so wrong that you need to scare me half to death?"

He was waving the controller at the TV, "They just announced that they suspect the Prime Minister has been poisoned ... that someone has attempted to kill her, and she's not been responding to treatment so far."

Looking at each other, a cold chill ran through them ... realisation hitting home... their suspicions were now fact. This was unbelievable.

About to speak, Derek shushed her. "Listen."

The story was repeated. The 'Breaking News' graphic board behind the newsreader and a scrawl across the bottom of the screen confirmed what was coming from her lips, announcing it to the nation. Taking a seat next to each other on the couch, they settled back to listen to the many expert opinions that followed. Although they were due to drive back to Sydney today, all thoughts of that and breakfast had vanished. It was just 07:00 Thursday.

* * *

For more than an hour the police and the forensic team had been turning Ranni's share house upside down. She wasn't impressed, but knew if she complained they would only make her life worse. She'd seen her share of police racial harassment in her younger days, and while that hadn't been in Australia, she certainly didn't want to upset these powers unnecessarily either.

Her housemates, Kathy and Graham, were even less impressed, and not being the one's officially under investigation were making their protests heard loud and clear, albeit to no avail. They all lived in the same house, so their rooms were also targeted. As one of the young detectives so smartly pointed out, "No room will be left unturned." And he was right.

The ungodly hour of their arrival, and the loud banging at the door was enough to wake the sleeping dead and every neighbour within earshot, she was sure. Now the mess as they went through every drawer, nook and cranny, Ranni couldn't stand to watch any longer as their normally neat and tidy home became a dumping ground. It was bad enough a team had come through just three days earlier, but she understood that reasoning. They were also a much smaller, pleasant group – and tidier. This morning there were six plain-clothes detectives and four people in the forensic team – she thought this was overkill.

Rodgers was sitting with the three house residents out on the back deck. Ranni had made them all coffee, including the arrogant 'D'. She would've preferred not to have offered the prick anything, but had thought better of it. Having given up the cause, Kathy sat silently staring into her steaming mug of coffee. Kathy wasn't a morning person at the best of times. She was more likely to be going to bed at 06:00, not getting up. Graham was much the same, particularly on weekends. However, today was a weekday and he had to be at work at 08:30, where she also needed to be.

Turning to Rodgers, Graham exuded nothing but politeness. "Sir, I have to be at work in an hour, can I go and get ready now please?"

"Where do you work?"

"Parliament House, sir."

"Doing?"

"Chef sir." Without flinching, Rodgers began making notes, taking down his full details.

After talking with a couple of the others, he agreed, "Fine, you can go, but don't leave town. We may need to talk with you further, later."

Ranni thought she'd give it a go too. "Sir, I really should be at work now. Can I go too please?"

"Sorry, not yet. In fact I think it would be best you call in sick."

Horrified, she jumped up from the table, unable to keep a lid on her anger. "But I can't. You do know what is happening in there today – don't you? In fact, I should've been there now."

"Too bad. What's happening in politics is not my concern right now. But I can tell you you're not going anywhere except with us this morning."

Her phone began ringing. Snatching it off the table, she walked into the garden. "Ranni."

"Where are you? Will you be long?" Nicole was panic-stricken.

"I'm really sorry. I've had a tummy bug all night and can't leave the bathroom for more than a minute," as she tried to feign a weakness in her voice.

"Well get here as soon as you can. I'll get someone from media in the meantime. I've got cops and forensic people everywhere in our suites as well and have had to move Francis to the bunker for now. He'll be meeting Hull in an hour. God knows which room. I just hope the cops are well and truly gone by then." Then in a more caring tone, she added, "Just get better soon and come in when you can. Thanks. Take care."

"I'm just so sorry. I'll be there as soon as I can pull myself together. I certainly don't need to pass anything on to anyone at work either."

Walking back onto the deck, fury burned from her eyes. If looks could kill, Rodgers would have died then and there. Storming back into the kitchen only to discover she couldn't even make another cup of coffee, Ranni sat on the sofa and looked at the mess surrounding her. Why? What had she done? It was like she'd personally tried to kill Carla Moore. Not one detective had given her any complete explanation for this morning's raid ... just a warrant that supposedly explained all. Where was that wad of paper? Looking around, she spied it on the breakfast bar. Resting her bottom on the high stool, she began reading.

* * *

No matter how significant, normally one story would outplay the others and if yours wasn't the lead, no one knew about it. But today even the media couldn't decide, rotating the four top stories every half hour. Carla Moore's poisoning and assassination attempt by person or persons unknown, not even a terrorist group yet claiming responsibility; a new cancer wonder drug was to be given to Carla Moore before it had been trialled on any other human in the world; Foreign Minister and former Prime Minister Keith Hull's resignation overseas and subsequent arrival back in Australia; a showdown looming between Hull and caretaker Prime Minister at the helm, Dick Francis in Carla Moore's absence, with rumours ripe that Hull was gunning for his Prime Ministership back. One thing was for sure, good or bad; everyone in the world knew where Australia was today.

Loving every minute, Coco was in the thick of it at Parliament House surrounded by the buzz and noise of hundreds of other media and camera crews, waiting in the reception hall for Hull and Francis to make their appearance. Charging on all cylinders, this was her at her best. The atmosphere was electrifying. Since Hull's untimely resignation the media had been touting a challenge for the top job, or a spill so catastrophic it would force another election.

The Australian public were divided, and while Opposition Leader Adam Scott's popularity had been considerably stronger for many months now, the swell was growing by the minute. The people wanted another election now – not in 18 months. Hull was also more popular with the people than Moore or Francis. Cartoonists and comedians were having a field day. Even though she was gravely ill there was no real sympathy for Carla Moore. They were still calling her Carliar, and Francis … who dances to the party tune.

Silence enveloped the media room as both men walked to the podium. Francis spoke. "Firstly, I'd like to mention the developments with Ms Moore." Concerned hums took over the room, and then hush. "This morning it was confirmed that she has been poisoned. The poison identified is polonium. The same, or similar substance thought to have killed Russian KGB agent Alexander Litvinenko in 2006. Because it's been ingested, polonium causes a cancer in the body. Doctors are now beginning treatment with a new Australian developed drug, which to date has not been trialled on human cancer patients, but has had outstanding success rates during it's recent trials. It is less invasive than other currently approved cancer treatments. The doctors have confidence in it. Both the TGA and I have approved it to be used in this one-off case. The drug has been developed by Australian company ChemThorpe, and if successful will be excellent for both Ms Moore and Australia. We are all praying."

Pausing briefly, the journalists began firing questions. "I'm sorry, but I am not taking questions on this matter." He continued, "We are here this morning on another grave matter. I don't have to tell you all how disappointed I am with Minister Hull's resignation. I had no prior warning of his grievances, or that he harboured a desire to resign. He's never personally raised his concerns with me. By airing his problems in the international media, in particular his lack of confidence with me and other senior party members, it leaves us with no option but to call a caucus meeting to determine the outcome once and for all. This will happen next Tuesday at 10:00. I'll now let Minister Hull explain in person his situation. Thank you." He stepped to the side of the stage.

There was deadly silence waiting for Hull to begin, each of his words hung in the air ... he was a seasoned speaker and a smooth operator. "I'm sure you all know by now the reasons why I resigned as Foreign Minister, but please let me explain it personally ... from my heart to you and the Australian people.

"It's only the second time I've resigned my position in public office, the first was when challenged and beaten by Carla Moore as Prime Minister of Australia, and now as Foreign Minister. This is the second saddest day of my working life. I was forced into this unfortunate situation because I could no longer do my job properly.

"In recent days my integrity has been publicly attacked, by both caretaker Prime Minister, Francis, and other senior ministers. Without their confidence, and the support of these key people, I can no longer do my job for the government or the people of Australia. I have not received an apology or explanation from any or all of them, even to this minute. Because of this I must take it that Mr Francis approves of these actions.

"This entire affair is beginning to look like a soap opera, and the government, as a whole, is becoming the laughing stock of the world. This is not how I work. It is affecting Australia's business, the economy, jobs and our good reputation and standing overseas.

"Yes, I felt very uncomfortable resigning while in Washington, but I had no choice. Many important challenges lay ahead on the world stage, and I did not wish to see Australia's international reputation tarnished by this ongoing saga at home. By resigning in Washington it meant that our Ambassador there could take over in my absence.

"As you have just heard from Acting Prime Minister Francis, now my caucus colleagues will decide on Tuesday who will be best suited to defeat Adam Scott in the next election. I personally do not feel Scott is Prime Minister material. But for sometime now he has been leading in the polls and is on track to take over.

"I want the best for my country – our country. I believe our future is best served with my Australian Labor Party, and I will do whatever it takes to see them succeed. Australia must be governed by only the best people; hence producing the best future for all. Before I conclude, I wish to thank my family for their support through all of this. I am flying home to Brisbane this afternoon and will be spending tomorrow and the weekend with my family and friends. I'd appreciate you leaving us in peace for now. I will not be taking any questions. Thank you all."

With that, both men departed post-haste amidst the myriad of questions being shouted from the gathered journalists.

Coco had to laugh, even though it was no laughing matter. They talked about a media circus, but the real clowns were the current members of the government. What a show. She'd never encountered anything like it here, or overseas. Then she remembered literally the huge fist fights in the Russian, Taiwanese and Italian parliaments in the past few years that had graced *YouTube*. But the worst had to be the Ukraine parliament, where not only fighting broke out, but smoke bombs and eggs were also thrown. Thinking of these episodes made the current Australian fiasco look like a child's tea party gone wrong. It was only being glorified now because nothing like it had ever previously happened in Australian politics. Let alone within a ruling party.

* * *

"Look, how many times do I have to tell you ... apart from what Vishnu told Wallace Davison, I know nothing about that polo whatever stuff. Wouldn't know it if I fell over it, what to do with it or anything else. If you want to know about it ask Vishnu. He's the scientific brain. But I'm positive he had nothing to do with it either." Ranni was exhausted with the persistent circle of questioning Rodgers and his teammate Boyce kept firing at her.

"Don't worry, we're asking him too young lady," piped Boyce.

Sitting back in the hard metal chair, she let out an audible sigh. She'd been in this pokey room at AFP headquarters for nearly two hours. It was pointless and frustrating. Her patience was wearing thin. Putting her hand against her forehead and her elbow on the table, she just glared at the scratches on the laminate top, creating a plethora of their stories in her mind. She was fed up to the eyeballs, and unless they came up with something new she wasn't going to say another word.

After five minutes, Rodgers stopped the tape and walked out of the room followed by Boyce. Dumbfounded by their actions, she cursed daggers at their backs, then slumped back, crossing her arms over her chest and began scrutinising the four walls for their stories in order to kill time.

Twenty minutes later they returned. She could go, but not

to leave town. "Don't worry, I won't be going anywhere ... I have too much work to do here, that is if I still have a job thanks to you turkeys." She stormed out.

* * *

"So you've used polonium?"

"Yes. As I've said we used it in some of our pre-test trials."

"Why? To see what affect it would have on humans?"

"No. That's absurd. We used it in some instances to induce cancer in the test animals. That's why we know ... well hope, that our new drug will be successful in Prime Minister Moore's case. Our tests in these instances showed a hundred per cent success rate. Provided it was before the cancer reached a certain stage. You have to understand polonium given like this also creates a different type of cancer."

"Have you still got polonium on the premises Mr Sinclair?"

"No. We only had a small amount for that specific testing and that would have been a good six months ago if I remember correctly. I'll get the files for you to check if you wish. It's all accounted for."

"Yes please. Any relevant paperwork would be appreciated."

"I can't let you take the files away though, we need them for our ongoing work and for the TGA. But I'm happy to show you the originals and you can watch them being photocopied ... if that helps?"

"If we both sign them, and someone can witness each page it will be suitable for court if necessary. Thank you." Commander Cross was impressed with Sinclair's helpfulness. Not once had he questioned anything, or faltered on an answer.

"I'll have all the files ready when you've finished talking with Vishnu." Leaving the door open, Cross heard him ask Melissa, his personal assistant, to retrieve all the files before ushering Vishnu in. "I'll leave you now," and Sinclair closed the office door. He knew it would be easier for Commander Cross to speak privately with Vishnu in his office, rather than the huge boardroom.

Noting Vishnu's shyness Cross was placid but firm with him. "Do you know why we are here?"

"I am concluding from the news that it is because my assessment was correct with Prime Minister Moore's illness."

"Yes partly ..." Cross continued along the same line as he had with Sinclair until, "Vishnu our forensic people found traces of polonium-210 at Ranni's house ... did you take it there?"

His eyes widened in disbelief. "No sir. Never. We are not allowed to take prohibited substances off the premises." He shook his head, "Are you sure it was from Ranni's house? She doesn't even smoke. I don't recall any of them smoking."

"What's smoking got to do with it?"

"Well polonium is commonly found in tobacco leaves. It's from the fertilizer they use when growing tobacco plants. This is why long term and heavy smokers often develop lung cancer, or emphysema ... because the smoke is ingested. Unless you are like me, in the chemical industry you cannot legally obtain the processed version we use in our tests here in Australia. What we use is strictly monitored too. While there are other ways of producing polonium, all take much time and effort. Someone would have to be very dedicated."

With no questions forthcoming from Cross, Vishnu continued pouring out his thoughts. "I don't believe Ranni would have anything to do with this. She was excited about working at Parliament House, and especially for the Prime Minister. As I have since discovered, Ms Moore was not well liked, but I do know Ranni was proud to be working for her. She was genuinely upset when she became ill, even calling me, very distressed."

"How often do you come to Canberra?"

"I have come every weekend since Ranni moved there. Just a couple of weeks."

"So you knew her before?"

"Yes, I met her at my friend's house a week before she moved."

"So in essence, you don't know her all that well."

"While I have not known her for many years, I do think I know her very well indeed sir. We have spent many hours together."

"Who's your friend? Where does he work, and how long as he known her?"

"Paul is my friend and he's a scientist here with me. I do not believe he knows Ranni well, she is a friend of his girlfriend."

The questioning continued for a while longer, before Cross thanked Vishnu and met again with Sinclair to review and copy the documents. Two hours later he began his return drive to Canberra – another three hours. If lucky, he'd be home by five.

* * *

While comparing notes the next morning with Rodgers, Cross received a call. "Ok. Thanks. Be there shortly."

"More?" queried Rodgers.

"Yep. Let's go."

Becky's smiling face lit up the room as they walked in. "Good morning gents." Knowing their eagerness, she paused briefly, "Do you want me to start with the good news, or the bad news?"

The expression on their faces was plainly visible; they weren't expecting any bad news. So to let them down gently she continued without allowing them get a word in. "We've more positive results from Ranni's place and Parliament House, so we are confident now that Moore was poisoned by polonium-210. However …" another indeterminable pause. "However, the traces at Ranni's place were only found in the kitchen and living room area. Nowhere else. So you know what that means."

They certainly did. "Can you confirm exactly where in Parliament House?"

"Yes. Moore's own office suite and dining room. Again that's another open book, encompassing many people. Sorry, we can't narrow it further at this stage sir." She handed the folder to Cross. "Good luck."

One step forward, two steps back, that's how it was beginning to feel. Depressing to be so close, yet no nearer to any particular suspect. Both knew their job was never an easy one and it was the challenge and satisfaction of weeding out the wrongdoer that kept them going.

Back in the office, Rodgers worked on the whiteboard, while Cross scribbled his own outline from their brainstorming on his trusty notepad. Two hours later they'd narrowed their profile and suspect list to two frontrunners, with another six 'maybe' accomplices. They began strategising plans for the teams' next moves.

23. STRUGGLES

After the press conference and doing her bit for Thursday's evening paper, she'd also re-jigged another foreword for the weekend magazine piece, including changing the title slightly, replacing 'or' with 'and'. It added a nice twist. Reading it in print now, Coco was pleased. Nothing had been cut. She enjoyed working with Paddy. He trusted her judgment and words. 'Annexation and Assassination' read well, even if she thought so herself. Relaxing in the sun at one of the many sought-after outdoor tables on the footpath at My Café in Manuka, Jonathon agreed. She was a master wordsmith. It had been a tumultuous week for both of them. It was pleasant now to have some time out enjoying coffee and breakfast together, albeit short lived.

"Hello you two." Looking up from the paper, they were greeted by the smiling faces of Derek and Beth, about to sit at the next table. "Nice to see you've survived the recent happenings. We've been wondering how you've coped. Good to see you have time to relax," chirped Beth, obviously delighted to see them.

They were not eager to talk, but both found it difficult to brush aside this basically harmless couple. "While I'd like to say I've been the busiest, I really think Coco's hectic work lifestyle trebles mine." Jonathon pointed to the magazine cover. "She certainly has a starring role this weekend, along with the big boys and girls."

"Oh, how wonderful dear!" exclaimed Beth, "We're so lucky to be in your company." Turning to Derek, she asked, "Can you get a paper too please darling?" as he was about to go inside to order their morning tea.

"The newsagent is just two doors down," informed Jonathon.

Unable to hold back any longer, Beth blurted, "So what's happening this week? Can you give us the inside scoop?"

Perplexed, Coco just stared while Jonathon was beginning to regret ever opening his mouth. "Sorry, how do you mean? Do you mean the PM and the caucus ballot?"

"Yes, what do they do? Do you have to do anything? You work for the opposition leader now, don't you?"

"Yes I do. And no, we aren't directly involved in it. It's internal politics within the ruling party only. Naturally we are concerned with the outcome. The focus is on my boss for his views and comments. If the results are not favourable an election could be called. That would mean a great deal more work for me then. Of course, Coco will be covering it for her boss. She'll be very much in the thick of it again."

There was no way of ignoring Beth's direct eyeballing. Coco had to reply. "Yes I'll be there with bells on." She spat half sardonically. Pulling a face, she tried to make light of it, but could see that as dippy as Beth came across, she wasn't stupid and really did want to know the inside workings.

Rethinking her reply, she said, "Well ... and this is only my take, so not gospel. Keith Hull is the most popular with the public, but he only has a few big players within his own party behind him. I doubt whether he'll win. In fact I'd be very surprised if he did. The people who know him best rejected him as Prime Minister eighteen months ago – June 2010 to be precise – that's when they voted Carla Moore in. While Carla is still in hospital and unaware of the past week's back biting, I doubt things have changed greatly since 2010, or this last week ... or that Hull has any additional support within those ranks. It's just a pity this has turned into such an international circus." Trying to politely bow out, she added, "That's why we're having a rest now – while we can."

Returning with the papers, Derek caught Beth's parting words. "Thank you dear, I do appreciate the explanation ... have a good rest. Looks like I have plenty to keep me busy now." The waiter placed their coffees and cakes on the table at the same time. "Thank you."

On leaving a short while later, Jonathon wished them a safe journey back to Sydney. "We've decided to stay another week. Because of the earlier events that you're well aware of, we didn't get to see nearly enough of Canberra. We've even booked to see parliament in action on Tuesday afternoon from the public gallery," said Derek delightedly.

"That one should be interesting. Enjoy your stay then." And they headed off up the street.

* * *

"Where are you – in Sydney or Canberra? … Great you're here. Can you come to the hospital please?" Vishnu was astounded at Dr Kelly's request. A chill ran through his body. His expression was blank.

"What is it?" Ranni asked.

"Dr Kelly wants me to go to the hospital … now."

"Well let's get going."

"But … but I've just arrived. And … and it sounded desperate. What if … what if there's a problem?" His heart was thumping out of his chest with panic.

Ranni shook her head, exasperated, "Oh for goodness sake just relax. If there's a problem, then it's better you're here to see for yourself. I bet you it's nothing. You worry far too much unnecessarily." She put her arm through his, and picked up her car keys and bag, coaxing him towards the door. His silence and petrified look was beginning to annoy her, but she focused on the positive in the hope it would transfer across to him.

The hospital was close – a mere fifteen minutes away. The girl on reception was expecting Vishnu, and paged Dr Kelly immediately. Positive? This wasn't a good sign. Vishnu began sweating, something he didn't normally do.

Dr Kelly was smiling, extending his hand to welcome Vishnu. Stunned, he quickly wiped his right hand down his jeans before taking Dr Kelly's. "Welcome Vishnu. Please follow me." Looking at Ranni, "You work for the Prime Minister, don't you?"

"Yes sir. I'm Ranni."

"You can come too, if you wish." This pleased Ranni immensely, as she almost skipped down the hallway behind the two men. The only annoyance was she couldn't quite make out what Dr Kelly was discussing with Vishnu ... it was like secret men's business.

There were two AFP security guards either side of Ms Moore's doorway checking their identification. Dr Kelly had second thoughts, "Ranni would you mind waiting here please ... for the moment anyway. I think I should check ... Ms Moore may not wish for you to see her as she currently is."

Not concerned, Ranni nodded in agreement. She was actually more anxious for Vishnu, squeezing his hand as he followed Dr Kelly.

Both men walked into the room, closing the door behind them. Vishnu was in awe. To be in the same room as the Prime Minister of Australia – his family and friends would never believe him. He wished he had a camera so he could prove it. He was oblivious to her condition as he dreamt away, only coming back to reality on hearing his name.

"Good morning Ms Moore. I would like to introduce Vishnu Sharma. He's the scientist who developed the new drug we've been treating you with."

Vishnu's heart was pounding like a drum. This was unbelievable. The Prime Minister was looking remarkable. Perhaps pale, but then again he'd always thought she looked extremely white when he'd seen her in photos or on TV. Perhaps it was the contrast to her brilliant red hair. He stumbled over his words, "Ah ... so very pleased to meet you, ah ... Ma'am." She smiled and nodded, but said nothing more.

Dr Kelly then continued, "How are you feeling this morning?"

"Still tired." Her voice was soft to begin with, slowly coming to life. "I've been to the bathroom on my own during the night and this morning, and managed to do a small amount of reading." Both men glanced at the stack of folders sitting on her bedside table.

"You're meant to be resting – not working. You must give your body time to replenish itself," scolded Dr Kelly. "It's been attacked by one of the worst illnesses known. Do I have to remind you? Your body was shutting down. You were dying. No one has survived this type of poisoning previously." Shaking his head, he felt like he was talking to a child.

"I know doctor, but I'm feeling much better. Thanks to your new drug Mr Sharma I'm no longer dying. I will beat this." Pausing briefly, she then informed him, "I need to go home tomorrow doctor."

Dr Kelly almost fell over. Hadn't he just finished telling her she needed rest and plenty of it for a while yet? "Do you have a real death wish?" He couldn't help himself. The soft and polite approach obviously had no affect on her.

"No. But that's what I will be if I'm not at that caucus meeting on Tuesday morning. I also need to talk with my other ministers. They need to see I'm alive and well, and capable to resume my duties. In fact, I will be sworn back in as controlling Prime Minister on Monday morning. It's all arranged."

He hated the fact patients could have telephones in their rooms. Without that she surely would've had no option but to rest and recuperate properly. It would've also been more difficult to be aware of the various events happening outside, and organise all this. While she currently didn't have a great deal of strength in her voice, he had to admire her tenacity and fighting spirit. Biting his tongue, he looked at Vishnu. "What do you think Mr Sharma?"

Again he was being put on the spot. He hated it. He didn't feel he could tell the Prime Minister of Australia what she could or couldn't do. Knowing Dr Kelly wanted some sort of backup, he tried to be diplomatic. "While we had almost one hundred percent positive results from our trial test of this drug, you do know it hasn't been officially approved by the TGA for testing on humans yet, don't you ma'am? If you don't recover fully before trying to resume your normal work schedule, I do not know what might happen. I do not know the effects, or side effects on humans – if any, yet either."

"I don't care. I'm alive, and getting well now. It's a gamble I will take. I must. You are both exonerated. I give you my word."

Knowing her reputation in parliament, and the public 'Carliar' opinion of her, Dr Kelly would have preferred to ask her for that promise in writing, and signed – but he wasn't game enough. It probably wouldn't stand up either. "Would you care to tell me when you've arranged to leave tomorrow? You seem to have everything else organised," he said smartly.

"Ideally I'd like to spend tonight at home. It's much more comfortable, and Greg is there to look after me."

Exasperated, Dr Kelly rolled his eyes, "I guess you've already organised that too? Even if I said no, you're going … aren't you?" She gave him a cheeky grin; he knew the answer.

"We have your number, but I'm confident I won't need it. Do you do house calls doctor?" she quipped. "If you want to check on me tomorrow, and each day, you're welcome."

"I still intend to check on you wherever you are. You do need monitoring … in fact every four hours at the moment. I will arrange for a shift of three nurses to be at The Lodge, or god forbid, Parliament House, if you must go in to work." He sighed heavily, "I will arrange for one immediately, so they can leave with you."

From the smile on her face as she relaxed back into the mound of pillows, he could tell this was one lady who was used to getting her own way.

Walking from the room, Dr Kelly told Vishnu he'd arranged for a copy of all the results to be sent to ChemThorpe.

"I am so thrilled that the drug appears to be working so well," Vishnu exclaimed to Dr Kelly. "The animals we tested had recovered within a three to five day period, and were usually fully clear within a month. If it works on humans as well as this too, it is brilliant news, doctor. Thank you so much. Mr Sinclair will be ever so grateful."

Then they saw Ranni. With all that had happened in the room, they'd forgotten all about her. Quickly explaining, she wasn't the least upset. "Don't worry Dr Kelly … it sounds like

I'll be seeing her soon enough anyway," and they all laughed. "Come on, let's go and celebrate another success over a long Saturday afternoon lunch," she suggested, grabbing Vishnu's arm. "Sure you can't join us doctor?"

"Sounds idyllic, but I have my hands full here." Shaking Vishnu's hand again, "Thank you so much young man. You've produced a miracle. I'm really pleased with your drug. It's truly amazing. I look forward to working with it more once the TGA approval comes through. These are exciting times. Have a wonderful weekend. I'll keep you informed."

* * *

Enjoying a late Sunday breakfast on the sunny veranda of The Lodge, Carla Moore looked thin and pale. Joined by Dick Francis and several other trusty ministers, they could clearly see there was nothing wrong with her brain, as she articulated her strategy for the upcoming caucus meeting.

Within the hour everyone was making phone calls, beginning with those they knew they could trust to keep quiet. Soon the team was buzzing, spreading the news. "Yes, Carla is alive and well. She's being sworn back in tomorrow. She's at The Lodge with Francis. No, the media and Hull do not know, and we'd rather keep it that way till tomorrow. Yes, we're meeting in her boardroom afterwards. Great mate … see you there tomorrow … knew we could count on you."

* * *

Kathy, Ranni and Vishnu were relaxing on the back patio. The scarce remnants of their smoked salmon salad lunch were crisping in the sun on the white china plates. Vishnu had surpassed himself. The girls were in seventh heaven, neither knew how to or even cared about cooking, relying on Asian takeout and Graham bringing home leftovers, or whipping up a masterpiece. Resting her outstretched legs on the chair across from her, Ranni took a long, slow sip from her wine glass. It seemed ages since they'd had a chance to relax and enjoy their surroundings. "That was excellent, thanks darling." She reached over and patted Vishnu's hand.

"Here, here," echoed Kathy.

"My pleasure ladies," he said, just as the doorbell rang. Two annoyed looks came from the girls. "Relax, I will see to it." And Vishnu disappeared.

Opening the door, he was surprised. Panic spread through his body. "Hello again Commander Cross."

"Good afternoon Vishnu, this is Federal Agent Rodgers, can we come in please? I have a few more questions. Is Ranni here too?"

"Yes. Yes, out on the deck. I thought you were going to tell me something had happened to Ms Moore."

"No. I don't know anything more about her condition. I assume she is still in hospital."

"No, she is at home at The Lodge. She dismissed herself yesterday, against the wishes of both Dr Kelly and myself." As they walked towards the kitchen, he asked, "Would you like a tea or coffee?"

"No thank you, we'd just like to talk with you all please."

As the two men walked onto the deck, neither girl could hide their annoyance. Sitting up straight, Kathy sarcastically forced a Cheshire cat grin. "And to what do we owe this pleasure, Mr Rodgers?"

Cross could see the contempt. "I'm Commander Cross, and I apologise for disturbing your Sunday ladies, but we have a few more questions please. We can do this civilly here, or we can take you back to headquarters if you'd prefer?"

Ranni sat up, lifting her sunglasses. "Shoot. I'm all ears. Then hopefully I will still have time to enjoy the rest of the day. If you didn't already know, I've had one hell of a week, and I've another ahead of me too. Fire away please?"

Both men were still standing, and neither lady intended offering them a chair.

Seating themselves, Cross began by telling them about the traces of polonium being confirmed for the second time in their house. When he began asking about the girl's cooking, Vishnu broke into uncontrollable laughter. "I'm sorry, but if I was to marry Ranni for her cooking skills, I would die of starvation before too long."

Noticing the officers glancing at the plates, he announced, "I'm not that brilliant either, but I'm certainly better than these two. They've been known to burn toast, and even boiled eggs."

Clinking wine glasses the girls chimed, "Cheers to that. And men looking after us for a change."

"Where's the chef? Graham?" asked Rodgers.

"He's staying at a friends place. But he wasn't at work on Friday," chirped Ranni. "They said he had the flu or something, and we're happy for him to keep it at someone else's house."

Getting the address, they thanked the girls.

As Vishnu showed them out he added, "Good luck gents."

"Thank you for your patience today. Enjoy the rest of your weekend," responded Cross.

Returning to the car, both men were positive they now knew the answer.

Five minutes later they were knocking at the green door of a low-set red brick house in Kingston. Like neighbouring Manuka, this suburb was expensive due to its closeness to the lake, Parliament House, many government offices, and the city centre. The land plots were large and many were now zoned for multi-story development. It was a mixture of new apartment buildings, immaculately kept gardens and renovated houses, and rented properties that stood out like a sore thumb for their unruliness. This was clearly a rented property, and a group house. A total of five cars were parked in the driveway and on the brown front lawn. One was a Subaru WRX, and there were a couple of reworked Skylines. Guessing they were probably involved in street racing, Rodgers copied the registration numbers of the cars. The rubbish bins were overflowing with beer bottles, and cardboard cartons were strewn along the path. It was hard to say if it was from a recent party, or general living.

Knocking again, they heard nothing. Thumping harder,

"Police. Open up," evoked a response. "I'm coming ... I'm coming ... don't break the door down."

A bleary-eyed half-naked male with shoulder length dishevelled black hair half-opened the door. "How can I help, officers?"

"We're after Graham Bratnell. Is he here?"

"No. Don't know 'im." As the door began to close, Rodgers stepped forward placing half his body in between. "Hey man I told ya, he ain't here."

"Well, we have information that he is here, or has been staying here. Let us in."

"You got a warrant?"

Rodgers looked back at Cross. "No."

He forced the door heavily against Rodgers, "Well get off my property then." As Rodgers had no choice he backed off, and the door slammed behind him.

Both men retreated to their car. Cross immediately called Green, giving him the full details to execute a warrant. "We'll wait here till you arrive. Any problems call me at once."

Driving around the block and pulling up near the house again, Cross repositioned the car so they could clearly view anyone coming or going more easily. In the meantime, Rodgers was running a check on all the cars. Graham Bratnell's car was there. They were in luck. Now they just had to wait.

The two-hours for Green to show up with the warrant seemed like a lifetime. Luckily, knowing Graham's appearance assured them that the only person to leave the house was not him.

Warrant in hand, Rodgers and Cross returned to the front door, while Green accompanied by Boyce went round the back. Knocking on the front door, it was opened immediately to reveal the same male, but clean-shaven, and fully clothed. The occupants had been watching the proceedings from the comfort of their lounge. They had a closed circuit surveillance setup linked to the TV. Naturally they'd turned it off before opening the door. Being mostly IT nerds or petrol heads, there were certainly no homely touches to be seen. However, there were two thin waifs of femininity clad in extremely short skirts sitting amongst the five assorted males in the living room. Scanning all the faces, Rodgers recognised none. "Where's Graham Bratnell?"

"Told you before, he's not here."

"His car is in the yard. So where is he?"

"Don't know man. We kicked him out Thursday night. He was off his face – stark raving loony. Don't know what he was on, but we don't do drugs. Despite what you think of me and me friends we don't have them anywhere around." They were all nodding in agreement. "He certainly wouldn't have been able to drive. He could barely walk. Don't think he even knew who he was."

"We're still going to have a look around ourselves." Rodgers shoved the warrant in his face. "Not going to waste this, seeing as you seemed happy wasting our time."

After letting Green and Boyce in the back door, he demanded, "If there's anything of Bratnell's here give it to us now. Unless you'd like us to turn the whole place upside down?"

Walking to one of the bedrooms the guy grabbed a small blue and grey backpack and handed it to Rodgers, "That's it as far as I know."

"Do you know any of his family or other friends … where he might go?"

"No. He doesn't talk much. He cooks, so he's handy to have around from time to time. He doesn't live here. Shares a place with two posh girls somewhere in Campbell." Seeing the look on the cops face, he added, "Never met them either. Told ya, I know nothin about him or 'em. He keeps pretty much to 'imself and personally we like it that way."

While Rodgers rummaged through the backpack, Boyce and Green were noting everyone's details. After checking out the rest of the house, yard and garden shed, Cross came back inside. Handing over his card, "If you see or hear from Bratnell, or anyone who knows of him or his whereabouts, I'd appreciate you calling me immediately. Thank you."

Taking the backpack, they returned to headquarters. Why couldn't people be more helpful up front? Instead of wasting three hours of their time they could've been focusing on actually finding Bratnell. It annoyed the team. They were back to square one.

Pulling up Bratnell's work file details, Rodgers noted that Kathy Green was listed as his emergency contact for next of kin. This required another visit to the Campbell house.

"I had no idea he'd listed me as his emergency contact. Never told me," Kathy said rather surprised. As this wasn't about her, she was being completely civil. "I first met Graham five years ago at the opening of the National Press Club restaurant. He was the chef there. A year later he was offered a job at Parliament House. That's where he met my previous house girlfriend – the one before Ranni. He told her he was looking for a place closer to work. Apparently he was living way out at Palmerston. He ended up replacing my other tenant a month or so later. I don't do huge checks on people if they come via friends. Plus he's always paid the rent on time, is clean and tidy in all common areas, that's what counts to me. Plus he cooks, as you know. That's a bonus. And being male, he's useful as a handyman from time to time. We don't see much of him out of work hours, and he's never had anyone stay over. I've often thought he might be gay."

"Do you mind if we go through his room without a warrant?"

"Fine by me. Anything to help find him." She smiled, "The rent's due next week."

His room gave them no more clues to his whereabouts or family. Checks on his background showed nothing. He had no record, not even a speeding ticket. His mobile was going straight to voice mail too. Every path led them to a dead end. The only choice now was to go public – a missing person – of interest. After all, it had been almost seventy-two hours since he'd last been seen – as far as they knew anyway.

* * *

After a full day out, footsore and weary, Derek and Beth were pleased to be back relaxing in the apartment. "I can see why everyone raves about the War Memorial. It's truly amazing. So many superb displays, I think I liked that big plane and re-enactment film best. I felt like I was there in the war with them. I wonder how they got the plane in there. Do you think they built the building around it? Someone said that part was new."

Agreeing with his wife, "Yes, 'G for George' and the other two big displays were excellent. But I'm sure the plane would have been assembled in parts inside the building. I'm so glad we decided to stay a bit longer. Cheers darling." From the comfort of the balcony chair Derek pointed the remote at the TV. The news flickered on. Seeing an image he recognised he turned the sound up and went inside for a closer look.

Calling Beth, "Isn't that the boy we phoned the ambulance for the other night?"

"Could be, but he had so much blood on his face and it was dark … it's hard to tell."

"I think it is. In fact I'm positive. I'm calling the police."

After telling them all he knew, Derek wasn't the only one surprised when Commander Cross knocked on the apartment door thirty minutes later. "You again?"

"Come in Commander. Would you like a tea or coffee?"

"No thank you, Mr Rosengold. I'm here because you phoned in about the missing man. Can you tell me more please? How do you know him?"

"I don't know him. As I told the girl on the phone, we were coming back from dinner and heard some groaning from under the bushes down the road there." He pointed out the balcony door. "He had obviously been bashed up. He was covered in blood. We called the ambulance and waited till they arrived. Then we left."

"When exactly was this? Do you remember?"

He looked at Beth for reassurance. "Round ten-ish Thursday night."

"Would you mind showing me exactly where please?"

Setting off down the street, they stopped just over a block

away. Underneath high green leafy bushes that formed someone's hedged fence line, Cross could see caked blood in the dirt. Without disturbing it, he quickly looked further afield. Calling Rodgers, he gave him the details to arrange for a forensics team.

"Thank you Mr and Mrs Rosengold. I'll wait here. Please go back to your apartment. I'll call you if I need anything further. Once again, you've been extremely helpful."

When the team arrived they cordoned off the area and began work. Cross had already spoken to the residents in the house. They were out on Thursday evening and didn't even know about the incident. In any case there were always noises, and they mostly ignored them now. The route is a main thoroughfare for residents to and from Manuka shops.

An empty wallet and mobile phone were found in the bushes a few doors down. Was robbery the only motive?

"Boss, I've just had confirmation from Canberra Hospital. An unnamed male in his twenties was brought in by ambulance on Thursday night. He's still there … in intensive care."

"Let's go." Cross and Rodgers departed, leaving the others to it.

Pulling up in the specially marked parking spot for emergency vehicles at the entrance to the public hospital, they introduced themselves to the receptionist. Within minutes a doctor was escorting them to the ward. Through the glass window Rodgers identified Bratnell.

They adjourned to the doctor's office. "As you can see gentlemen he's unconscious. He's been that way since his arrival. He's got severe head injures and his body was in shock. It was a violent attack. We placed him in an induced coma early Friday morning, but his vitals are getting weaker I'm afraid. You won't be able to talk to him for quite a while … if at all. Personally, I'd be surprised if he lives through the night."

Back in the car, Rodgers announced, "Well, whether she likes it or not, we've got to advise Ms Green of Bratnell's condition."

Shocked, Kathy, Ranni and Vishnu sat in disbelief as Cross and Rodgers gave them the facts.

"Sirs, I am thinking," said Vishnu. "Can you tell me again please what the men in the house said about his behaviour?"

"He was erratic, hallucinating, could hardly stand up. They thought he'd been taking drugs and told him to get out."

"Sirs, may I say something more?"

"Certainly. What?"

"If you found traces of polonium-210 here in this kitchen and in the Parliament House kitchen … Graham is the only person who has been at both these places, other than Ranni."

"Yes, we became aware of that this afternoon, that's why we've been looking for him."

"Well, the earlier symptoms he had at his friends house sound like they could also be linked to polonium. Perhaps he knew he was in trouble and was trying to kill himself."

"You could be right. However, while he's the prime suspect at this stage, we have no proof or motive for him even trying to kill the Prime Minister yet. We haven't been able to find any family either. Or anything about him, beyond his time here in Canberra. He's a mystery."

"If you wish to find out more you need him alive. Correct?" They nodded. "Then I suggest you arrange to have him treated with my drug too. The Prime Minister is alive and well. But it will depend on how much polonium he's taken, and also his head injuries." Vishnu raised his eyebrows, "That is my solution for what it is worth."

Cross liked this youngster. He was quiet, polite, intelligent and intuitive. He had a great future. "We'll get onto it straight away. Thank you again you three. Please accept our apologies and enjoy the rest of your evening."

Making a series of phone calls, several hours later Cross finally got approval to use the drug again, and the doctors of two different hospitals began talking with each other in order to treat and monitor Bratnell.

24. POWER

In his first class seat on the 06:10 flight from Brisbane to Canberra, Keith Hull sat in stunned silence, seething inside. Having rolled the Monday morning newspaper tightly he squeezed it hard, wishing it were the neck of Carla Moore. *'More Life for PM Moore'* read the headline.

She was his worst nightmare. A thorn in his side since he'd become the leader of the Labor Party back in 2006 – that agreement came with her as his deputy. He'd believed their publicity machine, that they made a good team. They'd swept into power in 2007; annihilating the sitting Liberal Party who'd held government for eleven years.

For three years he'd ruled as the most favoured Prime Minister of all times. But he'd been lured into Moore's web of deceit and lies, fooled by her cunning. Almost without warning she'd swooped like a vulture and snatched his job – yes, his Prime Ministership – from under him in June 2010. Then she'd relegated him to far-flung parts of the world as the Foreign Minister. Sure, he'd enjoyed his new role. Even his reputation blossomed on the world stage. This he knew annoyed her.

For eighteen months he'd successfully done his duty, but he was rarely home and being a family man, he missed his family and home dearly. When several faceless party members began a smear campaign aimed directly at him, he could no longer sit back and ignore the facts. While talking with close party colleagues in Washington DC last week he'd weighed it all up and made the only move he saw possible, and resigned as Foreign Minister, but not to retire or sit on the backbench. He wanted his rightful position as Party Leader and Prime Minister back. The polls showed the Australian public was fully behind him.

Ever since her narrow election win that was only secured

with the help of the Greens and Independents in August 2010, Moore has been losing favour with Australian businesses and the community. While Dick Francis was temporarily holding the top job it would have been easy to topple him, Hull had majority support over Francis. How he'd fare now that Carla Moore was to be sworn back in today, he wasn't so sure. He only hoped the party members would listen to the public opinion polls, instead of being hoodwinked by Moore's persistent lies.

Squeezing the paper once more, he pushed it hard into the magazine rack. Out of sight, but not out of mind. Taking a sip of the freshly brewed coffee, he squinted. Even it left a bitter taste in his mouth. This was not going to be a good day. He could feel it.

* * *

Paddy was lucky to have Coco on his staff. Without her inside information they would've been like all the other papers this morning. But for the second time in a week they had the scoop on Carla Moore's health update and movements. He didn't know how Coco did it, but he was glad she had. Keeping it under wraps overnight had been difficult, but now worth every cent.

Coco was pleased he'd agreed and not put her byline this time. She often wrote winning pieces without recognition. She didn't care. Strangely, it often made it easier for her to get information if she wasn't credited with obtaining it the spotlight remained off her.

She knew the PM's office would be busily sending out press statements first thing this morning, announcing Moore's fitness and reinstatement as Prime Minister. Smugly, she'd beaten them all to the punch.

Taking a mouthful of her coffee, she smiled luxuriating in her recent successes … sometimes life was so sweet. She'd been lucky over the last ten years … being in the right place at the right time. Someone was looking after her. Tomorrow she'd be fighting to keep that position. The media presence in Canberra had quadrupled in the last twenty-four hours. It seemed every country around the world had sent a representative or two to cover the caucus showdown tomorrow.

* * *

Shortly after the swearing in, Carla Moore posed for photos and read a brief statement thanking the doctors, the new drug, and the Australian public for their prayers and thoughts. "As I'm still recovering, please excuse me now. I have work to catch up on, plus I need my strength for tomorrow and all the days after, to do my best for my country and the people."

Returning to The Lodge with her were a dozen party faithful. The ones she could count on to gather the numbers needed in the caucus to rid her of Hull, hopefully once and for all.

* * *

Vishnu was excited. Almost jumping out of his skin. This was the opportunity of a lifetime. The TGA had granted him permission to work closely with Dr Ron Lopilato at Canberra Hospital on the treatment of Graham Bratnell. He'd have more contact with Dr Kelly and the Prime Minister's progress too. Mr Sinclair had also been thrilled. It was a dream come true – a break for ChemThorpe that no money could ever buy. "Of course you can stay there," he'd told Vishnu. "Your monitoring this first hand could be vital to the drug's final development. Grab it … grab it! You'd never normally get this chance."

Of course, spending longer with Ranni hadn't entered his mind. Like hell. She was over the moon about having him around. Even though both would be busy, it was going to be good sharing the day's events in person, and not via Skype or text message.

* * *

Tuesday morning was cold, wet and gloomy – a winter's day in the middle of summer. Looking out his hotel window, Hull prayed that the weather was a dampener for Moore, not him. Glancing at the breakfast tray his stomach churned in disapproval. Packing the black leather briefcase, he headed to his office in Parliament House. Hopefully, surrounded with friends he'd feel better.

The lines of media and interested public appeared to be at least two metres deep, and television breakfast shows were broadcasting live from tents pitched on the front lawns of Parliament House, as he was driven to the front entrance. Hull knew the media were espousing his prowess. The opinion polls supporting this were well and truly in his favour, over both Moore and Opposition Leader Scott. He smiled politely as the cameras followed his every movement from the car to the entrance. While microphones were shoved in his face, he reservedly declined to comment.

He knew in his heart he could take the Labor Party to a resounding victory in the next election, but deep down he suspected he didn't have enough believers in his own party to secure that victory today. Many had told him during his Monday calls, that it was better to present a united front behind Carla. To change leadership again showed instability. Only one vote more than her, that's all he needed, harbouring that hope, he'd prepared two speeches.

* * *

At times like this, Coco preferred recording the proceedings in addition to her notes. It was too easy to miss something important, especially if the action heated up – and that's what she expected today. It also refreshed her thoughts, placing her back in the thick of the moment, when recapping later.

In her usual efficient style, she'd already prepared an introduction and much of her base product. This way it was easy to fill in the atmosphere and statistical blanks quickly afterwards and get it off to Paddy.

Annually in Australia there's only one day when the entire nation stops work, and that is for the Melbourne Cup horse race. Whether on the Tab, with a bookmaker, or in the office sweepstake, everyone also has a bet of some sort. Today was the first time a political event had stopped the country. Legal betting on the outcome was also in full swing. Moore was highly favoured to win at $1.11, while Hull was odds at $10. Reportedly, one faithful punter had handed over $300,000 for a Moore win. People were even betting on what they'd both be wearing. Most were predicting black and white, for sombre and formal occasions. Hull was $3.25 to wear a black tie, and $4 for Moore to wear a plain white jacket. Personally, Coco thought Carla would strut out in red. Although it often clashed with her hair it was a powerfully winning formula.

Laughing to herself, she realised she should've made that bet. Watching Moore in a red jacket, white shirt, black skirt and red heels, walk down the corridor flanked by her party members in black suits, she was certainly making a statement. She was back in power and flaunting it. Today she meant business. Even Hull wore a red tie. It was obvious he and Moore had worked too long together. Like a married couple, they were dressing similarly even when not in the same room.

It was a painfully long wait for the media hanging about in the hallowed halls. It had been over an hour. Oh, to be a fly on the wall. What could be happening in that caucus room? Was it really that tight? Suddenly the doors swung open. There was much more to Moore – she'd trashed Hull seventy-one to thirty-one. How humiliating.

Always the perfect show pony, Hull walked out without uttering a word, just a smile plastered on his boyish face, trying to look gracious in defeat.

Beaming, the Prime Minister was clearly pleased, surrounded by her supporters. A simple 'thank you' was all she had for the waiting press. To hear the full details they had to hang around for the official press conference, scheduled twenty minutes before Question Time at 14:00.

After all that waiting, the press conference was an anticlimax.

Both were so civil it was almost sickening.

Hull, still sporting the supercilious grin, was humble. Thanking his supporters, his wife and family who were by his side, and the 'good' people of Australia. Coco's warped mind worried for the 'bad' people on Hull's list. Although he mentioned absolving his 'faceless' critics of the last week of any guilt over how they'd spoken about him. Sure – like hell. There was much more under this meek and mild godly-looking man. One never knew exactly what he was truly thinking.

She needed to focus on his words as he continued, "I knew today wouldn't be easy. I've fully accepted the caucus verdict. I will now dedicate myself to working completely for Carla Moore's re-election as Prime Minister.

"I've enjoyed working for the Australian people and I will continue in my position as voted by them as the Federal Member for Stocker. I'm not a quitter, and I will not be leaving. I will continue my work up to and beyond the next election.

"As I've said over recent days, these are difficult times for the Labor Party and I will do whatever is needed to ensure our future and success. I will faithfully throw my every effort into securing Carla Moore's re-election, and a Labor win at the next election."

Coco couldn't help thinking, what a back flip. It was a joke. Only last week he'd stated matter-of-factly that the party didn't stand a chance at the next election if Moore was still leader.

A recent survey had stated that Politian's were the biggest liars around, beating real estate and car salesmen hands down – well here it was in action. He may not be lying about policies and election promises like Carla 'Carliar' Moore, but he was lying through his teeth just the same. Did he honestly think anyone would really believe he was going to help her get re-elected as PM? The Australian public is not that stupid.

Moore's address was to the nation. She'd not been at the helm at the beginning of this debacle, and needed to reassert her authority and control. "I'm personally embarrassed about the events of the past week. They've been ugly. I know Australians have had a gutful of this nonsense, and I stand here today to assure you all that it will not happen again. The outcome is clear. The show is over.

"From today, my Government will be focused on work only. I understand many will have their doubts whether we can pull together, but I stand here to give you my promise that my Labor government will unite and deliver."

She mellowed while honouring Keith Hull's achievements as both Prime Minister and Foreign Minister, also announcing the new acting Foreign Affairs Minister.

Shock of shocks, she then admitted to having made mistakes in the past. "I will be a stronger and more forceful advocate in the future, ensuring we do achieve what the Australian people expect us to. We will be doing our very best to be worthy of winning the 2013 election. Everyone can be assured I am determined to resolve these past wrongs.

"After this last week, I am now impatient to get on with the job again … my job of building our nation's future. I am your Prime Minister and we are moving forward again. I am proud to serve the people."

The big unanswered question on everyone's lips was, 'could she be sure that Hull wouldn't stand in her way again? Would he set her free to do the job unheeded?' No one could guarantee that. Even she knew that.

Opposition Leader Adam Scott had a few minutes to get a word in before Question Time. Coco winked at JJ standing to the side of the stage. They would confer and enjoy a good laugh about all this tonight over a wine or three.

Scott was the most truthful of all, describing recent events as a stay of execution for Carla Moore, rather than a political victory. "Her challenge will be in uniting her people, and getting them all on the same path to run a competent government. Something she hasn't been able to do since taking power last year.

"Australia is a great country, but the rot that is systemic within the current government is dragging our great country down. Only my coalition team can give Australia the stability and competence required to succeed in governing the country correctly, and pushing ahead to the outstanding successes that are sorely needed."

Cheers erupted as he left the stage. Question Time was going to be interesting.

Racing home to JJ's, Coco turned the radio on, one ear tuned to the live broadcast while finishing her story for Paddy. Even though still very much a circus, Question Time was much tighter and more interesting since the three Independents had insisted on changes after the last election in 2010. Questions were now limited to forty-five seconds, and answers to four minutes. Always finishing at 15:30 this allowed for at least twenty questions per sitting day. The Speaker of the House ensured questions and answers were directly relevant and order was maintained.

Today, the first few questions from the Opposition Leader were personally directed at the Prime Minister, aimed at her lack of support from a third of her own party in the caucus results. How could she govern without the full support of her team? The House was in uproar.

Carla responded strongly and eloquently, but all were scripts Coco had heard a thousand times before about how her government was progressing with mining, carbon tax, immigration, family and education. Listening, one would never have suspected she'd been on her deathbed last week. Her recovery was remarkable.

Making a mental note that she must organise an interview with Vishnu and ChemThorpe immediately, she sent off a quick email to Ranni for his contact details.

The opposition continued attacking Moore's lies and lack of trust issues, from both before and since the last election. How she'd continually lied to all and sundry, even this morning on her back flip about Keith Hull. They even referred to Hull as a prima donna. Spot on there, Coco thought.

Remembering the Rosengold's were attending Question Time, she wondered what their thoughts were of the proceedings. One really needed to know a bit about politics and the players to have a true appreciation of the theatrics involved. It was a skill to speak so precisely off the cuff. Whether the statement held any real weight was inconsequential.

Droning on, they quipped how her government had not delivered the goods for the nation. Even Coco was becoming bored with the same old questions and comebacks. Echoing her sentiments, the Speaker announced, "The time allotted for this debate has thankfully expired." Laughter filled the House.

And to think, good taxpayers' money supported this circus. Perhaps when she retired she should think about running for politics. Money for jam, Coco mused.

Her email pinged – a reply from Ranni with Vishnu's details. He was still here in Canberra too. Terrific.

* * *

Just 32 hours since his first treatment and already Graham Bratnell was showing signs of improvement. While still in an induced coma, his vitals were stronger. Dr Lopilato was amazed. Discussing options with Vishnu, they decided to slowly bring him out of the coma overnight. Within twenty-four hours his own body would take over. It would be touch and go, but necessary.

Stationed at Bratnell's door was an AFP guard. Not that he was about to go anywhere in a hurry. His only visitors were doctors and police. No one knew the real reason for the police, not even Dr Lopilato. They assumed it was because of the bashing. Only Vishnu knew the truth. Commander Cross had requested he be notified as soon as Bratnell regained consciousness.

At home on the evening news, Vishnu was pleased to see the Prime Minister looking so well during the day's hectic events. Ranni reiterated the office happenings, adding that she suspected the PM was putting on a front. "She went home straight after Question Time, and I don't blame her. It was a chaotic day for all of us. And we haven't been sick."

He had to admit Moore was a gutsy woman. His drug was proving superior, but he was positive it wasn't responsible for creating another 'Wonder Woman'.

Over the next two days even Vishnu was astounded at the progress Graham was making. His drug was working quicker on humans than it had during his animal testing. This was excellent. Graham's real problem now was his head injury. He had acute amnesia. He didn't know his name, where he was born, worked, or why he was even in Canberra. He couldn't remember a thing, and recognised no one, including Vishnu, Ranni or Kathy. As he'd kept much to himself no one knew what to do except to hope that in time his memory would return. He was also unable to assist the police. Another roadblock.

Cross was irritated. Analysis of Bratnall's phone revealed a list of his incoming and outgoing calls. But none had produced a hidden family member, or a friend that knew him any better, or longer than Kathy prior to his time in Canberra. However, it did expose what Cross thought was somewhat unusual – an extraordinary number of exchanges between Bratnell and Keith Hull.

Reviewing the list, these covered a three-month period. There were several last Thursday after Hull had arrived back in Australia, with his final call to Bratnell lasting twenty minutes from 16:15. What was the nature of their relationship? Cross was puzzled as to why Hull would need to call a Parliament House chef so regularly.

With Bratnell's health improving, he chose to wait and hope that he would soon regain his memory. He preferred to question him first, rather than Hull.

Once Graham's health had improved, Vishnu needn't have stayed on. His drug had done its bit. With only one day till the weekend, Mr Sinclair had allowed him to stay on. It seemed pointless to endure a three to four hour bus journey back to Sydney to turnaround and repeat it twenty-four hours later.

Smiling at the prospect of a Friday lunch and long weekend with Ranni, he decided to check in on Graham one more time, before heading to pick her up.

"What are you doing here Vishnu?" Not expecting any conversation, Graham's greeting floored him. "Where's Ranni and Kathy?"

"Ahh … at work. It's Friday." Looking around, there were no doctors or nurses in sight that he recognised. "Can you tell me your full name and where you live?"

"Of course man. What's with the silly question?"

"Just please tell me. You've sustained severe head injuries, and it's just standard once you've regained consciousness."

"That explains the headache I suppose." A puzzled look came over his face "Do you work here?"

"Yes, this week I have been. Now can you please tell me your name, and where you live?"

Pausing he looked more serious than Vishnu had ever seen him look before. "Graham Bratnell, and at Kathy's house in Campbell. You know, man."

Vishnu began stressing. Where were the police when they were needed? They'd been visiting every morning till now. "I'll be back in a moment Graham." Having second thoughts, he asked, "Is there anything I can get you?"

"I'd love a Coke, man. But listen; do ya think I can go home? I really hate hospitals."

"I'm not your doctor for that. At present I don't think that would be wise though. I'm sure they'll need to run more tests first. Just wait, I'll be back soon."

As he left, he spoke with the guard to ensure Graham went nowhere. Walking to the entrance, he rang Commander Cross, who said he'd be there shortly. Sighing with relief, he walked to the vending machine and got a Coke, but was in no rush to return to the room. He didn't know what to say to Graham, and was afraid of messing up the police investigation.

While it was only ten minutes, it seemed an eternity till Commander Cross arrived. Together with Rodgers, they walked back to Graham's room, Dr Lopilato arriving almost simultaneously from the other direction. Outside the room they conferred about the patient's condition, agreeing that if his vitals were sufficient, the police could question him.

Vishnu gave him the Coke and apologised for having to leave. His priority now was spending quality time with Ranni. It had been a chaotic couple of weeks.

Cross focused the initial questioning on the bashing, which Graham claimed to remember nothing. This was feasible. His head injuries had occurred from behind. Showing him the wallet in a clear plastic bag, "We're assuming the motive for your attack was robbery. Is this yours?"

"Yep. Looks like it."

"Do you know how much money you had on you at the time?"

"Maybe fifty or so. I rarely have more than a hundred. Have ma Visa card. S'pose that's gone too?"

"Yes just a few papers I'm afraid." Noting his depressed expression. "No one has used your card. It would've been easier to find them if they had."

Relief flooded his face. "Good in one way, bad in another."

Showing him the *iPhone*, "We found this at the scene too."

"I own an *iPhone*."

"Yes we know this is yours. We've a list of your calls." Watching him closely, his expression gave nothing away. "Can you tell us who you spoke to last Thursday?"

"Ahh … not sure. Tis usually just me mates." Feigning no idea, "You said you had a list, so you must know."

"We do," said Cross matter-of-factly. Waiting for a reaction, again Graham showed nothing. He was a strange one, that's for sure. "Do you often have telephone conversations with ministers, or the Prime Minister?"

"Yeah, sometimes."

Cross could sense this was going to be like trying to get blood from a stone. He wasn't going to give them any more than necessary. "And why would that be?"

"It's ma job. When they're having an important meeting, or function and need catering."

"What catering needs did Keith Hull require then?"

"He was the Foreign Minister, he was always requiring this and that."

"He was no longer Foreign Affairs Minister last Thursday. He'd resigned before coming back to Australia."

"You are correct Commander. Go to the top of the class."

Cross wasn't impressed and didn't see the joke. "Well, why did he need your services last Thursday then?"

"He was just discussing an outstanding invoice."

"Was it resolved?"

"I don't know I've not been at work have I?" Graham retorted, clearly annoyed.

Doubting he was telling the whole truth, there wasn't much more Cross could do on this particular matter. "We also have other questions for you regarding the Prime Minister …"

Before Cross could finish Bratnall bit back, "Yes, I do her cooking too." For the first time he was showing real emotion.

"We're aware of that Mr Bratnell." Feeling he had the upper hand, Cross pounced. "You're aware that she was the victim of an attempted assassination then?"

His stunned silence was too long. Cross continued, "You're the prime suspect." Still no response, "Traces of the poison used were found in your house, and at Parliament House. Can you explain why please? It's a prohibited substance."

Graham glared at Cross, then retaliated, "What? Never! You're lying. It's not possible. Anyway why would I want to kill her?"

"We don't know Mr Bratnell … how about you tell us?"

"How would I know?"

"Because you're the only person who has been in both places, and also has the access and trust of the Prime Minister."

"I'm not the only one that lives in that house and works in Parliament House and works for the Prime Minister."

"We've already spoken with Ranni and Vishnu. You're the only one left." Cross felt he had him now.

"I'm entitled to a lawyer and I'm not answering any more questions until I have one."

"Have it your way. We'll wait."

Leaving him alone to contemplate his options, Rodgers and Cross adjourned to the corridor. They needed to talk with Hull, but Cross preferred not to send any of the others. He didn't want another Coco debacle on his hands. Heading back to the office, he left Rodgers to wait for the lawyer from Legal Aid.

Staring at the number and notes he'd made on his note pad, Cross wasn't sure how to handle it himself, or whether the call would go directly through to Hull. He'd never had reason to call a minister, let alone a former Prime Minister.

A million miles away, mulling over the best approach, his vibrating mobile on the desk, startled him. Snatching it, "Cross. Yes ... Really ... you're sure? ... That's certainly interesting ... Do you believe him? ... How come the sudden change of heart? ... Hmmm ... No, I haven't. This changes everything. Thanks."

He shook his head in amazement. The turn of events was mind-boggling. People are strange. He'd seen plenty during his career, but never would've considered anything like this happening here in Australia. Yet still unsubstantiated, he had to keep an open mind.

Discussing it at length with Rodgers on his return, they decided on the approach to use on Hull. Then Cross spoke with his counterparts in Queensland. Four hours later they met him at Brisbane airport.

He was impressed. The Queensland guys were organised with the relevant paperwork if required. After knocking at Hull's door, Cross turned around. Immediately, he was mesmerised by the view from the wide veranda of this replica old Queenslander style house. High on the hill overlooking the Brisbane River and towards the city, the dusky sunset sky blended from hot pink to inky blue, while the city lights twinkled like fairy lights ... it was breathtaking. Cross could easily picture himself enjoying a beer after work in the large deck chairs at the side. It looked relaxing.

The door opened. The teenage boy was polite, but looked surprised as the three suited men introduced themselves, asking for his father. Inviting them in, they remained in the hallway. A few minutes later, Keith Hull smiled equally politely and shook their hands. Ushering them into the study to the left he closed the large double doors. "Please, take a seat." There were four chairs placed equidistant across the front of a huge oak desk. The room was meticulous. Everything had a place, and everything was in its place, even the neat stack of folders on the right hand side of the desk. It said a lot about the man. It was reflected in his appearance too. Even at home Hull looked immaculate in casual beige trousers, brown boat shoes and a red Polo Ralph short-sleeved collared T-shirt. "How can I help you, gentlemen?"

"I believe you know a Graham Bratnell?" Cross began, carefully eying his expression.

"Yes. He's an excellent young chef at Parliament House. Why? Is there something wrong?"

"He was bashed and robbed last Thursday evening in Manuka." Hull, visibly shocked, gasped. "He was unconscious when brought to the hospital and placed in an induced coma."

Hull was silent waiting for the police to make their point.

"His mobile indicates you made several calls to him during the course of Thursday," continued Cross. "Can you explain the nature of these calls please?"

Keith Hull waited a minute gathering his words carefully. "I'm not sure exactly, but I do know I thanked him for his outstanding work. You've got to remember the past week has been tumultuous for me. There's no way you can expect me to recall every single phone conversation during this time."

"It's vitally important you do, Mr Hull. The last call he made before the attack was to you."

He gulped, "Is he getting better now?"

"Yes, he is recovering. Now, can you tell us any more please?"

"Not at the moment. I'm sorry."

"Perhaps you'd like us to refresh your memory?"

Hull was stunned, wondering what Cross was going to say next.

"You were arguing over a payment I believe."

Hull remained silent.

"He did some work for you, and you weren't pleased with the results. Correct?"

"You're telling the story Commander Cross. Please enlighten me further."

Slimy bastard thought Cross. Typical politician. Cross felt like punching him. Keeping his feelings under control, he continued. "As you wish."

Without any further explanations about Bratnell, he handed Hull a copy of the two search warrants. "This will explain it all."

One of the other detectives made two brief calls to a forensics team outside, and another in Canberra, before they began on the house and his Canberra office.

After reading the papers Hull called his lawyer, knowing there was nothing he could do but passively wait and see.

* * *

Coco was proofing the story before sending it to Paddy for the early morning edition. Her body and mind was still reeling in shock and disbelief, she was certain the entire nation would feel the same. On telling Jonathon, he'd immediately called Adam Scott, and then adjourned to the office. It was major. Everyone needed to be armed and ready.

Shaking her head, she couldn't fathom why a person in such an esteemed position would ever consider taking such a path? Especially one who went to church every Sunday, was a devoted husband, father, and trusted by the people in his electorate, in fact more than half the nation. It was a sad day indeed.

The headline was even more catastrophic. For Australia it was worse than 9/11, and the Bali and London bombings combined. *'Hull Hung over Moore'*.

Hull had taken his own life in a holding cell at AFP Headquarters in Canberra overnight. While he hadn't confessed to being behind the attempted assassination of Prime Minister Moore, his actions overnight as good as confirmed it. Cross had enough evidence to put him away for life, and deep down Hull had known it. All the prayers and family support were not going to save him now. He'd lost the favour of most of the caucus, and was now about to be the disgrace of the nation and his family. The only people who had really stuck by him, he'd let down. His actions and evil desires would be aired to the world. He wasn't fit to live and had taken the easy way out. But would it really save the embarrassment to his family?

The police had found traces of polonium in Hull's carry-on luggage, and at his office in Canberra. A significant amount of money had been setup in an offshore account for Graham Bratnell three weeks earlier, substantiating Bratnell's story.

Bratnell's confession had assisted Cross and Rodgers in placing the jigsaw pieces together. Lacing Prime Minister Moore's food, particularly her favourite cake with polonium over three days was the easy part he'd reckoned.

"Why did you want to be party to the assassination attempt?" they'd asked.

"The money of course. Plus she'd been a bitch to me from day one. Moore was always complaining about one thing or other. I think only Hull hated her more than me. His offer was too good to refuse. It appeared to be fairly straight forward and easy to implement."

However, Hull had refused to pay him the remaining sum agreed, because Moore hadn't yet died. Once she was dead, he would finalise the agreement. But Bratnell knew she was getting better because of Vishnu's new drug. Without telling Hull this, he'd weighed his limited options. He could try again when she returned to work, but figured it was too dangerous, and unable to leave town because of the ongoing police investigation, he'd eaten the remaining contents of the small container Hull had purchased overseas and given him. He'd decided it was his only way out. It was either that or run – but where? He'd had enough of running. It was a sad and lonely life. When the police had mentioned about recovering the small empty container, he'd spilled it all. He wasn't taking the rap alone. After all, it wasn't his idea and he didn't have the contacts or money to purchase such poison either.

The whole sordid affair was more than Coco cared to know about. She'd seen more than her fair share of atrocities during her young career, but this was too close to home. She'd never thought she'd see a day like it in her home country. For the first time she was finding it difficult to be unbiased. Hang it, it was the truth, the facts, she wasn't prepared to sugar-coat the truth just because Hull was a former PM. She'd seen too much of that over the years, where journalists were paid to keep quiet about the truth. Whether it involved affairs, drunken orgies, even one PM being homosexual, who appeared before the public with his beautiful former air stewardess wife, and two children. Once out of power they'd separated, and he'd moved in with his male partner, running a pig farm. To this day not a word has ever been printed or spoken about his sexual preferences. She dreaded to think the amount it must have cost him though. She was pleased that Hull's family hadn't attempted to bribe anyone, or seek an injunction.

* * *

Enjoying the late morning sun, Kathy, Ranni and Vishnu sat sipping their coffee on the deck. Like the rest of Australia they were stunned by the weekend headlines. Unlike Graham, they were free to enjoy the warmth of the sunshine.

Kathy broke the silence "S'pose we now have to find another housemate Ranni. Know of anyone?"

Staring straight ahead over the rim of her large coffee mug, her hands cupped for reassurance, she felt each mouthful warm her chest down to her stomach. Slowly nodding in agreement, Ranni's mind was still in shock. Then like a light bulb, she sparked to life, "Are we game enough to find another one that cooks?"

"Trust you to be thinking of your stomach." Kathy retorted. "But I think you're right there. Just not one that's a killer, hey?"

"How about another female? No competition for me then," quipped Vishnu.

"Yeah right. We better make sure she's older and ugly then," Ranni mock punched him on the arm.

* * *

"Just goes to prove you can never judge a book by its cover," stated Beth. "Who would've thought that about Mr Hull? He looked and spoke so sweetly."

"And to think I thought it was the owner of the *iPad* who was trying to kill the PM," reminisced Derek while they watched the morning breakfast program. "It's ironic that this was how he'd chosen to try and kill her though. How coincidental ... almost like he'd done the same research, or had been reading Coco's *iPad* too."

Having arrived back in Sydney two days earlier, they'd had lengthy discussions with Don and Sue about their little adventure. Will, and even Emma, were impressed with their grandparents' stories. They were certainly better than any bedtime tale. "When I go back to school I need you to come and talk to the class," said Will. "The kids will never believe me, that's for sure."

In his eyes, his grandparents were bigger than *Smallville's* Clark Kent and Lois Lane ... and so much better too. They were his family. Real people. Real heroes. Hugging Derek tightly, then kissing Beth, "I love you both so much. I'm glad nothing happened to you."

They were touched. Beth's heart sung as she smiled at her precious family. "Thank you Will, but we were never in any imminent danger, darling."

"Don't worry mate, we'll be coming to visit for many more years yet," Derek added.

25. REWARDS

Thirteen months later – 26 January 2013, Canberra, Australia.

The day couldn't have been more perfect. Not a cloud graced the azure sky. Rows of brilliant red and yellow flowers lined the white stone driveway, and a gentle breeze caressed the stately blossoming gums behind. Turning left as directed, the vibrant green grass reflected in the white walls of The Lodge. A row of white linen-covered tables stood like soldiers along the stone veranda. Squeezing Derek's hand tightly, Beth couldn't believe the sight before her eyes. Butterflies filled her stomach. She couldn't remember even being this nervous on her wedding day all those years ago.

Smartly dressed waiters in crisp black and white stood like penguins, offering drinks to the steady incoming stream of invited guests. Taking an elegant, champagne filled glass each, Derek turned to his adoring wife. "To you my sweetheart. Thank you for sticking by and believing in me all these years. I love you."

"I love you too. I'm so proud of you darling. Thank you." Her eyes were sparkling and heart dancing as she looked up at him. "I can't believe we're really here. Can you pinch me please, so I know I'm not dreaming?"

Taking the gold embossed invitation card from his suit pocket, Derek read it softly to her. "The Prime Minister of Australia, Mrs Carla Peterson, and Gregory Peterson cordially invites Mr and Mrs Derek Rosengold to attend the Australia Day Awards Presentation Afternoon Tea …"

Letting the words wash over her, Beth turned to survey the colourful apparel and elegantly coiffured surrounding guests. "Isn't that Coco and Jonathon?" she pointed.

Walking towards them, Coco smiled first, "Congratulations Mr Rosengold."

Before he could reply, Ranni and Vishnu were by their side. "Congratulations Vishnu." resounded from all, while a broad smile lit up his face. There was no hiding his pleasure.

"You must be so proud of him Ranni?" Coco said excitedly.

Both Ranni and Vishnu nodded eagerly in agreement, it was difficult to say who was more pleased. Almost forgetting his parents and sister walking behind, Vishnu turned and introduced them to the gathering group.

"Who would have thought that my son would ever be 'Young Australian of the Year'?" said Vishnu's father, beaming. "Australia truly is the lucky country for him. We are all so proud of him." Mr Sharma enthusiastically patted his son on the shoulder.

Even though it was true, Vishnu was clearly embarrassed by his father's statement. Thankfully, Mr Sinclair and his business partner Mr Goldstein arrived, saving the day. Vishnu introduced them around the group. ChemThorpe's work had also been recognised in the Australia Day Awards, for its outstanding contribution to medical science.

"Hey, when did this happen?" screeched Coco grabbing Ranni's left hand, admiring the huge single princess-cut diamond, standing atop a thin white gold band. "It's gorgeous. Double congratulations you two!" Cheek kisses abounded as everyone took turns at admiring her engagement ring.

"I thought I should make an honest woman of her," joked Vishnu. Looking across at his father's stern expression, he knew it would be a while before he'd understand Australian humour. At least he'd warmly welcomed Ranni into the family, and fully understood that they'd not be returning to live in India. He'd offered to buy his parents a house in Australia, but his father was too proud to accept. While his sister and her new husband remained in the same hometown, his parent's wouldn't move. Maybe one day they would all come. Possibly when Ranni had a baby. He was forever hopeful. In the meantime, they would visit them regularly. In fact they'd planned two weddings. One in Australia followed by the traditional Indian one. This way it would keep everyone happy.

When an extremely handsome man in a dark blue pinstriped suit handed Coco another champagne it left them all staring in wonder. Catching their glances, she announced, "Everyone, allow me to introduce my husband, Kris."

"You're the sly one ... congratulations! When did this happen?" blurted Ranni.

"At Christmas in London." Coco was beaming. They made a perfect couple thought Beth.

Changing the subject, Vishnu turned to Derek and Beth, "I'm so pleased you were recognised for your contribution in helping the Prime Minister too. Congratulations."

"Well, it wasn't really for that. I developed a reality TV show called *iPlot*," explained Derek. "Using clues on their *iPads* and *iPhones*, teams travel around the globe planning mock assassinations on high profile people, while also sabotaging or stealing each others' technology in order to beat the other teams. If and when they catch the celebrity target, the target has to pay to stay alive. The money then goes to charity. It's become a huge hit around the world. The UK, USA and Australia all have versions, and other countries have now bought rights too. We've raised millions for a variety of charities. That's the real reason for the Award – our fundraising efforts here in Australia in particular, where the majority has gone to cancer research."

"That's wonderful. Especially for cancer research, thank you. Unfortunately, I have very little time for television, but I must look out for it."

"I understand. Your work is much more beneficial to the people than mine I'm sure. Without it none of us would be here enjoying this highlife today."

Looking at everyone, Derek raised his glass, and the others followed, "Cheers and congratulations to a fabulous team. Thank you all."